For Mom, who accepted even when she didn't understand.

CONTENTS

1 A HEART OF CROWS

"Drew, what in God's name is on your screen?" I asked as I descended the stairs into the basement.

"Seems pretty self-explanatory, Abra," Drew shrugged, not turning away from his computer.

"What's he looking at?" Lorelei asked, craning her neck around her monitor, from which the sounds of orcs grunting and swords clashing emanated.

"I'm not sure how to say this, for many reasons," I said, taking at seat at my own computer, "but your husband seems to be watching ghost porn."

"Still?" Lore groaned. "Drew, can't you just watch, like, ten guys railing on a thirty-year-old dressed like a school girl or something? Like a normal person?"

"It's not ghost porn!" Drew objected. "I'm looking up how to have sex with a ghost."

"I wonder what I did in a past life to end up having this conversation," I muttered, rubbing the area between my eyes. "I'm going to regret this, but…why?"

"Because I fell asleep early last night, and he sat up until four in the morning watching shows on one of those hyphenated TV channels," said Lore, rolling her eyes.

"I saw an episode of this 'Realm of Hauntings' show," Drew sighed, as if he was explaining the most obvious concept in the world. "They had this lady on who said that she had multiple 'spirit lovers.' It was...I don't know, interesting."

"So naturally you took to the internet to research how you, yourself, could fuck a ghost." I said, my eyes rolling of their own accord.

"It's not like that," Drew objected.

"Yeah, Abra, geez," Lore said, clicking away at her mouse while the sword noises intensified. "You're making ghost fucking sound so seedy."

"Come on," Drew said, pushing away from his computer and coming around to our side of the room. At six-seven, he had to duck to avoid hitting the Christmas lights that were permanently hung from the ceiling. Their green and red illumination played off his shaggy beard and decades old Alice in Chains shirt, making him look like a giant elf from Santa's Seattle branch office.

"Come on?" I repeated. "That's your big defense? Come on?"

"You don't see the appeal? Drew asked, waving his arms between Lore and me. "To say you had sex across the boundaries of life and death?"

"Drew," Lore said, still mainly focused on keeping her Paladin from having its skull caved in by band of angry Tolkien creatures. "When we said we were going to have an open marriage, I thought you'd at least keep it to the realm of the living. I'll tell you right now, you'd better use protection, because I am not going to raise someone else's ghost-baby."

"You can't... that's not…Neal, come on, help me out here." Drew called back to Neal's corner, where he sat crouched over his drawing tablet. "I need some male backup."

"Yeah, Neal, you've been suspiciously quiet back there," Lore said, leaning around her monitor again.

"I am perfectly fine with not being a part of this conversation," Neal muttered, not looking up.

"Too bad, not an option," I said. "Seeing a ghost: terrifying or arousing?"

Neal looked up and set his tablet down on his lap, I imagine questioning the wisdom of remaining part of this friend-group.

"Well…," he finally said.

"Yes!" Drew yelled, jumping up in triumph. "Yes! See? It's not that weird!"

"I didn't say that," Neal interjected, his stylus tapping against the side of his tablet. "I mean...like, which ghost?"

"Which ghost?" Lore repeated, "You mean, like, Casper or

Hamlet's dad?"

"I'm disappointed, Neal. This is my disappointed face." I said, drawing a circle in the air around my head.

"No," Neal said. "I mean, like, you wouldn't just say, 'I want to have sex with people.' You'd specify *which* people. So, like, are we talking Earl the Janitor who haunts the abandoned steel mill, or like...Emily Dickinson?"

"Wait, Emily Dickinson?" Drew asked, his triumph fading before his eyes. "That's your go-to example of a hot dead person?"

Neal shrugged.

"No, I get it," I nodded. "But wait, so it's not the *ghost* part that bothers you, it's just that you want to save yourself for the *right* ghost? The thought of ectoplasm everywhere, you're just fine with that?"

"Well, I mean...just for the philosophical questions it would raise," Neal started to ramble.

"Sure," I said. "We all know that the best sexual encounters are the ones that create philosophical conundrums, but...."

"Hang on, I'll be back," Lore said, hopping up from her chair and gliding toward the stairs to the main floor of the house. She moved like a lithe pixie, the ridiculous height difference between her and her husband on display as she slid by him, barely coming up to his chest.

"I think we broke Lore," I muttered as she disappeared up the stairs.

"Please," Drew said, sitting back down, "she made it through the discussion over whether vampires count as asexual reproducers or not. This is nothing."

"So, out of morbid curiosity," I asked, against my better judgement, "which ghost would you fuck?"

"Janis Joplin," Drew said without hesitation. "There's no way that wouldn't be insane."

Neal and I nodded in agreement.

"So, we know Neal has a thing for wall-eyed chicks, and I'm into hippies," Drew said, running his hand through his beard. "Spill it, Abby."

A flurry of footsteps clattered on the floor above us.

"I'm on the 'ghost sex is wrong' side of the argument, remember?" I said, clicking an icon on my desktop to open an old haunted house themed adventure game.

"But, like, if you had to," Drew shrugged.

"Like, someone is forcing her to have sex with a ghost?" Neal asked. "This is taking a dark turn."

"Not like that, I mean--"

"Drew, I know too many ghosts for this to be a fun game for me," I muttered, randomly clicking through folders on my desktop.

"Like a famous ghost!" Drew clarified. "Marilyn Monroe, or Cleopatra or—"

Before Drew, the afterlife's first matchmaker, could list a third dead person, a moving white sheet flew down the stairs at us.

"Boo!" Lore blurted from under it, looking through two hastily cut eye holes. Neal and I started laughing, Drew just stared dumbfounded.

"What in the…." He started.

"This do it for you?" Lore asked, giving a provocative twist under the sheet.

"I…it…uh," Drew sputtered as Neal and I stifled laughter.

"Boo," Lore moaned, as seductively as one could boo. "Booooo?"

"Did you cut holes in one of our sheets for this bit?" Drew asked.

"Just an old one," Lore, under the sheet, shrugged.

"So, there's no way she's clothed under that sheet, right?" Neal whispered to me. I shook my head.

"Huh," Drew said, looking his besheeted wife up and down before hoisting her up with one arm and heading up the stairs, the sheet trailing after them.

"We'll be back," Lore called down, through peals of giddy laughter.

"Close the door and use your white-noise machine this time, please and thank you," I yelled after them, before turning to Neal. "Music. Music now."

Neal nodded and leapt toward the CD player, hitting play and cranking the volume. Drew and Lore were both athletic and vocal in their...let's be kind and say love-making...as well as rather descriptive in their sex-talk. I'm not a prude, but I still needed to be able to look them both in the eye later. The music blaring, I moved closer to Neal so we could actually hear each other.

"So, how's the new issue of *And All the Rest* coming?" I asked.

"It's...coming" he blushed. "I fear I kind of wrote myself into a corner at the end of the last one."

And All the Rest was Neal's online comic about a group of non-costumed, slacker superheroes fighting crime in Seattle. It was a passion project of his that he did in tandem with his graphic design work, making logos and ad banners that 'popped' and had 'wow-factor.' The dream, which was slowly being realized, was to make enough money from his comic to quit his soulless job or to get the attention of one of the bigger comic publishers. He'd do it, too. Neal was the most talented artist I'd ever met, and I knew it was only a matter of time until he became a big name.

"Well, you did have...them...all seem to die in the Space Needle explosion," I said. I'd almost slipped and said 'us.' For all of Neal's artistic talent, storytelling was, let's say, not his forte. The four lead characters in *And All the Rest* were all pretty clearly based on the four of us. But one time when Drew made mention of "his character," Neal got so flustered and embarrassed that he stopped drawing for two weeks until Drew told him that he just meant "his favorite character." Neal pretended to believe him and we all pretended to not know that we had a comic book about us, which is hard, because it's pretty awesome having a comic book about you.

"That's not the problem," Neal said. "It's more the relationship angle. I think I overplayed my hand with Red and Shade."

Yeah, he kind of had. Red was his avatar, Shade was mine. In his last issue, he had had Red confess to Shade, right before the climactic battle at the Space Needle, that he was in love with her. It was a dynamic that had been largely untouched in the preceding twenty issues, though "shippers" among his fan community were very committed to the idea of pairing them up. Unfortunately, Neal had realized too late that in giving them what they wanted, he had tipped his hand in the real world.

"It was just fan-service," I shrugged, trying to give him an out. "You have to give them what they want sometimes."

"Yeah," Neal nodded. "Hey, is that *Unwelcome*?"

"Yeah," I said, turning back to the eight-bit haunted house on my computer screen. "Wanna play?"

"Of course," Neal said, pulling his chair next to mine. "I think I can remember how to get through some of the puzzles, at least."

"You should; we played it enough. Remember the night we decided we were finally going to beat it?" I asked, smiling at the memory.

"I remember your sister coming downstairs with plates of waffles for us," Neal laughed. "Gwen couldn't believe we'd stayed up all night."

"And still didn't figure out the maze section," I sighed.

"Well, we have the internet now," Neal suggested.

"Blasphemy!" I yelled. "We're doing this the old-fashioned way, with lots of swearing and unnecessary death."

"Okay, bring it," Neal smiled. "All-nighter?"

"All-nighter," I nodded. "All we're missing is a two-liter of Surge and a pile of math homework we're ignoring."

"How about I get drunk on cheap rum and you continue to ignore that you have to open up the store at nine tomorrow?" Neal asked.

"Perfect," I said. And it was.

Unfortunately, we weren't sixth graders or even college students anymore. The "all-nighter" lasted until about 4 a.m. when both Neal and I fell asleep in our chairs pretty much simultaneously. We were, sadly, still stuck on the maze, the same pixelated hell that had confounded us back when we were twelve, playing a cartridge version of the game on my old Nintendo. I'd met Lore and Drew in college, but Neal and I had been inseparable since second grade. Lore and Drew only ever knew me as Abra, but Neal had met me before I was myself.

I found myself thinking about those early days, when I first started becoming myself, as I slid out of my chair at seven in the morning, careful not to jar Neal, who was slumped forward like he was trying to collapse himself into a ball. I walked upstairs to the main floor, hearing Drew and Lore both snoring away in their bedroom, door open and white-noise machine still humming. I crept up the second staircase, to the top floor, which was home to storage space, a bathroom that was usually full of spiders, and my personal quarters.

Lurching into my bedroom, I began my morning routine. I kept my pills on my dresser, in one of those little day-by-day organizers that old people use. Flipping open Saturday, I popped the two white Spironolactone tablets in my mouth, grabbed a drink from the water bottle I kept next them, and swallowed hard. My Estradiol patch wouldn't need to be switched until Monday. The grey-market website I ordered my meds from had delivered a new package the day before, so I was all set for another month.

I pulled on a pair of skinny jeans and a fitted black v-neck t-shirt, which was pretty much my unofficial uniform. Light was beginning to creepy in through the thin blue curtains that covered my room's only window. Once dressed, I stepped over to pull back the drapes and look out into the woods behind our house, the reflection on the glass giving me a not entirely welcome opportunity to look myself in the eye.

Neal knew me back when I made more sense to the world. When I went by a male name so dead that I have trouble remembering it and don't really care to anyway. We met in third grade, both of us playing alone on the playground. I'd love to say it was some cliched thing like we played GI Joe but I always wanted to play with Barbies, but nah, fuck Barbie. I loved playing all the same games he did. We used to get together (before video games entered our lives) and turn all our different toy-universes into one giant omniverse. Cobra Commander and Skeletor teamed up with Darth Vader to kidnap Optimus Prime, so it was up to Luke Skywalker and Cheetara to rescue him (okay, fine, you can probably guess who represented me in that scenario; I can't buck every stereotype). We went from friends to best friends to only friends, none of the other kids able to keep up with us as we spun increasingly complex rules for our playground games, or told odder and odder stories with our drawings. All the while, something was pawing at the inside of me, tap-tap-tapping on the walls of my skull, saying, "Hey, pay attention to me."

The voice got louder as the years went on. As action figure battles gave way to video games, which didn't give way entirely but transitioned to hanging out in each other's basements and getting high on really bad weed that my sister had procured for us, the little whisper became a shout, and then a pained, helpless scream. You need to understand, no one really talked about being trans back then, and no one understood it. I found out about the possibility that my outside and my inside could be different the same way that Drew found out about ghost sex: From a scandalous TV show I watched while home sick one day that had bragged, "We bet you can't tell which one of these beautiful women is actually A MAN!" And no, I couldn't. And neither could the audience. And just as I was beginning to feel like things were coming into focus, the TV host revealed 'the truth,' causing all of the men in the crowd to react with a chorus of boos and feigned retching.

Gwen was the first person I told what little there was to tell. Gwen was the person I told everything to, even before I told Neal. She didn't retch or boo, she put her arms around me and held me, for almost half an hour. We didn't say anything, until finally she whispered in my ear, "I was your big sister yesterday, I'll be your big sister tomorrow. Tell me how to help."

And help she did. She was in her first year of college at that point, though still living at home, I suspect more to serve as a buffer between our father and me than for financial reasons. She joined the campus' LGBTQ group as my proxy, gleaning what information she could and passing it back to me. After several visits with a therapist the group members had helped me locate (and which Gwen paid for), I accepted what I was. Unfortunately, I was still sixteen, and would need a parent signature for any kind of medication, which my aggressively Catholic father would never agree to. But Gwen, who was a Computer Science major back when that made her the only female student in her department, knew things. The internet was still in its childhood at that point, but there were already places to procure things that you couldn't get elsewhere. Gwen found reputable (for such sites, at least) online pharmacies, and consulted with her group to determine dosages.

About the time I was waiting for my first package of meds to arrive, I realized I'd need to tell Neal. We'd never kept secrets from each other before. He'd told me earlier that year that he'd realized he was finding himself attracted to both men and women, news which I had received by saying, "huh" and asking him to pass the Fritos. I told Neal my news in my basement, our usual hangout spot. Gwen stood at the top of the stairs, in case our father had somehow roused himself from his latest drunken stupor and decided to see what "his boy" was up to.

I told Neal in one giant burst, all of the information I had accumulated over the last two years spilling out of me like molten lava. I probably gave too much information on my plans: New name? (TBA at that time) Medication? (yes) Surgery? (no) Dressing in women's clothing? (eventually) Do I like guys now? (No, just women). Scratch that, I *definitely* gave too much information. He took it all in in his usual stoic way, nodded, slapped one hand on my back and pulled me in for a quick embrace. Neither of us said anything after that, at least not on that subject. We turned on the good ol' N64 and started up Goldeneye, Gwen coming down to join us as a third player about thirty minutes in.

There were other people I told, not a lot, but some. Some were disgusted. Some called me an abomination. Fuck those people. Some were over the top supportive, telling me I should instantly be out and proud, offering to take me out shopping for dresses and heels, wanting to make sure everyone saw them with their cool new t-girl friend. Fuck those people, too. Gwen and Neal were the two who reacted like I'd hoped they would. Your real friends don't give a damn. They don't love the man or the woman; they love the person.

Drew, Lore, and I drove to Cluster together. Neal, who had emerged, groggy, from the basement shortly before we left, would join us later. He had a meeting with the owner of a truck dealership who wanted him to design a new logo for their Christmas sale.

"You and Neal beat the maze?" Drew asked as he drove us, his enormous old Suburban groaning down the road.

"No, not yet," I said, glancing in rearview mirror. I looked better than I had in the window reflection. At least my makeup was done and my hair looked like an organized clump of roots now.

"Well, you sure were up late," Drew muttered.

"Drew!" Lore hissed. Drew made a grunting noise and dropped the subject, pulling the SUV into Cluster's parking lot.

Cluster was my pride and joy, my dream come true. All through college I was told that being an English major would be the road to a dead-end job as a barista or a secretary, but there I was, a business owner. Because of, not in spite of, my degree. In a roundabout way, at least.

In its original incarnation, Cluster had been a three-shop strip-mall with an insurance agent's office at one end, a coffee shop in the middle, and a two-bay car mechanic at the other end. All three had long since gone out of business by the time I acquired the strip. A few walls knocked down and a lot of trips to the big box hardware store on the edge of town, and what was once three stores was now one big, messy clusterfuck. What had once been the mechanic shop had become a used music area with a performance space for local bands to perform. The coffee shop still served coffee, but was also a gallery for local artists (including Neal) to sell their works. The third section, which had housed the insurance agent at one point, had become my lair: A store that sold cool shit. And that's pretty much as defined as it got. Vintage toys? Only if they didn't suck. Used video games? Not the shitty ones. Random old machinery that no one knew the purpose of? If it looks awesome, bring it on in. It was called Cadabra's Corner, and Neal had designed the sign for it, with a caricature of me wearing a purple witch's hat and cloak.

"What do we have for today?" Lore asked, unlocking the doors between the sections and turning on the store's lights.

"We have Monkey Don't playing tonight at eight," Drew said, looking at the clipboard on the wall behind the music store counter. "So bring your earplugs. You still doing makeup today?"

"Yeah," Lore said, grabbing her fold-out table from behind the coffee store counter and setting it up in the main seating area.

"Okay, great," Drew said. "I'll run the coffee bar while you're out here. Anything special in your section, Abra?"

"Yeah, I'm running a special where I don't call someone an idiot if they ask why a twenty-year-old action figure costs more now than when it was new." I said. "Today only."

Drew laughed and went to start turning on the lights in the music section. While being an English major had somehow led to me owning my own business, it *didn't* prepare me to actually run it. Thankfully, both Drew and Lore had earned business degrees, something which I had once mocked them for. They never let me forget that, especially the last few months, when Cluster had been consistently in the black. My used awesome stuff store, being one of the only vintage item shops in town, brought in a fair amount, but it wasn't until Drew started booking bands and Lore started doing the costume makeup demonstrations that she had become moderately internet famous for that the money really started rolling in.

I went to my counter and shuffled a pile of loose Star Wars figures off to the side. I would make sure to get around to sorting them, but without weapons or other accessories, they weren't going to bring much. I would probably just end up throwing them in a box with a '$20' tag on it and calling it good. After switching on my register, I reached up to the shelf behind me and touched the beak of the monocle and top hat wearing plush crow that lived there, as was my daily ritual. A sign hung around his neck that read, "Snooty Crow is not for sale. Don't ask." A most ineffective sign. Next to Snooty was a small, framed photo of college-aged me standing next to a woman with light brown hair and a smile that shamed the sun. That one didn't need a sign.

"Our walls are looking a bit bare," Lore said, looking around her section of the store. "Do you know if Neal has anything he's ready to display yet?"

"I don't think so," I said, straightening out my shelves before the customers arrived to transform them into chaos again. "I mean, he's got some stuff finished, but...I don't know. I think he's depressed. He's been kinda shut down lately. He seemed okay last night, but beyond that...."

"Yeah, I was glad the two of you stayed up all night," Lore said. "I've been worried about him, too. I know he kind of cycles through these things, but...."

"Yeah," I sighed. Neal's depression was largely under control but had a tendency to flare up and hit him like a wrecking ball. When that happened, he drew into himself like a threatened armadillo.

"Is he still seeing that girl?" Drew asked, coming over from the music bar to join our conversation in the door between my section and the coffee shop.

"Sofie?" I groaned. "No, thank God. They broke up about a month ago. But I don't think that's it. He broke it off, not her."

"Praise the Lord," Drew muttered. "I miss Dan."

Lore and I nodded in agreement. Neal, who was good looking by any standard as well as almost universally easy to get along with, had never had much trouble finding dates. He did, however, have an immense amount of trouble telling good people from terrible people, and terrible people from terrible weird people. There was the guy who made blankets out of the fur of roadkill (Conner), the girl who was arrested drunk in a cemetery at a stranger's funeral and made Neal bail her out (Hope), the girl who told him that she was only dating him because she didn't want to be a lesbian anymore and thought he was hot enough to "turn" her if they had sex (Tracey...still a lesbian when last checked in), the guy who declared he didn't like music, any of it, at all (Ryan), and the girl who bragged about getting her neighbor's dog put down by lying and saying it bit her (Sofie). That had been the past year.

But before that, there was Dan. Dan had come right before Roadkill Conner, and had lasted a good two years. A *really* good two years. Dan was normal, almost to a fault, but in a sweet, good natured way that made you like him even if he thought that polo shirts were acceptable daily wear and listening to the Eagles wasn't something he needed to explain. Neal had met Dan at Cluster, while hanging one of his paintings, a re-creation of a popular panel from an issue of *And All the Rest.* It turned out that Dan was also an aspiring comic book artist, and asked if Neal could look at some of his work. Neal, flustered by the square-jawed, all-American Adonis standing before him, agreed with a series of noises that could generously be called words.

What followed was a romance and relationship that pushed blood into even my cold, dead heart. Neal and Dan were inseparable, and for the first time, Drew, Lore and I didn't mind one of Neal's dates tagging along with us on our adventures, or just hanging out with us in our basement. It turned out that Dan had supremely undersold his own talent. He was already a popular artist online and had published a handful of comics through an independent label out of Seattle. He and Neal helped each other grow, their work improving at a rapid clip over the course of their relationship. They seemed to amplify the good parts of each other. Lore once asked me if I was jealous that my best friend wasn't spending as much time with me anymore. I wasn't; I was happy to finally see him happy. It didn't happen enough.

But then came the bad day. Neal, who had last been seen happily departing for a day alone with Dan, showed up back at the house, his face fallen and his voice hollow, telling us it was over. He wouldn't say anything else. Even a year later, Drew and Lore couldn't believe what had happened. It made no sense to them. I feared, however, that I understood.

As if aware we were talking about him, Neal chose that moment to call my phone, the custom ringtone I'd chosen for him (Rainbow's Man on the Silver Mountain, because Dio rocks, duh) blaring from my pocket.

"So you gonna sell some trucks?" I asked as I answered the call.

"Guy wants both Santa *and* Jesus on his banner. Along with a Ford F-350," Neal sighed.

"Can Santa be driving and have Jesus in the back?" I suggested.

"Shouldn't Jesus be driving?" Drew asked, loud enough for Neal to hear over the phone. "Isn't there, like, a whole song about that?"

"But it's for Christmas," Lore objected. "Jesus would still be a baby, right?"

"Neal, I'm going to put you on speaker," I said, tapping the speaker button, "we're going to help you get to the bottom of this."

I heard Neal laughing on the other end of the line.

"Tonight, how about," Neal said. "Listen, Abra, I noticed your stock was getting low. There's a row of old junk stores out here by the dealership, do you want me to go on a hunt?"

I glanced around my shop. He was right, I had had a good month, which had left my shelves rather bare.

"Yeah, if you want," I said. "We'll try to suss out this Santa and Jesus Road Trip Adventure thing of yours in the meantime. You were right to come to us with this."

Neal laughed, told us he'd see us later, and hung up.

"Why didn't he get the lecture about acceptable merchandise?" Drew asked. "The last time you sent me out, I got like a half-hour long training session on what you define as 'cool shit.'"

"*Neal* already knows his cool shit," I shrugged. "*You* brought me Episode 1 cup toppers."

"They're from Star Wars," Drew protested. "You said Star Wars sells."

"Drew, they're from Episode 1," I groaned, waving my arms like an air traffic controller. "And they're grotesque. No one wants to drink out of a child actor's severed torso. Episode 1 cup toppers are the bane of the vintage toy community. They're like a curse: You can't sell them, you can only trick someone else into taking them from you. I'm pretty sure there's just, like, five sets of those toppers that have been playing musical chairs through every vintage toy store in the country since 1999!"

To illustrate my point, I gestured to the set of four toppers, still sitting on my shelf, with a sign under them that read, "PLEASE STEAL."

"Happy thoughts, Abby, happy thoughts," Lore said, swishing from my left shoulder to my right with a little dance step, trailing her fingers the whole way. She drifted over to the shelf, picked up one of the toppers, one in the shape of a blue fly alien, and set it on top of my head.

"Well, okay," I said as Drew and Lore cackled. "That's one down, I guess."

I managed to keep it balanced on my head all the way back to the counter, where I took it off. A lady doesn't wear her best hat inside.

Business was slow that day. We knew it would change at night, once the screechy but locally-beloved band Monkey Don't started belting out covers, but it was nice to have some quiet. Unfortunately, quiet seems to bring the assholes out.

"So, that crow up there," one such asshole said, pointing up over my shoulder. "How much?"

I inhaled. Everyone gets one.

"I'm sorry, but it's not for sale." I said, with my brightest smile (though my friends always told me it looked more like I was baring my teeth).

"Yeah, but...how much?" the man winked. Oh buddy, oh. It didn't help that he had the greasy, smarmy look of a guy whose main hobby was telling feminists on the internet that they should get raped to death.

This time I just pointed at the sign.

"I just think my daughter would love it," the man said, ignoring me. "It's her birthday soon and she's been sick."

I really meant to invest in a neon sign that said "BULLSHIT" that I could turn on when needed. I believed in ghost sex more than I believed he had a daughter. Every jackass who wants to haggle claims that they are buying for their kid. Because there's nothing children love more than old, used toys.

I tapped the sign.

"Jesus, what's the big deal?" he sneered, his pleasant demeanor falling away. "It's just a stupid stuffed crow."

The bullshit light would have gone on again. There was no way someone getting this insistent thought that Snooty Crow was just another stuffed animal. He knew exactly what Snooty Crow was, he just hoped I was an idiot. I was *not* an idiot.

See, Snooty Crow had a rather dark history. He was a second-tier character on a live action kid's show that was moderately popular when I was growing up called *Spinwheel.* The show was mostly terrible, featuring a happy-doofy star named Mr. Spin generally being a Robin Williams rip-off for a bunch of puppets who were there to teach you important lessons about sharing, telling the truth, and, in one ill-advised but well-meaning episode, not ostracizing people with AIDS. The bright spot in the whole mess was Snooty Crow, a fancy-dressed crow puppet that would appear at the window after a big musical number to condemn the constant silliness around him. In reality, he was a pretty direct knock-off of the Muppet's Sam the Eagle, but British.

Snooty Crow was the only reason Gwen and I watched *Spinwheel.* Gwen had received the plush crow sitting over my shoulder for her eighth birthday, and he quickly became a constant participant in our games. Unfortunately, things took a grim turn when the news began to report that police had raided the house of the actor who played Mr.

Spin, and it turned out that Mr. Spin's hobby when he wasn't teaching puppets not to pet strange dogs was producing large amounts of child pornography in his basement. Unsurprisingly, *Spinwheel* was immediately pulled from the air and all of its associated merchandise stripped from store shelves overnight. Then the real purge began. Parents around the country began seizing their children's *Spinwheel* toys and sending them to the landfill or, in more dramatic cases, holding multi-family bonfires to dispose of the tainted merchandise. Our own mother, who was well-meaning but prone to whatever panic the media was pushing that day (I wasn't allowed to play Dungeons and Dragons as a kid, but on the plus side, I still have my soul), demanded that Snooty Crow go into the trash. With some of her characteristic quick-thinking, Gwen had grabbed an old plush penguin instead and shoved it into the trashcan, showing mom only the black, fuzzy back. The real Snooty Crow was then placed in the remains of an old laundry shoot in the back of Gwen's closet, only to come out when both parents were away.

"I'll give you twenty bucks," the jackass at my counter offered. "That's five times what it is worth!"

Bullshit. Due to the purges and Snooty Crow not being especially popular outside of my sister and me, Snooty Crow plushies could push three grand on eBay. And this asshole damn well knew it. I could practically see him drooling.

"No," I said. "Can I interest you in some Episode 1 cup toppers?"

Jackass' face twisted into a snarl.

"Oh fuck off. Keep your stupid crow!" He yelled, heading toward the door, past a mildly amused Drew and Lore. We would have let him go, too, but then…."

"Fuckin' tranny."

Drew, who was roughly the size of some minor land masses, who made extra cash during college performing in a local 'pro wrestling' league as a lumberjack themed villain named Maul Bunyan, who looked like a semi-shaved Kodiak bear, stepped between the jackass and the door.

"Excuse me?" He said, his voice bellowing from deep within him. He towered a full foot over the pitiful little weasel.

"I--I just…." the man stammered. He was interrupted by Lore gliding between him and her husband.

"Hi!" she said in a cheery voice. "My name is Lorelei. I do fantasy makeup tutorials online, I collect fairy figurines, my favorite color is electric teal, and if you ever say that word to my friend ever again, I will fucking end you. I'm not joking. I will end your miserable existence. I will spill every feeble, worthless thought and dream you have ever had all over the floor of this shop, and then I'll listen to ABBA while I mop it up. I will turn you into a cautionary tale they tell at the ER. I will make everyone who ever loved you cry at the thought of what I've done. My husband will know when to quit. So will I, but I won't. I will keep going until you are red mist on my tiny little hands, and if you don't believe me, it's only because you don't know me, and you're an idiot. Now get the fuck out of our store and never show that gross amalgamation of features that passes for your face in here again."

The man stood in stunned silence, Lore still looking up at him with an angelic smile. He looked like he wanted to say something, but some not-dumb part of his brain, deep, deep down, told him not to. Instead he just snorted, kicked open the door and ran out.

"Buh-bye, dickface," Lore called after him before hugging me.

"I...I could have gotten that," Drew chuckled.

"Of course you could have," Lore said, patting one of her husband's ham-sized biceps.

"Yeah," I said, clapping him on the back. "But then we wouldn't have gotten to see a grown man almost wet himself when confronted by a girl who weighs a buck-five on Black Friday."

"Exactly," Lore curtsied. "Punch his dignity, not his face. You okay, Abby?"

"Yeah," I waved her off. "It's nothing I haven't heard before."

"Well, you shouldn't have to," she said, hugging me again. "Now get over here, I need a model."

"Can't you use Drew?" I sighed.

"I used him last time," Lore said. "Come on. I promise I won't do cat makeup this time. How about... a crow?"

I shrugged and sat down in the chair across from her at her table. These were friends worth having your face painted like a fantasy bird for.

"Okay," Gwen said, backing away from the camcorder. "Action!"

My sister and I had a hobby on rainy days. We'd make our own movies using dad's old camera, based on scripts we'd throw together on the spot. One of the rules was that we had to make them up right before filming. If an idea had been percolating for more than five minutes, it was discarded.

"You're out of time, Queen Fantastica!" I bellowed, in the deepest voice my nine-year-old larynx could produce, waving a laser gun made of cardboard at her.

"No I'm not!" Gwen declared, waving an old wrapping paper tube painted silver in my direction. "I can control time I've just decided!"

"Your new time control powers can't save you from...having to listen to Vanilla Ice CDs forever!" I yelled, followed with my best evil laugh.

"Noooooo!" Gwen screamed, dropping to her knees and grabbing her hair with both hands. I loved my sister so, so much in that moment. I didn't know many other thirteen-year-olds who would want to spend hours filming idiotic movies with their younger sibling. I knew even fewer who would throw themselves so completely into it.

"What the fuck are you two doing down there?" a voice bellowed from upstairs. Gwen sprang into action, ripping off the metallic purple cape she had been wearing and throwing it over the camcorder.

"Just...playing," she responded as our father, still wearing his khakis and tucked in polo shirt from work, stormed down the stairs into the basement.

"Playing what?" He snapped, glaring at me.

"Just...like…," I stammered.

"We were playing GI Joe," Gwen answered for me. "I was being the Baroness."

Dad's glare shifted back and forth between the two of us.

"You're too old for that," he declared, calmer, but no less intense. "Both of you. And you…."

He looked right at me, and I thought for sure this would be the time he finally did it, when I'd finally feel his fist slam into my face. I was sure of it. I could feel him, teetering on the edge.

"You need to find someone to play with who isn't your sister," he growled. "It's gonna make you into a pansy. And not that little weirdo you hang out with all the time, either. Jesus, boy, sometimes I feel like I've failed you."

What he really meant was that I had failed him. He snorted like a boar and started back up the stairs, shaking his head.

"You okay?" Gwen whispered as our dad's footsteps faded. I nodded, looking down at my lap. The cardboard laser cannon I had been holding before dad came down the stairs was sitting on the ground beside me, and I suddenly felt incredibly foolish.

"Hey," Gwen said, putting a gentle hand on my chin and lifting my head up to face her. "Don't listen to him, okay?"

"Okay," I whispered. "I'm just…. Never mind."

"I always mind," Gwen said, one of her favorite lines. "You just what?"

"I'm just scared!" I blurted.

"Of what?"

"Of him," I admitted. "I know he loves us, but...he gets so mad. Sometimes it seems like he never stops *being mad. It just seems to, like, build up. And then something else happens, and he gets madder, and it just builds on top of that and--"*

"I get it," Gwen said, hugging me.

"I worry what happens if he gets so mad he can't hold it in anymore," I said, tears starting to fill my eyes.

"I do, too," Gwen said, wiping away a drop running down my right cheek.

"What if he hurts us?" I cried.

"He won't hurt you," Gwen declared.

"Why not?" I asked, through tears.

"I won't let him," she replied. "I want to tell you a secret, okay?"

I nodded, dripping tears all over both of us.

"Dad's scared, too," Gwen whispered. "I don't know of what, but he gets angry because he's scared, and I don't think he knows why either. But he's scared, and that means I can keep him from hurting you, okay?"

"W-why?" I stammered.

"Because," Gwen winked, "I'm not scared of anything."

My nine-year-old brain didn't question the logic, and instead just tumbled into her arms and let my big sister make all the bad thoughts go away. It also didn't question why she hadn't said "he won't hurt us.*" It wouldn't for a long, long time, either.*

"So," Calliope said, between sips of her coffee as she sat across the bistro table from me, "explain why you're a crow."

"Because I'm helping Lore show that you, too, could be a crow for the low, low price of ten dollars," I said, glancing at myself in the mirror mounted on the wall across the room. Lore, who was busy turning another customer into Moon Cat (which is, apparently, like a regular cat but blue), had done a fabulous job of making me into a crow. The black makeup had formed a mask that covered my forehead and faded down my cheeks in a gradual black-blue gradient. A sharp point resembling a beak trailed down my nose, and silver feather embellishments framed my eyes. To better display her work, Lore had pulled my hair back into a thick black braid, and added a black feather for effect.

"I think I'll pass today," Calliope said, tossing her flowing mane of chestnut hair behind her shoulder.

"Your loss!" Lore, who had shockingly good hearing, called from the other side of the coffee shop. Calli pressed her lips into a passable facsimile of a smile.

Calliope, who I probably don't even need to tell you had picked her own name, was my longest relationship, but what we were on was a date only in that it was down on our calendars.

I don't date a lot. Why, you ask? Here's why: I'm going to make you do a little work, because people are always asking me to back up my claims with hard evidence that is seldom required from others. So, here's your assignment: Start with the population of the world. I'll save you some time, because I'm generous; it's about 7.6 billion. Now winnow that down to the number that lived with me in Brahmton, Washington. I'll save you a little more time, it's a much smaller number. Now, as I've mentioned, I am only into women, so take that number and divide it in half. With the resulting number, it starts getting trickier. Remove all of the women who are only interested in guys. I'm assuming your number is much more manageable now. But we're not done. The leftover number is the women who are lesbians, bisexual, pansexual, or some other configuration that includes other women. But--and this is a big one, and much trickier--now you must subtract from that number all of the women who don't consider trans-women to be "Real™ Women," who think of us as men who are either mentally unwell or actively trying to infiltrate the female world. Once you've separated all of those lovelies out, you'll need to remove all of the women who are already in relationships, who aren't interested in relationships, who aren't into monogamy (because, surprisingly, I'm kind of old fashioned), who act like they are into relationships but, on the third date, ask if you would be interested in a threeway with the husband that they had failed the mention who wants to "spice things up" (for God's sake, please remove them), women who think Kirk is better than Picard, women who brag that they don't own a TV, and women who just plain find my personality and/or appearance repulsive, and you are left with....

Calliope. I'd met Calliope when she had signed up to be our entertainment one night two years ago. She was a self-taught yet incredible pianist with a low, sultry voice who sang songs in a way that laced the air itself with sex. When I watched her perform that first night, I was entranced. She was beautiful, graceful, and, I discovered after Drew and Lore built up my courage enough to speak to her, trans.

She was the first trans person I'd met. Gwen had acted as my liaison with the support group at her (and, eventually, my) college, so I'd never spoken directly with any of them. There had been rumors of other trans-people when I'd gone, but they were all smart enough to keep their heads down. Calliope, who was two years older than me, had met other trans-people, but not since she'd moved to Brahmton. Our mutual fascination with each other smoothed over all our differences. She was everything I wished I had been. While I look like someone threw Jack Skellington and Wednesday Addams into a particle accelerator, she was curvy, petite, elegant, and passed so well that, if she hadn't announced herself, I would never have guessed she was transgender. She had high cheekbones, ice blue eyes, and warm, toasted brown hair that I loved to feel under my cheek when we lay together in bed. Touching her felt like embracing silk-wrapped velvet, and being touched *by* her was electric.

Unfortunately, once I got past her looks, her musical talent, and the fact that she fucked like a succubus, I started to notice that she was also wildly unhinged. At first it came off as free-spirited hippie nonsense. Waking me up at three in the morning to go do chalk drawings in the parking lot. Showing up to a nice dinner out wearing a child's princess Halloween costume. Harmless silliness. Then things started getting weird in some oddly dark directions. Drew once described Calliope as the Manic Pixie Dream Girl that would be featured in a David Lynch movie. She'd greet me at the door in a full-blown rage because it was the solstice, and I "should know what that means!" She had a death mask made of an old boyfriend, who was still very much alive, and kept it in her bedroom, "so he could watch." She once booked us an AirBnB that we stayed at for three days before having to leave abruptly in the night after she confessed that it *wasn't* an AirBnB, it was the home of one of her former girlfriends whose vacation schedule she knew and whose key she still had. She yelled at birds. All birds. For my birthday, she gave me an oil painting she had painted; It was her as a corpse, decomposing.

After what was easily the most bonkers, sexually intense year of my life, Calliope told me she didn't feel like we were right for each other, and that she needed someone more adventurous. There were no words for how relieved I was.

I told her I understood, and we agreed that we should be friends.

She got out of bed, got dressed, and then on her way out, proposed to Lore and Drew that they have a threeway wherein all three of them would pretend to be me.

And now she was sitting across from me, the picture of demure grace, sipping her coffee.

"So how has your month been, Abby-Cadaby?" she asked, using her old pet-name for me that I always loathed.

"Pretty boring," I shrugged. "The shop is doing well, and Drew let me help make Thanksgiving dinner. No one got food poisoning, so I'll call it a win. How about you? It's been a while since you've been in to play."

"Yes, well," Calli said, biting her lip, "I do hate to sound like a snob but...you do keep that piano around as a joke, right? Because no music is ever going to come out of it. I need a proper instrument, sweetness. Find me one and I'd love to come back and play. For you."

I really, really hated myself for still being almost overwhelmingly sexually attracted to her.

"And Black Needles?" I asked.

"Doing wonderfully, Abby. Am I going to see you in again any time?" Calli smiled. "I did enjoy working on you."

Calli ran one of two tattoo parlors in Brahmton, and, despite the seeming lack of wisdom in letting such a person approach you with a needle-gun, she was amazingly talented. She had done my one and only tattoo, a Sacred Heart with two crows inside of it, based only on an old, faded sketch on a VHS box. The ink work was sharp, and the plume of red shading that surrounded it vibrant and alive. If I wanted another tattoo, even knowing Calli as I did, I wouldn't have gone to anyone else. But I didn't. I had the only one I ever wanted to carry with me.

"When I think of what word I want on my infinity symbol," I said. Calli laughed. Infinity symbols with inspirational words were the Episode 1 cup toppers of the tattoo world.

"I do miss laughing with you," Calli said, tossing her hair again. "I'm seeing someone now. He's a lawyer, but we have to keep it quiet because his wife doesn't like me. He's very...strong...but serious. You knew how to laugh. So how about you, Abby-Cadaby, anyone new in your life?"

"Well, there's this lady from a phone commercial that I had a super inappropriate dream about the other night, but otherwise, no." I said, picking up my cup more out of habit than to actually take a drink.

"Aw, sweetie," Calli cooed, reaching out and running a soft hand against my face. "You should be with someone. You're so sweet, and when you aren't wearing crow makeup, you're pretty cute. What about that hot artist boy that follows you around like a puppy?"

I sighed as dramatically as I could.

"You know his name. And he doesn't follow me around like a puppy," I grumbled. "And I've told you before, I'm not--"

"Yes, yes, I know," Calli said, her hand fluttering in a circle in front of her. "All I'm saying is that if I had someone who looked at me like that--especially someone who *looked* like that--I sure wouldn't let something as trivial as gender stand in the way. But if you're not going to...do you mind if I give him a shot?"

"Yes," I said, not even trying to conceal my horror. "Yes, I mind very much."

"Hmm," Calli hummed with a sly little smile. "Maybe ask yourself why that is."

It was mainly because I was afraid Neal would wake up in a bathtub full of ice missing his kidneys, but whatever Calli needed to believe to keep away from him was fine by me.

"Well, I must be going," Calli said, her flowy purple dress billowing around her as she jumped up from her seat. "Same time next month?"

"Sure," I nodded. She gave me one more smile that affected me in ways that I'm not proud of, and then disappeared through the front door of the shop.

"That lady weirds me out," Drew said, emerging from behind the counter to clean up our table. "Every time I talk to her, it feels like we're meeting in a dream.

"Calli's harmless," I said, to both of us. "She's just...eccentric. Besides, it's nice having another...one of me...to check in with from time to time."

Drew nodded and then paused, looking down at the table like he was studying a Where's Waldo page.

"Hey, uh, where's the other cup?" He asked.

"What?"

"Calli ordered something, right?"

"Yeah," I said. She had gotten the same thing I had, a latte, served in a wide-mouthed mug that said "bliss" on the side of it in fancy script. The same type of mug that I had in my hand, but it's twin wasn't sitting at the empty spot at the table. Without a word, Drew and I both turned and looked out the front window, just in time to see Calli, oblivious to us, raise the purloined mug over her head, smash it to the ground, and then let out a deep and joyous laugh. After that, she got into her car and drove away.

"Well," Drew said, with a nod. "You're cleaning that up."

Yeah. Probably.

Out of breath, I pounded my ten-year-old fist against the smooth, red door, not even thinking about the bell next to it. I didn't know what I was going to say if his mom or dad answered. I didn't even really know what I was going to say if he did. Too dehydrated to cry, my eyes burned. It wasn't until I was there on Neal's front porch that I noticed I had left my shoes at home and water had begun to soak from the damp ground up into my exposed socks.

"Hey!" Neal said, excited to see me as I opened the door. "I was going to call you. My dad rented Jurassic Park. You want to watch it with us?"

I barely heard him, and the first words that came to my brain tumbled out of my mouth.

"My mom died."

"Neal?" Neal's dad, a large, jovial man, called from somewhere in his house. "Who is it?"

Neal looked back at me. I shook my head rapidly.

"No one," Neal called back. "Just...someone left a toss-on paper. I'll go throw it in the bin, then I'm going to walk down to the park and play for a bit, okay?"

"Okay!" It was Neal's mom who answered, thankfully without coming to investigate. "Take a coat though, it looks like the rain might come back. Don't want you to catch cold."

"Okay!" Neal yelled back, and then gestured for me to wait as he closed the door only to emerge a minute later with two coats and a pair of old rain boots.

"These are my old ones," he said, handing me the boots and the spare coat he was carrying. "Might be a little small."

They weren't. Neal was always a full head taller than me, so his last-year coat and boots fit me like this year's. I zipped the old coat up over me. The Seahawks logo was embroidered on it, his dad's desperate attempt to try to get his son interested in football. It hadn't worked.

Neal and I walked the block and a half distance to Thorton Park. It was built on the grounds of a large, free-standing crag that had once been used as a Native American lookout point. A narrow path ran up the side of the rock that would take you to the top. At night, the top of the plateau was usually occupied by teenagers drinking and/or making out, but during the day it was empty. It was that day, at least.

Neal and I walked right to the edge of the crag, to the spot that had, at different times, served as our military watchtower, our crow's nest, and the Death Star's command center, among others. It was a little lookout point that jutted up over the tree-line just enough to provide a spectacular view of our decidedly unspectacular town.

We stood, looking out over the vista, still in silence, until it became too much.

"What...what happened?" Neal asked, his voice shaking almost as much as mine did.

"I don't know!" I blurted. "She was in the kitchen making lunch, and then we heard a crash, and Gwen and I ran in and she was on the floor and she wouldn't say anything, and it was like she was asleep but we couldn't wake her up and my dad ran in and started yelling and then he called 911 and they came but they couldn't help her!"

I lost my breath and began panting and wheezing like a dog after a run. I tried to force more words out, but nothing could get through. There wasn't much more I could tell, anyway; it would still be at least a week before I learned the word "aneurysm" or what it meant. Neal opened his mouth to speak, but no words came out of him, either. Instead, he did what he never would have done with an audience, lest we be labelled a 'pair of faggots' like my dad sometimes enjoyed calling us. He put his arms around me and hugged me, awkwardly, as I sunk down onto the grass. My body managed to find a bit more moisture, and the tears began to flow again. His did, too.

In later years, I'd feel bad about having put so much on another ten-year-old, but at the moment, I hadn't known what else to do. The police were still at my house when I had left, though the EMTs and firemen had long since departed. I didn't have to be sneaky, I just...left. Gwen, fourteen at the time, had run up to her room and slammed the door, screaming for me to leave her alone when I knocked on it, which had never happened before. My father was sitting in the living room with two detectives who were desperately trying to get him to answer some questions, but couldn't get anything through over the loud, bleating sobs coming out of him. He cried like a man who had forgotten how to. Amid the chaos, my body had just walked itself out the front door and down the road to Neal's house. I had no recollection of deciding to do so.

Neal and I sat there and cried for what seemed like forever, but was probably just half an hour. When we had both worn ourselves out, we moved apart, and sat looking down at the town.

"I'm sorry about your mom," Neal whispered. I nodded. "She was always really

nice to me. I bet she's in heaven."

"I hope so," I said, surprised at how steady my voice was now.

"When grandma died last year, my dad said that people who die don't even know it happened, they just wake up in heaven. Or.... But, yeah." Neal stammered.

"That must be scary," I said. "To be just making sandwiches and then you're talking to God."

"Maybe God wanted a sandwich?" Neal said, and then blushed. A look of relief came over him when I started laughing.

"I guess they don't have McDonalds up there," I said, feeling the tears welling up behind my eyes.

"I don't think they would," Neal said, and then started laughing along with me. Even for ten-year-olds, the jokes weren't funny, but the feeling was...normal. And normal felt amazing.

We stayed up there another half hour, telling increasingly stupid jokes and alternating between laughing and crying before returning to Neal's house. By the time we got back, Gwen was there waiting for me, along with Neal's parents, who both swooped in and wrapped me in an enormous hug as I came to the door. They sent Gwen and I home with an extremely impromptu casserole that Neil's mom had prepared.

When we got back to my house, my father was sitting in his chair, beer can in hand, facing the TV like he usually did, but with nothing on it. He looked up at Gwen and me, and without a word or even a sound, turned back to the shiny black screen.

Neal came in around five, much later than we had been expecting him.

"Hey, slacker," Lore called from her makeup chair, between clients. "You get lost?"

"Uh, no," Neal muttered. "Just...is Abra around?"

"Back here!" I called out from behind my counter. "I sold the Fortress Maximus! I'm $500 richer!"

"I knew that thing would move," Neal said, walking back to Cadabra's Corner. "It had both of its heads and everything."

"Well you helped find it, so--" I started, then actually got a look at him.

"Are you okay, Neal?" I asked. His face was blotchy, like he was trying to go pale and blush at the same time.

"Yeah...yeah, I'm fine," Neal said. "You're a crow?"

"I'm a crow," I nodded, crossing my arms. You didn't just wash off one of Lore's creations. "So what did you want to see me for?"

"So, I went to that old junk mall, out by the highway?" Neal said, inhaling. "I... found something."

"You mean Rag Pickers? Ugh, I would have told you to skip them," I said. "Nothing out there but old appliances and hepatitis. What did you find me?"

"It's not for the shop," Neal said, sounding like he was about to tell me that he'd found my corpse, that I'd been dead all along. "I-I really need to just show you. I'm sorry. It's back at the house. Sorry. I shouldn't have brought it up yet."

"Oh," I nodded, studying my friend's unusually serious face. "Okay."

"Hey Neal!" Drew called from all the way back in the music section. "The three of us worked out your Santa/Jesus/truck problem!"

"Oh yeah!" I said, remembering the hour-long discussion we had had around the heads of confused customers. "So, what you have to do is have the truck pulling Santa's sleigh instead of reindeer, with Santa in the truck and baby Jesus riding back in the sleigh."

"Now I know what you're thinking," Lore jumped in, from the corridor that ran through all three sections of Cluster. "Shouldn't Santa be in the sleigh? No, and here's why: It's irresponsible to leave a newborn infant--"

"Even the King of Kings," I piped in.

"--in a vehicle all by himself." Lore finished. "So Santa is driving the truck, which is pulling the sleigh, which has Jesus riding in it."

"And before you object that it's probably dangerous to have a baby in a sleigh by himself, too, let us get to our next suggestion." Drew said, holding his palms up.

"Put Mary and Joseph with Jesus in the sleigh," Lore said. "He's far too young to be leaving with a babysitter, even one as trustworthy as Santa Claus, so the whole Holy Family can enjoy a sleigh ride led by St. Nick and a good ol' American built pickup truck!"

"I bet you're going to ask why we can't put Santa in the back and have Mary or Joseph drive the truck," I said, as Neal opened his mouth to say something that never came. "But come on, think: They were alive way before cars were invented. They don't know how to drive. But Santa is eternal, so I imagine he has had to have learned sometime in the last hundred years."

"So, there you go," Drew proclaimed. "Santa's sleigh, with the Holy Family riding in it, pulled by a pickup truck driven by Santa Claus. You're welcome."

"Well, actually," Neal mumbled, blushing, "I was just going to go with something like this."

He reached into his green messenger bag and produced a sketchbook with a rough drawing of the ad, Santa kneeling next to baby Jesus in the manger with "The reason for the season" in calligraphy over it. The Ford F-350 was at the bottom of the ad, two holly branches framing it.

"Neal," I said in a grave voice. "You are my best friend. There is no one in this world I love more than you. But today...today, Neal, you've hurt me."

"You've hurt *all* of us," Drew scowled. "Very disappointed."

"Oh come on," Neal laughed, as Drew, Lore and I went back to our sections of the store.

"Very disappointed!" Lore yelled.

We shunned Neal for the next ten minutes and then let him out of the artist doghouse. I had him help me sort through a small box of old crap I'd been ignoring for months, separating out the few saleable items from the dross. We talked and laughed as usual, but there was still something off about him

Monkey Don't showed up early for their set and blasted punk covers of non-punk songs well into the night, to the point where we literally had to pull the plug on them before we violated the town's noise ordinances. By the time we finished escorting the last of our customers out and managed to corral the mess they had left, it was well into Sunday. When we finally stumbled back through the door of our house in one big clot, the four of us were beyond exhausted, both physically and mentally. I hated that my mind kept drifting back to the dickwad who wanted to buy Snooty Crow and his parting shot. No matter how long it had been since I had transitioned, no matter how well I passed, no matter how much I tried to convince myself that I no longer cared what idiot strangers thought, someone always managed to slither in and get under my skin. I hated that some random asshole whose name I didn't even know could strip away my dignity and my humanity with minimal effort. Calli always told me to get over it, let it roll off my back, rise above it. Her ability to do so was one of the many things I envied about her. I knew I shouldn't let words hurt me. And it wasn't so much the word that had gotten to me, it was the attitude. The look. "You are wrong. Your existence is wrong. Nothing I could do to you would be wrong, because you're not a valid human being."

I hadn't told Neal about what happened, because I was trying to convince myself it wasn't a big deal, and because I knew how he'd react. Targetless rage was not a good look on him. I loved that I had friends that were willing to stand up for me, I just felt awful that they had to.

"Hey," Neal said as we stood in the entryway, Drew and Lore already having waved goodnight and shuffled off into their room, "about the things I found at the dirt mall…."

"I want to know, I really do," I said, my eyelids having trouble staying up. "But can it wait for tomorrow?"

"Yeah," Neal nodded, "that's just what I was about to suggest. G'night, Abra."

"Hey, wait, walk with me a second," I said, gesturing for him to follow me up the stairs. He nodded and came with, the old steps groaning under our feet.

"What's up?" He asked, halfway to the second floor.

"I just.... Are you okay?" I asked, leaning on the railing. "You just seem not yourself lately."

"If only," Neal sighed, sliding down and sitting on a step. I joined him.

"What's going on?" I asked.

"I don't know," Neal said, his eyes pointed down into the dark at the bottom of the stairs. "It's just...like, I feel...okay, you know those shows that are really good, and everyone loves them, and they can't wait for the next episode, and the network keeps renewing the series? But then the writers tell all their stories, and the actors are kinda checked-out, and the fans are losing interest and talking about how the show has gone downhill, but the network keeps renewing it, and the stories start becoming thinner and making less sense, and no one wants to admit that it has gone on too long, so it just keeps going, for no real reason? I feel like that. Like a show that no one remembered to cancel."

"Neal," I whispered.

"It's not like that," he waved his hand. "I didn't mean to sound like that. I'm not suicidal, I'm just...alive and not really sure why."

I put my arm over his shoulder and let him lean into me.

"Is this...is it because of...," I stood on a precipice that, once jumped off, I couldn't return to. I knew I needed to take the leap, had for a while. But first and foremost, I'm a coward, and those closest to me are the ones who pay for it.

"Is this about what happened with Dan?" I asked, a question adjacent to the one I needed to ask.

"No," Neal gave a thin smile. "And yeah. Abra, you're fading like a dying lightbulb, you need to get to bed."

"Nah, I'm good," I said, snapping myself to attention, unaware of how thick the tendrils of sleep had grown around my brain. "Look, let's head down to the kitchen and pour a bunch of coffee down my throat. Cluster is closed tomorrow, anyway, so we can sleep later."

"Abra, it's okay," Neal laughed, bumping his shoulder against me.

"No, it's not," I said, my legs protesting as I stood up to head back downstairs. "Come on, let's talk!"

"We will," Neal smiled. "But later. I'm exhausted, too. And I'm okay, Abra. I just need to crawl out of my own head for a while."

"Alright," I sighed. "But let's not make this one of those things we put off forever, okay?"

"Sure," Neal nodded, taking my elbow and walking me the rest of the way up the stairs to my door.

"You still have stories to tell, Neal," I said as I flipped on my light. "And your fanbase is fiercely loyal."

"Goodnight, Abra," he smiled as he pulled the door closed for me. The light from my room glinted off the moisture in his eyes for a split second as the door closed, leaving him in the hall and me alone in my room. I flopped myself, still fully clothed, sideways onto my bed, fully intending to not move until morning. But before sleep could have its way with me, a quick shuffle of movement from the floor caught my eye. Sitting up, I saw a folded piece of paper had been slid under my door, a clean white rectangle on the warped hardwood. Pulling myself off of the bed, I staggered over and picked the paper up, unfolding it.

It was a quick but well-drawn sketch of a large pickup truck, being driving by Santa Claus, pulling a sleigh with Mary, Joseph, and baby Jesus riding in it. Above them, fancy script read, "Merry Christmas, motherfuckers!"

"Who's going to crush this?" I yelled in my best cheerleader voice, dancing around an increasingly red-faced Neal as I pumped my fists in the air. "Neal is!

Neal! Neal! Neal! Neal!"

"Okay, okay okay!" Neal laughed. "I'm psyched, I'm psyched!"

"I don't think you're psyched enough!" I said, switching to a wrestling announcer voice. "In this corner, getting ready to go out on his first ever date with a dude, looking like a million bucks and ready to blow the minds of everyone at the subtly-named Second Annual Freemond College GSA Rainbow Ball, weighing in at like seventy-five pounds, the Artist of Destruction, the Artist of Seduction, Neal Tate!"

"Woooo!" Lore and Drew both yelled from the other side of the dorm room Drew and I shared. Drew was shoved into a tux that looked like it was about to burst off of him, and Lore looked amazing in a plain black dress that came to mid-thigh, her hair, hanging over her right eye, freshly dyed electric teal.

"Guys, I'm good," Neal laughed. "I don't need any more psyching."

"Naw, this is a big deal, man," Drew said, clapping Neal on the back with one of his ham-sized hands. "What's your date's name again?"

"Tristan," Neal said, blushing again. "I met him in my anatomy drawing class."

"Yeah you did!" Lore yelled, holding her hand up for a high five that, eventually, Drew had to claim.

"And he's meeting us there?" Drew asked, straightening his tie.

"Yeah," Neal replied, looking at himself in the mirror for the first time since we'd finished assembling his outfit like Cinderella's pet mice. He was wearing a black suit with a dark green vest and bowtie, a rental which we'd helped him pick out a week before. His hair was trimmed and dyed its usual jet black. He'd put in simple black ear studs to replace the skulls he usually wore.

"Whaddya think?" He asked.

"Well, I'm not the best judge of male attractiveness," Drew said, "but…."

"I am!" Lore chirped. "And right now, you look like you're cosplaying as the general concept of sex. Damn, dude!"

Neal looked in my direction, expectantly.

"I…," I stammered. "You look very nice, Neal. Tristan won't know what hit him."

"Speaking of," Drew said, looking at his watch, "we'd better get doing."

"Abby, are you seriously not going to come with us?" Lore asked, tilting her head to the side like a confused puppy. "This is like...your thing. You helped plan it and everything!"

"I'm good," I said with a smile.

"Lydia will probably be there," Lore said in a sing-song way. Lydia was a girl from my Fiction Writing class whom I had made the mistake of exchanging flirtations with in front of Lore. We did eventually date for about a month, but it

was hardly anything to write home about.

"Then I'll spare her having to see me dance," I said. "I'm good, you three go have fun."

Lore made her face look like a Tragedy mask and mimed a single tear rolling down her cheek.

"Okay," she said. "Well, if you change your mind...."

"Uh huh," I nodded as she and Drew left the room.

"Hey, Neal, hold up a second," I said as he was sliding out the door.

"Yeah?"

"You got this," I said, looking him in the eye. "I know you're more nervous than you want to let on, but you got this, okay? And if he turns out to be a dud, come back here and we'll play Starcraft all night and say mean things about him."

"Thanks, Abra," Neal laughed. He paused in the doorway, like he wanted to say something, but then turned and left.

The room empty, I flopped down into my desk chair and opened up ebay, checking on my auctions. I had several scholarships, but a large part of my college career had been financed by selling used toys on the internet. I had a handful of GI Joe figures up for bid at the time, most sitting at about $10 but one up around $50. The tens would catch up; they always did. I knew how to sell even back then, maybe the only gift I'd ever inherited from my father, who had made his living selling furniture for commission.

About half an hour after my friends had left, I had moved from watching my auctions to half-heartedly painting a pewter gaming figurine silver, which was, in retrospect, somewhat redundant. Part of me wished I had gone to the dance with them, but the other, louder part of me (the part that remembered my crippling social anxiety and utter lack of coordination or rhythm) knew I had made the right decision. Still, it would have been nice to get out of the dorm for something other than class.

As if reading my thoughts, the phone rang.

"Hello?" I said into the cordless handset.

"Abra, it's Lore," her voice said over the phone, distorted by loud techno music in the background. "You need to get down here."

"Yeah, no," I said, slumping back into my chair.

"Yeah yes!" Lore snapped.

"Whoa, okay, what's going on?"

"Tristan didn't think it was a date," Lore hissed into the phone. "He showed up with another guy. He thought he and Neal would just 'hang out' at some point in the evening, whatever the hell that means."

"Oh, fuck," I groaned as my heart sank into my abdomen. "Poor Neal!"

"Damn right 'poor Neal,'" Lore said. "Drew and I are trying to cheer him up, but he's doing his stoic Zen-master thing. So put on something pretty and get your butt down here!"

"I'll be at the Field House as soon as I can." I sighed.

"Good!" Lore exclaimed. "Hurry!"

I only had one thing that counted as 'pretty,' a dark chocolate brown dress that my sister had handed down to me because she said it went with my eyes better. I scrambled to peel off my hoodie and jeans and throw it on along with a pair of leggings before realizing that the only shoes I owned were two pairs of Converse, the beat-up ones and the really beat up ones. Putting on the nicer of the two, I rushed out of the room and down the hall to the stairs, ignoring the sarcastic wolf-whistles of two of my transphobic hall-mates on the way out.

Although it was only about a ten-minute walk across campus to the Field House, it was also February, and not a warm one. The night was clear and crisp, and stung my bare arms as I hustled down the foot paths toward the Rainbow Ball.

"You can slow down," a voice called as I reached the center of campus, a large, currently deactivated fountain with a less than impressive rose garden around it. I looked over and saw Neal sitting alone on one of the benches overlooking the fountain's pool.

"Neal," I panted, without enough breath to form a second word yet.

"Holy crap, you got dressed up," he laughed. "Lore called you, huh?"

"Yeah," I said, taking a seat next to him. "And yeah."

"Well," he exhaled, "can I do firsts, or can I do firsts?"

"That guy is an idiot," I gasped, catching my breath. "You're going to--"

"It's okay," Neal said, putting a hand up, "Lore and Drew already gave me the pep talk. Lore wanted me to find a new date right there at the dance, but I think one rejection per night is pretty much my limit."

"Yeah, but, you did it, you know?" I shrugged. "You put yourself out there. You just put yourself out there to a crappy guy. It's all easier from here."

"I guess," Neal smiled. "Can we take a moment and talk about you getting dressed up?"

"Oh shut up," I elbowed him. "It's not like I've never dressed nice before."

"You've dressed nice," Neal said, "but you haven't dressed up."

"Yeah, well," I said, feeling my face flush, "shut up."

"You look really nice," he said, quietly. "Thanks for coming out to rescue me."

"You'd have done it for me," I shrugged. "But you would have come along to make sure it went well. I'm sorry, Neal, I didn't consider that things might go south."

"I understand, Abra," Neal assured me. "And I'm really fine. There will be *others."*

"Damn right there will be," I said. "Lore was right, you probably could have hooked another there at the dance. You're giving me *grief about how fancy I look? Sheesh! This dress is, however, not warm, so if we could meander in the direction of shelter…."*

"Sure," Neal nodded. "Hey, the dining hall is open all night, you want get something to eat?"

"Yeah, I could go for some cardboard pizza and stale fries," I said. "You want to stop by the dorm and get changed first?"

Neal paused and looked out over the still water of the fountain's basin.

"No," he finally said. "But here."

He pulled off his suit jacket and laid it over my bare shoulders. I opened my mouth to thank him, but he was already ahead of me, moving toward the dining hall. So I just enjoyed the new warmth that was wrapped around me and ran to catch up.

I woke up to the most heavenly smell on Earth: breakfast foods cooking. If I get to heaven and God doesn't smell like pancakes and bacon, I'm going to be extremely disappointed. I bolted up from my bed and then stopped cold as I noticed the large, blue-black stain on my pillow. I had fallen asleep as a crow. I grabbed my clothes for the day and swung into the bathroom. Lore's hard work was now a smear of blue with a top coat of ink black. I looked less like a crow and more like a Smurf committing a hate crime. A large amount of washing later, I was ready to face society again (though my sink paid the price).

"Good morning," I called as I ran down the stairs.

"Abra!" Lore yelled from the kitchen, "It's breakfast day!"

"It sure is!" I exclaimed, sliding past Drew at the stove, tossing a pancake. The batter he used was his mom's secret recipe, but I could never remember which mom.

"I figured it was the only way to get everyone out of bed today," Drew said, flopping the pancake onto a platter that was already piled high. "Coffee's on, and there's bacon in that foil-covered tray."

"That might be the hottest thing you've ever said," Lore told her husband, sliding up behind him and goosing him with one hand while she grabbed a strip of bacon with the other.

"Holy crap, is it breakfast day?" Neal yelled, rounding the corner into the kitchen.

"It sure is! Drew's winning 'best roommate' today!" I said, filling my plate with pancakes and bacon.

"Glad I can serve a purpose for y'all. But if I can be serious for just a split second," Drew said, lowering his head, "while you enjoy these pancakes, take a second to think a good thought about my mom. It's her recipe."

Drew kissed his fingers and extended them to the sky. That answered that. Drew's mom Cassandra, a bubbly, outgoing woman who greeted everyone with at least three hugs and wanted to hear the life story of everyone she'd ever met, had passed away three years prior after a short battle with ALS. His remaining mom, Loretta, who was quieter and more reserved than her spouse had been, lived alone one town over, near the college, where she taught biology.

"To Cassandra," I said, raising my Garfield coffee mug.

"To Cassandra!" Everyone agreed, mugs and orange juice glasses lifting high.

"So, is the rib marinade you make her recipe, too?" Neal asked, filling his plate with pancakes.

"No, that comes from my other mom," Drew said. "Pretty much any of the breakfast and baked goods came from Cassandra, Loretta did all of the main courses and sides."

"Well, if you ever follow through with your plan of opening a restaurant, you know I'll be there," Neal said, sliding into a seat at the table. Drew turned beet red.

"Well...not really a restaurant," he muttered, looking at his feet. "More like...I dunno, a bakery? With breakfast food and coffee."

A look exchanged between him and Lore did not go unnoticed. I decided to change the subject for them.

"So, what was the mystery object you found out at Rag Pickers yesterday, Neal?" I asked between bites of bacon.

"Um, it's...I think maybe you'd prefer I just show you in private," Neal mumbled, turning the same color Drew had.

"I appreciate it," I shrugged, "but I'm curious now. This is a safe space, Neal; come join our trust circle."

To illustrate, Drew, Lore and I formed a haphazard ring with our arms around the table.

"Okay," Neal chuckled. "I'll be right back, it's in my room."

We waited while Neal clomped through the living room, down the hall and then back again. He emerged holding an enormous, ragged cardboard box.

"Hey look!" Lore exclaimed, "Neal found us a big box of the hantavirus!"

"That's probably not far from the truth," Neal said. "I'm going to set it down away from the food. Abra, you want to come look?"

I sure did. Setting down my coffee, I slid away from the table and joined Neal on the floor, next to the box. At first glance, it wasn't anything special; just a standard box full of junk store garbage. There was an old hairbrush, a few water damaged paperbacks, what looked to be some VHS tapes, a dented-up jewelry box--

My blood froze. The jewelry box was upside down among the mess, but there was something startlingly familiar about the part of it I could see. I glanced back at the brush, which I realized I'd seen before, too.

"Neal," I said, my chest tightened.

"What's wrong?" Lore asked, coming over from the table.

"If I turn that box over…?" I finished.

"Yeah," Neal whispered.

"Okay, hold still," Gwen said, running a foam brush under my left eye. "We're almost done. This is called a smokey-eye look."

"And that's a good thing, right?" I asked, keeping my face as still as possible. I wasn't allowed to look in the mirror until she was done. "Smoke in the eyes doesn't strike me as something you'd want."

"Yes, it's a good thing" Gwen groaned. "You're going to look great."

"Yeah," I sighed, "and then I'm going to have to destroy all of your hard work and go back to dressing like a dude before Dad decides to wander upstairs."

"I know," Gwen conceded. "I know it's hard. Soon, though. Soon you'll be out of the house and you can live however you want all the time. Until then, I'll try to give you as many 'girl times' as I can. And don't worry about Dad; the Rangers are playing a double-header today, so he's dead to the world. Last I saw, he was firmly bonded with his recliner and already had three empty cans next to him."

That was *pretty good insurance. If there was a very unlikely fire and Dad could have saved either Gwen and me or the Texas Rangers, the folks at Arlington would be letting him throw out the first pitch at the next game. He even sprung for the special cable package that let him watch all their games, even though we lived in Seattle Mariner country. As I recalled, the Rangers were playing the Mariners (or, as my Dad called them, "The fucking Mariners! Bunch of faggots!") that day, which further ensured he was planted for at least four hours.*

"Okay, done. Voilà!" Gwen said, stepping back and spinning my chair around to face the mirror on her vanity. I lost my breath; I looked amazing. For the first

time ever, I saw the me I saw in my mind staring back at me in the mirror. My hair was much shorter then (Dad wouldn't stand for his 'son' having long hair "like some hippie faggot." Dad had favorite words.), but she had swooped it over to the side, and worked it into a more feminine style. I was wearing the A-line chocolate brown dress that wouldn't officially become mine until my next birthday.

"What do you think?" Gwen asked, biting her lip. "Is the eye-stuff too much? I can tone it down a bit if you want."

"No," I said, barely above a whisper. "It's...wonderful. I... it's me. That's me in the mirror."

"It sure, is, sis," Gwen said, leaning in and kissing my cheek. "Is it okay that I'm a little mad that that dress looks better on you than it did on me?"

We both laughed and kept staring into the mirror, amazed by what we were seeing. Maybe if we hadn't been so entranced, we would have heard the phone ring downstairs. Or the door to Gwen's room open.

"Gwen," a slurred voice called from the now open door. I froze. I was in full view, there was nothing to hide behind. Gwen stepped in front of me.

"Dad!" she yelped. "What...what's up?"

"Your boyfriend is on the phone," Dad slurred, then looked over Gwen's shoulder. "What the fuck is going on here?"

We were both frozen. My mouth hung open, but no words even tried to come out.

"Get that shit off you," Dad shook his head. "You look like a fucking retard."

Before we could even think about responding, he staggered away, back down the stairs. I started to sob as soon as his footsteps were no longer audible.

"Hey," Gwen implored, hugging me. "Hey. He's an asshole. He's a drunken asshole who's mad that the world doesn't work the way he was always told it would work. Don't listen to a goddamn thing he says."

I nodded, trying to stop the tears that were causing globs of mascara to run down my face. Gwen kissed my forehead.

"Here," she said. "I was going to give you something before Dad interrupted us. It belonged to Mom, and I want you to have it."

She reached into her jewelry box and produced a silver necklace with a butterfly pendant, a small blue topaz set at its center. Gently, she placed it around my neck, and clasped it.

"Remember who you are," she said, nose to nose with me. "Even when you can't look like this, you're still you."

I nodded and watched her walk back over to her jewelry box to close the wooden lid, the abalone "GEC" inlay flashing in the vanity light as she did.

I sat on the kitchen floor holding my sister's jewelry box. Part of the inlay on the lid was chipped away, but the groove still remained.

"What does GEC stand for?" Drew asked.

"Gwendolyn Elise Collins," I said as tears started to run down my cheeks. "My sister. This was my sister's jewelry box."

"Shit," Drew whispered. "Why was it at a junk store?"

"When my sister...when what happened, happened," I said, crying harder despite my best efforts. I motioned for Neal.

"Abra's father gathered up all of her sister's things and threw them away," Neal continued from my stopping point. "He and Abra weren't speaking at that point, and he just dumped it all before she could go through it. We only found Snooty Crow because it was hidden in a little compartment their dad didn't know about. Junk store stuff, it, like, circulates. Dealers buy it in lots, sell what they can, dump the rest on someone else. It has probably been bouncing from person to person for years."

I was still holding the jewelry box, which was now empty, no doubt ransacked before being tossed into the junk crate. The silver butterfly pendant felt suddenly heavy against my sternum, where it had rested every day since Gwen had removed it from this very box and placed it around my neck.

"Abra, there's…more." Neal said softly. Setting down the jewelry box, I looked back into the tangle of my sister's old possessions. A purple and blue lamp that had sat on her desk, a faded pink My Little Pony with most of its hair long since combed out, her "Mathlete of the Year" award from eleventh grade. The random, sundry scraps of Gwen's existence, moldering away in a junk store cardboard box.

"The tapes," Neal whispered. I had registered the VHS videos, about ten lined up along the side of the box, but hadn't thought much about them. I figured they were my sister's scant movie collection. Ghostbusters, Airplane!, Aliens, The Breakfast Club, a few others. But when I picked one up, I didn't discover a professionally printed label. Instead, I saw a plain white sticker with a quick ballpoint pen drawing of a Sacred Heart with two crows inside of it.

"Hey," Lore said, looking over my shoulder, "that's your tattoo! From the tape you have. I didn't know there were more of them."

"There were," I said, picking up another tape and finding a similar drawing. A smile formed on my face through the tears. "But I thought they were gone forever. Holy shit."

I sat there in shock, looking over a series of tapes of our homemade movies that I thought had ceased to exist long ago. The one tape that I had saved, the one I had given to Calli to base my shoulder tattoo on, featured Gwen at about ten as an evil sorceress and me at about six as both her hunchbacked sidekick and the valiant warrior who was on a quest to stop her. It was only luck that I had happened to have it with me, it having been accidentally placed in a box that I took with me to college, allowing it to avoid the purge.

"We've gotta watch these," Drew exclaimed. "That other one was gold. I mean, uh, when you're ready to watch them, of course."

"We will, definitely. Neal...I can't thank you enough for finding this. This is amazing." I said, being bombarded with about every possible emotion all at once. I put down the tape in my hand and picked up another, from the far end of the row. Turning it over, I paused at the label.

"Huh, that's different," Drew mused, seeing the same thing I did. The drawing on the label was similar but not the same. The Sacred Heart was still there, but there was only one crow inside it, and instead of being feathered and slightly sarcastic looking, like the ones on the other tapes, it was just a crow skull.

"Yeah," I said, still studying the drawing. Keeping the tape in hand, I flipped through a few of the other black plastic rectangles. Most of them had our standard two-crow drawing, the crows being Gwen and me, and the Sacred Heart representing our family. It had been Gwen's idea, after Snooty Crow became hidden contraband. It was our first (certainly not our last) big secret together, and she called us the Society of the Heart of Crows. The symbol came first. I never claimed we were normal kids.

Only on the last one had the drawing switched to the crow skull version.

"I don't know what this is," I said, mostly to myself.

"You're going to have to find something to play it on, first," Drew said. "Our old VCR crapped out years ago. Maybe we could stop by a thrift store, or…?"

"I actually have a VCR back at Cluster," I said, still staring at the tape. "I use it to make sure old tapes that come through work."

"People buy old VHS tapes?" Lore asked.

"Just the Star Wars trilogy. It's one of the only ways to get the original cut," I explained.

"So...do you want to go now, or…?" Neal asked.

"Yeah," I said, then shook my head. "No. Shit, I got to get into a better head-space first."

"Sure, we get you," Drew said. "So what do you want to do?"

"Finish breakfast," I said, setting the tape back down in the box. "This is incredible, but nothing is worth cutting Breakfast Day short."

"So say we all," Lore said, heading back to the table. "Pro tip: If you eat a piece of bacon at the same time you eat a bite of pancake, you'll kiss God."

"You're my favorite theologian, Lore," I laughed, returning to my seat and cutting off a piece of pancake. Neal sat down in the chair next to me, giving me a look while Drew and Lore devoured their breakfasts. I gave him our childhood secret signal, a rolling blink starting with the left eye and moving to the right. It was our "aloha," and in this case, it read, "I'm okay."

Dad didn't come to Gwen's college graduation. The two of them had had a huge blow-up the night before at a party thrown in her honor after Dad had made a crack about her degree being mostly his accomplishment, since he was the one who 'made' her. What resulted was a fight that topped the already impressive list of their battles, during which I seriously considered coming out as trans, because after "you drunken, Neanderthal piece of shit, the whole world doesn't deserve to be miserable just because your dick doesn't work anymore," I doubted anything would seem shocking. By the time we reached "you're nothing but an uppity little rotten cunt," most of the other guests had dispersed, leaving only dearest Dad, Gwen, Gwen's boyfriend Brock, Neal, and me. Brock, who, at the time, seemed to have the personality of a golden retriever, attempted to step in and play peace-maker, which just led to both *parties getting pissed at* him *until he, too, wisely stormed out.*

"Better get used to seeing that!" Dad barked, gesturing at the door slamming behind Brock. "You may think you're hot stuff, but there's no man on earth who is going to put up with your bullshit!"

"Should we...go?" Neal whispered to me as we stood plastered to the wall behind my father, watching him turn redder and redder, his face and cranium being taken over by his own bulging veins, visible through his thinning brown hair. I shook my head.

"You get a little degree, take a few cute little classes, and now you think you're something goddamn special," Dad continued. Gwen, steel in a party dress, didn't waver, but she didn't retort, either.

"You're nothing special," he spat. "You're nothing at all."

And then, eighteen years of silence, cowering, and cowardice all came to an end before I even realized what was happening.

"Shut the fuck up, you worthless old man," I said, not yelling or whispering, just steady. Neal, who had witnessed my father's rage before, gasped beside me. Gwen's eyes bulged and her face fell. My father turned like a panther sizing up its prey, fists clenched and veins throbbing. An awful thought drifted into my head, from the ether: What if he died? What if he just had a stroke or a heart attack right that minute, and just died, right there in front of us? Would we laugh? Would we cry? In sadness or joy?

"The fuck did you say to me, boy?" He snarled, getting close enough to my face that I could smell the alcohol on his breath. Every instinct in me told me to run, to beg forgiveness, to say "nothing" and look at my feet. Yet, instead....

"I said you're a worthless old man, and I'm tired of listening to you," the words tumbled out of me. "And nothing Gwen or I will ever accomplish has anything to do with you, because--"

At that moment, for the first time, my father did what he'd always threatened to do. What we'd always feared he would. It was a clumsy shot, and weak, his gnarled fist popping into my left cheek, the side of my face blossoming into a quick burst of pain. I took one step back, his blow not carrying much momentum. Thinking about it now, I wonder if it was starting even then. It only took a second for me to turn back toward him, but instead of the rage-fueled beast, I saw my father backed against a wall with Gwen standing in front of him. She didn't have a finger on him; she didn't have to. She had tapped into some almost otherworldly power. Her anger had suddenly abated, replaced by a cold, terrifying calm.

"Never. Again." She growled, her voice smooth and low. "Do you understand?"

Our father's face faltered, the rage still boiling, but something new creeping in, too.

"You don't--" he started, before being stopped without so much as a gesture.

"Never again," Gwen repeated, no different than the first time. "The two of us will be gone in two months. She'll be off to school, and once that happens, I'll leave, too. Until then, if we're in a room, you're not. Do you understand?"

Dad's lip spasmed, and I knew what it was that was infiltrating the anger. For the first time, I saw the fear Gwen always told me was there. If he'd noticed the pronoun Gwen used, he wasn't addressing it.

"This is my house," he blurted, trying to recapture some of his dignity. "I paid for it."

"And it will be all yours again, soon. All yours, all alone." Gwen said, tilting her head. "Until then, you get to enjoy different parts of it than we do. Do you understand?"

Dad stared at her. The anger had been replaced by fear, but hate remained.

"I ASKED IF YOU UNDERSTOOD!" Gwen suddenly shouted, loud enough to rattle the windows.

"Yes," Dad said, barely above a whisper.

"Good," Gwen responded, back to her calmer tone. She craned her neck to look around his head to Neal and me. "Let's the three of us go for a walk."

We didn't need to be asked twice. Sliding past my father, standing right where he had been the whole time, still fuming, we followed Gwen out the front door, pausing only for her to grab her faded blue messenger bag.

We spent about a block walking in total silence, save for our footsteps on the wet pavement. Finally, as we reached the crosswalk, Gwen spoke.

"I'm sorry the two of you had to see that," she said, her voice shaking. It was then that I first noticed she was crying. I hugged her as Neal made some paraverbal noise to indicate that it was okay.

"We'll be free soon," I whispered to my big sister as I held her. I wasn't used to being in the comforter role. "We're almost there."

She nodded, sending tear drops spattering onto my shoulder. Pulling away from me, straightening her dress and wiping her face, she turned to Neal.

"Decision time, Neal-before-Zod," she said, keeping her voice steady. "I'm guessing you've had enough of the Collins family for one night, so you can head home if you want. But my sister and I are going to go get high on the old playground, so if that doesn't sound unbearably grim to you, you're welcome to join us."

"We are?" I asked, getting a nod from Gwen in response.

"Sure," Neal shrugged, and the three of us walked the additional four blocks to what had once been called Yancy Park. Yancy park had never been impressive, even in its heyday, but ever since the town council voted to close the park and sell the land, it was little more than an overgrown field with a rusting play structure jutting out of the middle of it, along with a giant "FOR SALE" sign that, years later, had yet to bear fruit.

"Okay, this is all I have on me," Gwen said, digging into her bag and producing a Ziploc with three small joints. "So make it count."

The first puffs were glorious, not for the chemical effects but for the release that the simple ritual provided. The chemical effects were pretty nice, too, though.

"Much better," Gwen said, sitting down on the edge of one of the play structure's platforms and taking a drag.

"So, you just walk around with these?" Neal asked, removing his joint from his lips. "Isn't that...dangerous?"

"Not usually," Gwen shrugged. "I put them in there specifically for this. This was my plan even before the blow up. I had a feeling we could use some release even

if the party didn't implode."

"You packed three of them," Neal mused. "I'm...thank you."

"You're one of us, Neal," Gwen said and I nodded in agreement. "I thought you'd have realized that by now. You're family. Sorry."

"Better than the one I have," Neal sighed. "I know it's nothing compared to your dad, but at least he acknowledges your existence. Ever since I was about 13, my parents just kind of...drift...around me. I can't remember the last time we said more than three words to each other."

"To the family we make!" Gwen declared, taking a long drag and releasing a sizable cloud of smoke.

"To the family we make!" Neal and I parroted, trying and failing to produce similar clouds.

"Okay, but there's something we need to talk about," Gwen said, giving me the 'head tilted down, eyes up' look that I'd been seeing since I was born.

"What?"

"You need a pick a fucking name!" She yelled. "Seriously, I don't want to call you...you know...but I'm getting tired of referring to you only using pronouns. Back me up, Neal."

"It's...a bit tricky," Neal mumbled, looking down.

"I can't decide!" I blurted, throwing my hands in the air. "You know me; I spent a whole year deciding whether to buy an Xbox or a Playstation 2, and then I panicked and bought a Gamecube. I don't want to end up with the Gamecube of names! You only get one shot at this."

"What's your shortlist?" Gwen asked. "We'll help."

Jenny. Ezri. Jada. Sophia. Moira. Hannah. Abigail. Jacinda. Mary. Johanna. But I didn't feel like sharing. Every time I got close to declaring one my new name, I suddenly decided it was stupid and retreated back.

"I...I don't have one," I muttered.

"Okay," Gwen said, puffing at her joint. "Well, then I'm going to call in Big Sister Privilege and help you. Your name is now...Abra."

"What?" I asked, stunned. "Abra? Like Abracadabra?"

"Well, I was thinking more like the character from East of Eden,*" Gwen shrugged, "but now that you say it, yes: Abra as in Abracadabra. As in, abracadabra, I just gave you a new name."*

My mouth hung open, trying to think of an objection.

"If you have a better name, this is the time. Trial by fire, kid." Gwen said. "Speak now or forever hold your peace."

My mind a blank, I turned to Neal.

"I... kind of like it," he said, still looking down but meeting my eyes.

I still felt I should object just on the grounds that I hadn't had any input, but it was strangely catchy.

"Okay," I said, finally. "I guess I'm Abra."

"Nice to meet you, Abra," Gwen proclaimed, sticking out her hand, which I took and gave an exaggerated shake. Neal and I did the same a moment later. The three of us stayed out on the playground long after the pot was gone, for what seemed like at least two hours, talking about everything from my sluggish transition to Neal's feud with our high school art teacher. Gwen skillfully avoided having the conversation turn to her future plans, instead entertaining us with tales of the adventures she and her dormmates had had during her first two years of college. At midnight, Neal decided it was finally time for him to head home and said his goodnights, leaving Gwen and me to walk back to our house just the two of us.

"There's another thing we need to talk about," Gwen said on the way back.

"What?" I asked.

"Neal."

"What do you mean?"

"No," Gwen snapped. "Don't play dumb. You're better than that. You know what I mean. You and I can both see the way he looks at you. You should have seen him after Dad punched you. Half of why I stepped in was to keep him from murdering our father. How is your cheek, by the way?"

"Pretty good," I shrugged. "Dad's not great at punching."

"Well, anyway," Gwen said, "you know this isn't a new thing, right? That boy has looked at you like that for a long time."

"Yeah," I sighed, looking at the ground. "I know."

"So, what are you going to do about it?" my sister asked, stopping us in the middle of the sidewalk.

"I don't know," I said, honestly. "He's my best friend. But I don't--."

"I understand," Gwen put up a hand. "But do you love him?"

"Yes," I answered, without hesitation. "But not like that."

"Abra," Gwen put a hand on my shoulder and looked at the ground. "There may come a day--no, I think there will *come a day when, because you love him, you'll have to make a real hard decision. Because he won't."*

As usual, my sister was right, but at that moment, as much as I loved her, I hated her for it.

"I've been thinking about your *And All the Rest* problem," I said to Neal as we walked toward Cluster. Drew and Lore were taking the day to drive up to Comstock to see Drew's mom, Loretta, so the two of us decided to go examine the mystery tape on our own.

"Oh yeah?" Neal said.

"Yeah," I nodded. "So, back a few arcs ago, you had that minor villain, the one who could mimic anyone?"

"Visage, yes."

"Yeah, Visage," I said. "Well, could you say that Red had been kidnapped and replace with Visage, and he was trying to sow discord in the group by confessing feelings to Shade?"

"I could," Neal nodded. "It's not a terrible idea. Still feels like kind of a cop out, though. Lore had an idea, but it's bold, and I'm still processing it."

"That's...most of Lore's ideas," I said.

"Yeah," Neal replied. "Hey, you're not still, like, into her, right?"

"Nah, not for a long time," I waved him off. Drew and Lore had met after I had asked Lore to come study in our dorm room for a final in a class the she and I shared. My plan was to study with her, ask her out for dinner afterward, and then go from there. It... did not play out that way. I was mostly fine with it, but then a few years later, some weird feelings had bubbled up and suddenly I was all about Lore again. Thankfully, though, that stupidity wasn't long-lived.

"I mean, I understood it," Neal shrugged. "She's awesome and she looks like some kind of moon-pixie."

"Well...," I paused, "yeah, wait, that's exactly what she looks like. Wow, I didn't even know I was into that."

"What about Calli?" asked Neal. "I heard the two of you were having coffee the other day."

"That's just our monthly trans-lunch," I responded. "And no. No no no. No."

"You're still, like, painfully attracted to her, though, right?"

"Yeah," my shoulders slumped. "But once you get past her looks and the immense amount of Olympic-level sex we had, we're just different people. I'm a hopeless nerd, and she's…a fashion-obsessed reality TV junkie who occasionally commits felonies. But anyway, why am I being grilled here? What about you? Anyone new since Sofie?"

"Nah," Neil shook his head. "There's a girl at the front desk of one of the churches I do design work for who always flirts with me, but that's about it. Unless something magic happens, I think Sofie put me off dating for a while."

"Fair enough," I nodded. "What about...I don't suppose you've heard anything from…Dan?"

Neal's face grew dark.

"Let's leave that one be," he said, lowering his tone. Taken slightly aback, I nodded, and we walked the rest of the way to Cluster in silence. His mood had shifted back by the time we got there, using the back entrance and leaving the doors locked and the windows closed since we had decided not to open the store that day. Walking back to my sanctum, Neal grabbed a chair from the coffee shop area and dragged it in. Moving my chair from around the back of my counter and setting up the little TV/VCR combo that I had long ago rescued from the garbage, I reached into my messenger bag--blue, like Gwen's, but a different one--and produced the mystery tape.

"I'll only ask this once," Neal said, standing next to me, "are you sure you're ready for this?"

"I'm sure," I replied. "Or, at least I'm sure I'm never going to be *more* ready. Besides, this is probably just her singing along with the radio or something. It's just...going to be nice to see her again.

"Okay," Neal said, taking a seat as I inserted the tape. "But, it's not like I'd think less of you if you need to turn it off at some point."

"I know," I said. "Thank you for doing this with me. I don't think I could have watched it alone, and Drew and Lore didn't know her like we did."

"They missed out," Neal lamented as I pushed play and took a seat next to him.

A quick burst of tracking static over a black screen gave way to my sister backing away from the camera, sitting on her bed.

I started to cry, my resolve not as strong as I hoped it was. She was older than she had been in the tapes we had made as kids, college age by the looks of it. She looked just how I remembered her, sitting on her bed with its faded blue and purple comforter, an old Discman resting on a pillow next to her. She had on a severely distressed tank with screen print of Shepard Fairey's "Andre the Giant has a Posse" design, one of her favorite tops.

"Hi, camera," Gwen said, looking directly into the lens. I'd forgotten her voice, even though I thought I'd remembered it. A sweet but sharp tone that told the world she wasn't looking for a fight, but she'd been fucked with for the last time.

"Jesus," Neal whispered. "I forgot how pretty she was."

Pretty was underselling her. While we both got mom's raven hair and brown eyes, I was stuck with dad's pasty Irish complexion and sharp, pointy face. Gwen got both Mom's rich, caramel skin and her soft, graceful features. She had never had a shortage of admirers. There were probably scores of horribly written poems about her scattered in comp books throughout the state.

"So," Gwen continued, talking to the camera, "I need to talk to someone, but I can't afford a shrink for myself, my friends are stupid, my dad's a drunk asshole, and my brother--"

On the screen, Gwen grabbed her hair and started swearing.

"Shit!" Shit shit fuck!" she yelled. "Sister! My sister. Fucking shit, Gwen, you know this."

She proceeded to hit herself in the forehead several times. I wanted to reach back through time and tell her it was okay, that she was learning, that we were both learning, and that no gender-slip could ever cancel out everything she had done for me. My heart hurt watching how upset she was getting.

"My sister," she said, calming down again. "Can't talk to her. So, someone told me once that it helps to tape yourself talking things out, so you can watch it later, and that's how pathetically desperate I am right now. So."

I shouldn't watch this, was my first thought, but my selfishness won out. After losing her years before, my sister, or at least a tiny scrap of her, was back.

"So," continued Gwen on the tape, "where am I? I still live at home with my asshole father because I can't afford a place of my own yet, because I don't have a job, because I just graduated with a computer science degree that my advisor assured me is 'the next booming field,' but apparently someone forgot to tell Brahmton that. My friends have all moved away. My sister, whom I stuck around for, has now gone off to college herself, and I'm just...alone."

My heart ached even more. My first year of college, I had been too busy to come home much. I figured that Gwen was happy to have some time away from her dorky little sister. I never imagined she would be lonely.

"Except for Brock, but it's not fair to put everything on him. He can't be my only friend." Gwen played with the edge of her comforter as she spoke. "When he finishes up next year, he wants us to move to Portland, where his family lives. I... I think he's planning on proposing to me after he graduates."

The insides of me twisted like a dishrag being rung out. That never happened, and he didn't graduate.

"And I think I'll say yes," Gwen continued. "He's a good guy, sweet...kind...."

Neal clamped a hand onto my shoulder, and I dug my nails into my thigh.

"No, he's not who I pictured myself with when I was in high school," Gwen shrugged, "but what are my chances of *actually* meeting Chris Cornell, right? Brock loves me, and that's what matters, and--"

Gwen paused and looked down at her own knees, folded under her on the bed. When she looked up again, tears were running from her eyes.

"Oh, fuck this," Gwen's voice wavered through tears. "I'm talking to a fucking camera; why can't I just be honest? Fine...I'm pregnant."

In that moment, after the words, spoken years ago, slipped from my dead sister's lips, the whole universe collapsed on itself. Everything folded in, moons, planets, galaxies, the reality beyond reality, every last thing swirled and condensed again, and again, and again, down to the size of a single atom, which then split and detonated within my skull.

"Abra, did...what?" Neal stammered. Gwen on the tape was crying, and I couldn't make the words come to answer Neal's half-formed question. No, I had never known she was pregnant. She had never told me, and there was nothing on her autopsy report. Based on what she was saying, the tape had only been shot a few months before her death.

"I'm not ready for this," Gwen cried. "I like kids, but I'm not ready. Brock doesn't know. He'd want me to keep it; he wants a family. I do, too, but...not like this. I know what I need to do, but...holy fuck Catholic upbringing fucks you up! I wish I could tell Abra. We don't hide things from each other, but this...I miss my sister. I want to tell her so many things, but it's hard because I don't want to hurt her."

There was a burst of static that startled both Neal and me. The screen went black for a second and then a picture reappeared.

It was Alex Rodriguez, then shortstop for the Texas Rangers, swinging at a pitch and sending it "all the way to the moon" the announcer yelled. I jumped at the VCR, mashing the fast-forward button, hoping that it was just a blip, that the rest of Gwen's tape was still intact. But instead, all I saw was a super sped-up version of a mediocre Ranger's game from 2002.

"Oh, fuck," Neal whispered. "Are you fucking kidding me?"

"No," I laughed, the manic laughter of a broken woman choosing not to scream. "No, it makes perfect fucking sense. Perfect, absolutely perfect sense."

"Jesus, Abra, I'm sorry," said Neal, walking to the TV and turning it off for me.

"It's fine," I gasped, though peels of broken laughter. "It's fucking perfect."

I looked down at the ground.

"You win, you dumb motherfucker," I yelled, all the way to hell. "You fucking win again."

Neal wrapped his arms around me as my insanity-cackling finally turned to tears. From the hottest depths of the underworld, I swore I could hear laughter.

I had officially met Brock shortly after the blow-up at the graduation party. I had seen him there, but we hadn't had a chance to actually talk. He had apologized profusely to Gwen for trying to get involved in family business, and Gwen, being Gwen, forgave him. They had been dating for about a year at that point, and while I had heard plenty about him, Gwen had been reluctant to bring her boyfriend around the house. I can't imagine why.

I met the two of them at Revive, *a small coffee shop not far from where Cluster would eventually be located. I rode my bike, chaining it up on a rack next to where Brock's pristine black Acura was parked.*

"Hey hey!" a booming voice greeted me as I entered the shop. "Finally I meet the famous Abra!"

It took a split second to remember that that was me now. Brock got up from their table at the back of the coffee shop and came forward to meet me. He looked like the standard-issue human being (Model: Caucasian, Male). He was very fit, neither tall nor short, and had blonde hair cropped into a conservative crewcut, sitting above a face that could best be described as "there." He looked like the kind of person God makes on days when He's "just not feeling it." But I tried to give him a chance, I swear.

"Hi, you must be Brock," I affirmed, in my most pleasant voice, which probably came off more as 'creepy' than anything. A quick flash of discomfort, one that I (and I assume all trans people) knew well, crossed his face. It was the spark of "EEK! What IS that?" that sneaked out right before the "I'm enlightened and totally okay with this" curtain fell back into place. Gwen had insisted that I should come as myself, which I did, in bootcut jeans and a fitted tee with a hood. Brock, she assured me, was "cool." Well.

"Nice to meet you," Brock said, almost crushing my hand as he shook it. "We'd

better get back to the table, before your sister gets all, 'What are you two talking about over there?'"

The voice he used to imitate Gwen sounded like it should be coming out of some sort of bird-monster. My first instinct was to not like him, but I tried to push past it, knowing that I still had enough of a shred of "brother" in me to be predisposed to hating my sister's boyfriends.

"Hey, sis," Gwen said, standing and hugging me as I got to the table. "I ordered your usual."

She tapped the side of the latte sitting in front of the empty chair. Thanking her, I took a seat.

"I don't get how girls can drink that froofy stuff," Brock laughed. "Just good ol' black coffee for me, thanks."

To illustrate, Brock lifted his cup to his lips, took an exaggerated drink, and then smiled like he was being paid a generous sum by the Black Coffee Council. When he went back for another drink, I shot a look at Gwen, who responded to my non-verbal "what the fuck?" with a non-verbal "Isn't he great?"

"So, Brock," I said, trying to keep upbeat, "Gwen tells me you're majoring in engineering?"

"Hell yeah," Brock exclaimed. "It's in my blood, you know? My dad, my brother, my uncles...all engineers. I'm gonna make bank. Nothing pays better than engineering. Gwen's never going to have to work a day of her life."

He punctuated this by leaning over and planting a sloppy kiss on my sister's cheek. I waited for her to respond, but she just smiled.

"Gwen's got a degree in computer science," I interjected, feeling like I was playing the part of Gwen in this conversation.

"Well, sure," Brock shrugged. "I mean, she can work if she wants, I guess. But she won't have to. *She can just stay home if she wants. Keep those stress-lines from getting any deeper."*

Oh, okay, *I thought*, Brock is about to get his ass kicked by my sister. That'll be fun to watch. *I waited for Gwen to respond.*

And waited.

And waited.

And waited. And when I couldn't wait any longer, I opened my mouth to say something. A light pat on my knee from my sister stopped me.

"Brock really loves video games," Gwen interjected. I stared at her, stunned.

"Oh, yeah, I forgot Gwen said you were super into video games," Brock grinned. "Have you played the new Madden?"

The rest of the interminable conversation covered the Seattle Seahawks, a time he and his bros got "so wasted" in Canada, half-remembered Simpsons quotes, the

Seahawks, how rich his family was, a (thankfully) brief pitstop at being "totally okay" with "the whole gay thing," the Seahawks for a third time, and how comic books are for children. Peppered throughout was a smattering of more impressions of my sister, who was apparently constantly nagging him in a screechy witch voice. The whole time, I waited for Gwen to say something, to put him in his place, to draw on the same cold steel that I had seen at the graduation party. But it never came. She just sat there, pleasantly, bursting out in forced laughter whenever she sensed that I was about to say something for her. By the time we left the coffee shop, I was confident in my decision to not like Brock.

Brock had a class back on campus, so he bid us "later" and drove off in his audacious Acura, leaving my sister and me to walk back home.

"Well…?" Gwen asked as we departed, me pushing my bike next to her.

"Gwen," I faltered, "I... I love you, you know that. And--"

"He was nervous today!" Gwen snapped. "He's not usually so…'on', but he was nervous to meet you because he knows how close we are."

"Okay," I nodded. "But I don't like how he talks to you."

"Like what do you mean?"

"The weird voice," I answered. "And the mimicking you. Acting like you're some nagging shrew."

"That's just his humor," Gwen waved off. Her voice was beginning to take on the edge that I had waited for during our coffee meeting. "We joke around with each other."

"I didn't hear you making any jokes like that," I muttered.

"Abra!" Gwen snapped. "He's a nice guy! Stop looking for things not to like about him. I get it, he's a much, much different person than you are--"

"I don't care if he's a different person than I am," I exclaimed. "I care that he seems like a different person than you are! Seriously, what the hell do you have in common?"

"I would have thought that you of all people would understand that having things in common isn't the be all and end all of relationships," Gwen seethed. "Yeah. He's different from me. But he's the right kind of different for *me. He has a lot of good qualities, and I'm sorry he wasn't showing them today. But I like him, and he's going to be a part of my life, so if you can't make yourself like him, you at least need to come to peace with that."*

I was pissed, and turned to make some cutting remark when I noticed the tears in Gwen's eyes.

"Okay," I said, shock draining the anger out of me. "Okay. Look, I didn't mean to make it sound like I hate the guy. I want you to be happy, and if he makes you happy, then...I'm happy."

"I know he didn't come off well today," admitted Gwen. "I think by next time he'll have calmed down a bit, and you can really get to know him."

"Okay," I agreed.

In the future, I would look back on that coffee as the first moment I truly knew there was something wrong. The next time I saw Brock, I certainly got to know the real him.

"That's some heavy shit," Drew said, from his computer. "I can't believe your dad taped over it."

"I wonder if he even looked at what was on the tape before," I mused. "Probably just needed a spare VHS, went up to Gwen's room and found that one. Maybe she left it in the camera and he decided it was blank."

"You okay, though?" Lore asked, leaning around her monitor. "That's a lot to take in."

"I'm fine," I asserted. "It was really good seeing her again, even if it was...yeah. If nothing else, I think we finally solved one of the lingering mysteries of that whole travesty."

Drew, Lore and Neal nodded. We never really knew what the catalyst for what happened was, and I would be lying if I said it didn't bother me. But now we had a better idea.

"Anyway," I continued. "Enough about me. How was your mom, Drew?"

"Good," Drew blurted. Another mystery look passed between him and Lore. More and more curious. "Didn't have much time to talk, had a lot of papers to grade."

"How about you, Lore," I asked. "I feel like we haven't had a chance to talk a lot lately."

"Other than the comments section on one of my makeup tutorials being overrun by trolls telling me to 'show my tits or STFU,' everything has been good," Lore replied. "But you're right, we should hang out more, just the two of us. It's been a long time since we had a good ol' fashion Monstrosity Hunt."

"Absolutely," I agreed.

"I try not to take it personally that I'm never invited on those," Drew said, explosion sounds emanating from his computer.

"Neal isn't either," Lore shrugged. "It's an AbraLore thing."

"Fine, fine," Drew muttered. "But Neal and I aren't going to invite you on the super awesome thing that we're going to be doing at the same time. It's a DrewNeal thing. A Dreal thing. Dammit, our names don't push together well."

"What awesome thing are we doing now?" Neal asked, looking up from his tablet.

"We'll figure it out," Drew said. "But it'll be awesome. Speaking of, how are the adventures of *And All the Rest* coming? You haven't posted a new page in a while."

"I know," Neal sighed.

"Still trying to dig yourself out of that hole?" Drew asked.

"Kinda," Neal admitted. "Lore and Abra both gave me ideas. I can't decide which to go with, though. So I'm drawing first pages for both and seeing what works."

"You should go with mine," Lore sing-songed. "It gets you out of your hole without retconning, and would free you from a lot of chains."

"What was your suggestion?" Drew asked.

"I--" Lore started, before being cut off by Neal shaking his head. She stopped and made a "lips are sealed" gesture.

"Jesus, am I the *only* one here without some weird secret ritual with someone?" Drew grumbled.

"Well, you and I fuck a lot," Lore offered. "So there's that."

"That is true," Drew conceded. Drew and Lore always made me smile. Being hyper-progressive, when they got married they insisted that monogamy was not going to be a societal prison that they would live in, and declared their marriage open and free. To my knowledge, neither of them had ever acted on that freedom.

"Speaking of...not that...but other secret rituals," I interjected, "Neal, take a break: it's maze time."

"Hell yeah," Neal said, turning off his tablet and dragging his chair over next to mine.

"How long have you been working on that damn thing?" Drew asked.

"Technically, since we were twelve," I responded. "But not, like, constantly. Off and on. I had the old Nintendo version back then, but it got lost in the shuffle somewhere. Hell, I guess it probably made it to Rag Pickers. I downloaded an emulated copy last week. Shh, don't tell the FBI."

"And you won't just look at a strategy guide?" Lore asked.

"Strategy guides are for the weak," Neal stated.

"Hey, I use strategy guides!" Lore protested.

"We've been working on this too long to just read the solution somewhere," I said. "We need to do this the old-fashioned way."

"Okay," Drew muttered. "You two go ahead and wander your asses around a semi-haunted maze. I've got robot Nazis to kill over here."

"To hell with your anti-Semitic robots," I declared. "Maze time."

Neal and I waited while my emulated copy of *Unwelcome* started up. We had a save file that started right at the entrance to the infernal labyrinth, which at least saved us from having to go through the first half of the game every time.

"Okay," Neal said as I clicked the 'forward' arrow at the bottom of the screen to enter the maze. "Right?"

"Sure," I said, moving the cursor over and clicking to turn right. "This is great, but it was still more fun with actual controllers."

"Aye," Neal nodded. "Okay, go straight, how about?"

"'Kay," I clicked the arrow to go straight, leading us to a corridor with a tombstone in it that, if clicked, informed you that the tombstone was "old and too worn to read. No doubt the final resting place of another lost traveler."

"Something has to happen with that tombstone, right?" I asked.

"Yeah, but we've tried everything," Neal sighed. All the possible actions for your character to take to interact with an item were listed at the bottom of the screen. We'd tried 'hit,' 'push,' 'examine,' 'take,' and everything else that made sense. The problem with *Unwelcome* was that the designers and artists working on it had done a great job of creating a rich, 'lived in' environment. Everything could be interacted with in some way, which made it hard to know what was game-critical and what was just there for flavor.

"Okay, we'll leave it alone for now," I decided. The other problem with *Unwelcome* was that the game had a time limit in the form of an unstoppable demon who was hunting you through the whole thing. If you ran out of time, it ate your soul, and you had to start over at your last save. There was no time to sit around and ponder.

"How about right again?" Neal suggested.

"Sure," I tapped the cursor on 'right.' "I hope *you're* keeping track of this."

"Only latently," Neal admitted.

Two hours and much swearing and jumping around later, we were no closer to seeing the end of the maze. Drew and Lore, however, had been highly amused by our antics, enough to stop their own games and watch us like spectators at a sporting event.

"Okay," I grunted through my teeth. "Left this time."

"Oh! Left!" Lore said, in her best sports announcer voice. "She's going with left for this one. It's a risky move, but that's what this game, nay, this life, is all about."

"Have we seen this area before?" Neal asked as we progressed into the next corridor of the crudely rendered, pseudo-3d maze. This section had a large tapestry on the wall that I didn't recall seeing, either. "This seems new."

"Do we have a breakthrough, folks?" Drew yelled with John Madden-level intensity. "Could this be it? Do you believe in miracles?"

"What do you think we should do?" I asked Neal. "Hurry, I think we're almost out of time!"

"Uh, examine it!" Neal blurted. I selected 'examine' and clicked the tapestry.

"It's an old tapestry." the game declared.

"Gee, thanks, game!" I yelled. Just then, the screen turned red and then displayed a picture of a glowing-eyed, horned demon.

"Your soul was delicious," the screen stated. *"Better luck next time."*

"Fuck!" I yelled, dragging the word out in to about ten syllables. "Fuck fuck fuck!"

"Fuck!" Neal agreed.

"Oooh!" Drew and Lore both winced. Lore took up the announcing duties. "And there you have it folks, that's it for this round. Our brave team, the Brahmton Basement-Dwellers, has taken their lumps again, leaving them with a record of oh-and-sixty-thousand or so."

"Laugh it up," Neal chuckled. "Back at it!"

"Back at it!" I agreed, raising my arm triumphantly in the air. This game wasn't going to beat us.

"You've got to admire their tenacity," Drew said, dropping his announcer voice. "But I'm hungry as hell. I think Wife-a-tron and I are going to go grab something to eat. Want us to bring you two back some burgers?"

"That actually sounds great," I admitted. Neal nodded in agreement "My purse is by the door. I should have some cash."

"Nah, it's on us," Lore laughed. "We have to pay you for the entertainment somehow."

"I won't argue with that," Neal said. "Thanks!"

"See you soon," Drew called as he and Lore headed up the stairs.

"Those two being a bit mysterious lately?" I asked once I heard the front door close and Drew's truck start.

"Yeah," Neal looked down. "I noticed that, too."

"So many secrets," I feigned sorrow. "So many secrets. What is happening to our little group? What will become of our heroes now?"

"They'll solve this fucking maze, I hope," Neal exclaimed.

"You ever worry that once this maze is done, there's like another three-fourths of the game or something?" I asked. "Like, what if this is a mid-level puzzle and we're just idiots?"

"That thought *has* occurred to me, yes," Neal confessed. "I've also wondered, what happens when we actually finish this thing?"

"You mean the maze? I dunno, more monsters and 'bring item A to location B' puzzles, I'm guessing."

"No," Neal clarified, "I mean, like, when we beat this maze, we have to celebrate somehow, right? We've been working on it since we were kids, we've got to do something."

"At this point, I imagine the joy of seeing the end of this pixelated hell is going to bring on a thirty-minute long orgasm, but after I clean up from that, sure." I said. "What do you have in mind?"

"I don't know," Neal said. "It seems too big to just say we'd go out for celebratory pizza or something."

"Right. So, trip to Paris it is," I nodded.

"Not unless you've found a bag of money you haven't told me about," Neal laughed. "What if we thought smaller and just went to Seattle for the weekend or something?"

"That...actually sounds like fun," I decided. "Just go and live it up. Do all the stupid touristy things, go to a Mariners game just to piss off my father in hell, hang out on the waterfront...yeah, I can get behind this plan."

"We can go somewhere nice, too," Neal said. "Like for dinner. They have a ton of nice restaurants."

"Well, I'm loathe to dress fancy," I said. "But for you and the maze, sure."

A flash of that old look crossed Neal's face before he forced it away. He'd gotten good at that in the years since Gwen had confronted me about it. So good, in fact, I had decided that he was probably past any feelings he might have once had and decided we didn't *need* to talk about. I found myself very easy to deceive. But, occasionally, the old look danced on by, like it had just done, and it both broke my heart and tapped at my conscience. I knew what needed to be done, but it was, for many reasons, the last thing I wanted to. So, once again, I took the coward's way out and let it lie.

On the screen, the maze started up again.

"You know," Neal sighed, "Seattle sounds fun and all, but sometimes I worry we're never going to get out of this stupid thing."

"I'm just saying, the Goonies' lives definitely suck now," Drew said, reclining on his bunk.

"You mean, like, the actors who played the Goonies?" Neal asked while he and I half-played a game of Quake on our computers.

"Naw, man, I mean, like, the characters," Drew sat up and leaned over the rail. "Just...what's it got to be like to have had that kind of adventure that young in life? They weren't superheroes or aliens or anything, they were just normal kids who had a crazy experience, but how do you live with that?"

"I kinda get that," I said. "Like, now that they're all grown up, do they get together and say, 'hey, fellow goonies...remember that time we all found a fucking pirate treasure? Well, I'm a shift manager at Applebees now'? How could you go through life listening to Doug from HR *talk about his 'crazy weekend' on the golf course when you had foiled an evil crime family as a kid?"*

"Right," said Drew. "It's like, how are you not constantly asking yourself 'is this really all there is for the rest of my life?' You'd have to become some sort of vapor-locked person."

"I don't even want to hear what you two have to say about ET*," muttered Neal. I was about to respond that Elliot almost certainly grew up to be some unhinged conspiracy nut, but the sharp, tinny tones of my cellphone's ringtone (a midi version of* Paint it Black*) interrupted me.*

"This has to be Lore, right?" I muttered, grabbing the flip-phone from my desk. "Everyone else who would call me after eight is in this room."

"Lore has got night class," Drew shook his head as I checked the green and black display. No name came up, but a very recognizable number.

"Oh what the living fuck," I blurted.

"What is it?" asked Neal.

"It's my dad's number. Why the fuck is he calling me?"

The phone continued to ring in my hand. I hadn't spoken to my father--not a single word--since the night of Gwen's graduation party. Against my better judgement, I mashed the "answer" button.

"Hello?"

"You need to come home. Now." My father's voice groaned on the other end. He sounded tired, even for him.

"I don't have time for this," I sighed. "You're drunk. Don't call--"

"Gwen's dead!" Dad yelled.

What happened next was a messy blur of noises and light. I remember screaming. I remember babbling to Neal and Drew about what had happened. I remember Neal having to pretty much carry me to Drew's truck--the only vehicle we had access to. I remember Drew not knowing what to say, so instead just keeping his eyes on the road and going as fast as he could without adding three more to the night's body count. I remember Neal sitting in the back seat with me, holding my hands in his and crying along with me.

There was a single police car outside my house when we got there, its lights off. Neal and Drew asked me if I wanted them to come with me, and I remember shaking my head, so they waited in the truck as I staggered out and up the walk to my childhood home, which now seemed like an alien structure on some distant planet.

The door was unlocked, so I just went in. My father was sitting at the kitchen table, a youthful man with a clerical collar sitting next to him, two stone faced detectives questioning him. His face was drenched with tears.

"Excuse me," one of them, a tall man with silver hair, called out, heading towards me from the kitchen. "You can't be in here."

"That's my son," my father said. "It's okay."

The detective looked me over, furrowing his brow. I became acutely aware that I was in full girl-mode, the first time I ever had been like that in that house. Outside of my sister's room, at least.

"Oh...okay," the detective said, trying to keep the confusion out of his voice. "Martinez, why don't you take Mr. Collins out to the car to look at some photos. I'd like to ask this one some questions."

"You got it," Detective Martinez, a stern-looking Hispanic woman, said. "Come with me, Sam. I can pull up the pictures we need you to look at on the laptop in our car. You need a coat?"

My dad, followed by the silent priest, shook his head as he was led past me, and then stopped, his face twisting into a scowl as he stared at me.

"For fuck sake," he said, looking me up and down, his face wet and twisted. "Why the hell couldn't it have been you?"

"This way, Mr. Collins," Detective Martinez insisted, shooting me a sympathetic look as she walked past.

I have another task for you. I want you to look up how long it takes to strangle someone with your bare hands. I'm not going to tell you; I had to look it up, so do you. Suffice to say, it's not like in the movies, a quick closing of the hands, a gurgle and pop, then unconsciousness and death, all over in ten seconds. Take that number you found, that number that may not seem large at first blush. Find an object that has a little bit of weight to it, but not too much, something easy to lift. A two-liter bottle of soda, a somewhat sizable hardback book, whatever. Now hold it in your hand, palm facing down, arm outstretched. Set a timer equal to the number you just looked up, the number of minutes it took my sister to die in the hands of someone she loved.

Your arm starts getting tired pretty quick, doesn't it? Keep holding it. Think about how the seconds seem to move slower. Think about how you could, if you chose, let go at any time, how there is nothing forcing your hand to keep doing what it is doing. But don't; keep holding it. Think about a human throat in your hand, instead of whatever object you picked up. And not just any human throat, the throat of someone who you claim to love. Someone who took care of you when you got the flu. Someone who learned to love football so she could spend more time with you. Someone who spent months knitting you a sweater for Christmas in your favorite colors. Someone who was going to spend the rest of her life with you. How heavy is that thing in your hand getting? Wouldn't it feel good to let it go?

As the muscles in your hand get tighter, imagine you are looking into her eyes, deep brown eyes, watching the panic in them as the light fades. Watching tiny blood vessels burst and you could just stop and let go of that thing in your hand but you don't you just keep holding it and watching. Watching as the life ebbs out of her, watching as her incredible ability to solve any computer problem, her love of making nachos on summer days, her habit of swearing in traffic, her affinity for trashy horror paperbacks, her need to win every argument, her jokes that could make you laugh yourself to tears, her perfectly done cartoon voices, her ability to parallel park in one shot, her love of singing along to the radio and changing the lyrics of songs to be about her life, her fire, her passion, her vulnerabilities, her hopes and dreams and fears and loves and joys all extinguishing and you're still fucking holding on and don't you dare stop.

Your arm starting to hurt? Is it at the point where it would be easier to let go than it is to hold on? Let go and heal, let go and move on? But you don't. And that's how she died. That's how the woman who helped me learn to ride a bike, the woman who didn't make fun of me when I cried at *Bambi*, the woman who showed me how to set the marshmallows in my hot cocoa just right, the woman who never got tired of being called in to finish difficult video game levels, the woman who read me the Lord of the Rings books and let me read her the Harry Potters, the woman who stayed up with me and said mean things about the first girl to dump me, the woman who spent her entire life using herself as a barrier between my father and me, the woman who let me be myself even when it was hard for her to understand, the woman who loved me when no one else would, could, or should have, that's how she died. With the hands of a worthless viper of a man wrapped around her throat, tight enough that they could identify his fingerprints from the bruise pattern. She died in the hands of a man she had been foolish enough to give her heart. He could have let go at any time. It would have been easy--easier, even. He chose not to. We never found out for sure why he did it, but seeing the video, I could guess. When her autopsy was done, Gwen wasn't pregnant. She had taken care of it, and I would bet he found out. Is that thing in your hand fucking heavy yet?

I only saw Brock one more time, being arraigned in court. He pleaded not guilty, but never made it to trial. A day later, he hanged himself with a bedsheet. I hope he's still swinging in hell.

You can let go now.

2 THE KINDERGARTEN TEACHER'S WOLF

The shaggy-haired student speaking from his desk had a face that gave my fists erections. I don't remember ever seeing him look anything other than insufferably smug, and his voice sounded like an unwanted tongue to the ear felt.

"So, here's the thing," he continued his rambling diatribe, speaking about our class' most recent reading assignment, Giovanni's Room. *"I don't think Giovanni really exists."*

"That's...an interesting theory, Brandon," Professor Paulson (who let her students call her Olivia) said, sounding almost sincere. "Elaborate?"

"I think that Giovanni is, like, just a figment of David's imagination," words continued to slobber out of Brandon. From my TA chair at the front of the room, I shot Olivia a look, which she responded to with a wry smile.

"Like," he continued, "he's got all these homo thoughts--"

"Excuse me," Olivia said, her voice still cheerful, but her eyes conveying her message.

"Okay," Brandon sighed. "All of these homosexual *thoughts. But he knows he shouldn't, so they just built up and formed this, like, constructed identity separate from himself. Like, okay, have you seen* Fight Club*?"*

My eyes rolled in my head like marbles in a centrifuge.

"Again, that's a very interesting theory," Olivia praised, in the sweet, gentle way only she could pull off when faced with such an idiotic series of ideas. "But I'm not sure if it's true to the author's intent. What--"

"Why does that matter?" Brandon interrupted. He was a favorite student of Professor Campbell, also the dean of the department, who taught critical theory down the hall. You know, 'the author doesn't matter, the text doesn't matter, only your interpretations matter, and nothing is true or false or right or wrong except

people who say that there are things that are true or false or right or wrong, now let's get back to our discussion of why Runaway Bunny *is an allegory for the plight of the working class being pursued by the overly paternal industrial complex, and anyone who says otherwise is a hopeless simpleton.' That kind of bullshit.*

"I think it matters because--" Olivia started, before being cut off again.

"Because you're insisting on sticking to the same surface-level readings we learned about in high school," Brandon snapped. "I'm sorry, someone tell me to shut up if I'm wrong, but I'm sick of this! We learn how to have real discussions in other classes, and then we come to this one and get told to limit ourselves, to put the training wheels back on! This isn't what we're paying for."

"Shut up," I voiced, from the front of the room. The other students turned their heads back and forth between Brandon and me, waiting for what would happen next.

"Excuse me?" Brandon asked, glaring at me.

"You requested we tell you to shut up if you were wrong," I said calmly. "You're wrong. About a lot of things. About critical theory, about the quality of your poetry, about William Carlos Williams being superior to TS Eliot, about Giovanni's Room. But mainly you're wrong about Professor Paulson's request. She is not asking you to 'limit yourself,' she's asking you to discuss the text, the actual text. In this class, author intent matters. In this class, the text matters. She's asking to put away the bullshit fever-dream theories you cook up to make yourself feel so very, very smart and actually engage with the work. Because that's *what we're all paying for. Not to hear you try to cram a book into a box you built with your mind, not to hear two self-serious jackasses like you and me have a pissing contest. So, let's both shut our gobs and get back to discussing this very important piece of early queer literature."*

Brandon was scowling, but silent. The rest of the class was talking to each other using only their eyes.

"I'd like to discuss the room itself as a metaphor," Olivia chimed in, like nothing had happened. The students, all but one, snapped to attention and started flipping through their books, like a meaningful contribution to the discussion was going to tumble out of the pages. Brandon, however, continued to glare at me.

The glare lasted all the way to the end of class. On our way out, I felt a firm hand on my arm, stopping me. I turned and saw Brandon, eyes blazing.

"Can I help you?" I asked, trying to sound calm but, despite being surrounded by other people, actually a little afraid.

"You know," he said, ignoring the question, "don't think you're fooling anyone. Everyone knows what's going on. You walk around like you're something special, but you're just a little lapdog for the Kindergarten Teacher. Enjoy your special

treatment while it last; she's on her way out."

"Fuck off," I groaned, wrenching my arm free and continuing down the hall. I was spending a decent amount of money to learn fancy words and ways to express my thoughts, but sometimes the old classics were the best fit. I tried my best to ignore the blare of Brandon's onomatopoeic laughter behind me.

Brandon and me bickering had become the background noise of Garrnet Hall, home of the Freemond College English Department. We'd been sparring ever since he went on a lengthy rant during a small-group workshop in our fiction writing class about how it was ridiculous that he had to waste his time reading the rest of our stories, when his writing was "on a completely different level." Well, actually, that's not true; our feud really started a month or so before that, when someone informed him that the girl he'd been clumsily flirting with was transgender and sent him into a tailspin of toxic masculinity. But there was something different that day; it didn't seem like our usual sniping.

"Don't listen to him," a whispered voice came from behind me, as the last students disappeared down the hall ahead of me. I turned to face Olivia. "You're more of a lap wolf *than anything."*

"Sorry for overstepping today," I said, sincerely. I'd been as much of a disruption to her class as Brandon had.

"Don't worry about it," Olivia shook her head. "It is sometimes nice to have someone around who can...say the things that I can't."

Olivia was, and would always be, my favorite professor. At just shy of 50 years old, she was the most enthusiastic, energetic, joyful person I had ever met. She started every day of the year with a five AM run through campus, and ended it sitting in the English department common area, sipping her coffee as the day wound down. She invited all students to join her at either of these, but I was the only one who ever took her up on it (thought I'll admit I made a lot more coffees than morning jogs).

Unfortunately, the very reasons I loved her were the same reasons she was treated as a joke in the rest of Garrnet Hall. This was the English Department, you see. You were supposed to be droll and serious, quick witted and biting, at all times maintaining the necessary dividing wall between faculty and student, so as never to slip from your pedestal. The less human the students saw you, the better. There was little patience for a woman who was passionate and excitable when discussing 18th century British literature, or one who would take up 'valuable class time' relating to her classes stories of her own time in college, or tales of her perennial Summer trips around the country to visit used book stores. The department's toxic mindset trickled down to the students, who had begun to equate serious and biting with wise and learned. I wasn't sure when her nickname, the Kindergarten Teacher, developed, but I knew exactly why.

"It just...bothered me," I sighed as we walked through the halls and down the stairs to her book-packed office.

"Your heart is in the right place, Abra," she said, taking a seat behind her desk. "But it's alright. I know how I'm seen. I know what they call me. But I decided long ago that I had to make a choice: I could either change myself to be a person that they liked but I hated, or keep being the person they hate but I like. I'm guessing you know something about that."

"I get it," I nodded. "Just pisses me off."

"Oh, me too," Olivia said, pushing a lock of her light brown hair away from her face as she lifted a colorful coffee mug to her lips. "I just cope in different ways."

"How?"

"Every night I smash old fluorescent light bulbs and scream at God in the alley behind an abandoned IHOP," she stated, setting her coffee mug down and looking me straight in the eye.

My mouth opened to say something. What, I don't know.

"I do yoga and listen to angry music, Abra!" Olivia burst out laughing. "But you wondered, didn't you?"

"I did," I laughed. "I...do. That IHOP thing seems a bit too...specific."

Olivia gave me a quick wink and took another drink of her coffee.

"You sure you want to hunt here?" asked Lore as we pulled up to Rag Pickers in Drew's borrowed Suburban. I was glad that Lore, at least, had maintained her driver's license.

"Yeah," I nodded. "It's been on my mind ever since Neal found the box of my sister's stuff."

A week had passed since the discovery. It had been low-key around Cluster in the preceding seven days. Drew had booked a few local bands, lighter stuff than Monkey Don't, and Lore had done a few more makeup days. They were both still being oddly evasive about something, but I hadn't figured out what, yet. Most of our energy was being spent planning for our annual event that was coming up on December 15, the following Thursday.

"You're wondering if you'll find anything else of Gwen's, aren't you?" Lore asked as we climbed out of the truck.

"Maybe," I shrugged. "Neal said he gave the place a pretty thorough going-over after he found that box. But who knows?"

"Yeah, but see, that's my worry," Lore explained. "What if we're doing our Monstrosity Hunt, and I find something I think is a winner, and it turns out it's, like, your dead sister's favorite super-racist porcelain figurine from childhood?"

"I think you're pretty safe," I laughed. "But if you find an old jean jacket covered in metal studs and 'edgy' patches, let me know. She went through a brief but memorable punk phase."

"Your sister sounds awesome," Lore snickered. "I really wish I could have met her."

"Oh, the two of you would have been unstoppable," I said, picturing them as friends for the first time. "Seriously, I cannot overstate how instantly you would have become best friends."

"You miss her like crazy, don't you?" Lore asked as we pushed open the smudged glass door to Rag Pickers.

"Every damn day," I sighed. "Every damn day, there's like, this brief, split second, usually right when I wake up, but not always, where I catch myself thinking, 'I should call Gwen today' or 'I can't wait to tell Gwen about that'. Then I feel like an idiot for still having that tiny fragment of my brain that keeps thinking it's going to wake up from this mean, pointless dream."

"Aw, sweetie," Lore hugged me and leaning her head into my neck, eliciting stares from the two large old men in camo hats at the front counter. I paused to remind myself that I did *not* have feelings for Lore, but her slender frame pressing against me was providing a rather compelling counterargument.

"I'm okay," I whispered as she embraced me. "Now stop before you accidentally remind those old dudes what a boner is."

Lore laughed and punched me in the shoulder.

"Okay, okay," she said. "Me and my dumb, unintentionally erotic forms of providing comfort. Let's go find some awful crap! Meet here in thirty!"

The two girls at the front of the store no longer groping up on each other, the guys at the counter went back to watching a static-occluded football game on a tiny TV next to the register as Lore tore off into the dirt-mall. The point of a Monstrosity Hunt was simple: Find the most hideous, outrageous, disgusting, repulsive, outlandish, inexplicable or otherwise just plain 'worst' item that you could. Whomever was judged to have found the 'winning' item had to buy the other person lunch. In cases where Lore and I couldn't agree on a winner (which were not that common), Neal and Drew were called in to be guest judges. They, however, never understood our hobby. Spending half an hour of your time intentionally searching for a horrible item didn't make a ton of sense to them.

Rag Pickers was kind of an embarrassment of riches, as far as our game went. Often dubbed the Dirt Mall, Rag Pickers was actually a series of about forty separate vendors with their own stalls housed inside of a building that was once a Montgomery Ward. Two stories tall with a staircase that was just a non-functioning escalator, Rag Pickers should have been a flea market fan's paradise, but had increasingly become an indoor landfill where people tried to make you pay for their garbage. There was almost nothing usable (forget useful) to be found at any of the stalls, mainly just broken appliances, scratched up records, and well-soiled stuffed animals (along with numerous Episode 1 cup toppers). And, of course, my sister's personal belongings once she was no longer burdening our father by being alive.

The days after Gwen's death were a whirlwind of awfulness. Brock was, unfortunately, not dead yet, and the state was preparing its case against him. My father and I were interviewed, separately, by people who may have been detectives or prosecutors, or Santa's motherfucking elves for all I knew. My brain was pretty much a slurry at that point. Whomever they were, they warned me that the case would probably turn ugly. They had seen these things before. They had Brock pretty much dead to rights, what with his fingerprints being embedded in Gwen's throat, her body being found at his apartment, and him being found sobbing next to it. So his goal, they told us, would be to avoid the harshest possible penalties, which Brock's extremely-well-paid lawyers would attempt to accomplish by framing the whole thing as a "crime of passion," and my sister as "no angel." They'd dig up anyone who had something negative to say about her. Old boyfriends, teachers who didn't like her, people she looked at sideways in grade school, anyone who might say something that would imply that she wasn't Mother Teresa. Everything would come out, they warned. Any test she had cheated on, any parking tickets she had left unpaid. "Sex-stuff," especially, they cautioned. She ever send a nude photo to Brock or anyone else? Be prepared to see it. Experiment with another girl in college? Get ready to hear that story. Have a sibling who is, as the interviewer put it, "a shemale"? Yeah, that's going to come up. Anything that would subtly imply that, while it wasn't a *good* thing that dear, sweet Brock did (and how very sorry he is that *it happened*), maybe it wasn't the *worst* thing, either. I mean, did you know she had a tattoo?

Fortunately, before any of that could transpire, golden boy wrapped a length of sheet around his own miserable neck and then did the only worthwhile thing he'd ever done in his life. He shit himself while hanging there, too. The detective who delivered the news to me, Detective Martinez, the same woman who was there the night of Gwen's murder, made sure to mention that, and I'm eternally grateful to her for it.

Walking up the old, dead escalator to the second floor of Rag Pickers, I wondered if I would stumble upon any of Gwen's other possessions. Neal said he did a thorough sweep of the place after finding the one box, and I believed him, but what if some object that Neal wouldn't have recognized caught my eye? I really didn't want to break down in the middle of a junk dealership.

I didn't go to my sister's funeral. I wouldn't have been able to keep it together. I don't mean I would have broken down in ugly sobbing, I mean I would have broken down. My mind during those next few weeks was shot, barely held together and threatening to burst apart at any moment. Neal, Drew, and Lore were the ones who convinced me not to go, another thing I'm eternally grateful for. I wasn't ready to say goodbye to Gwen yet. Eventually, I did visit the niche at the cemetery where her urn was entombed. It was an unremarkable little square of concrete with a brass plaque bearing her name, a second plaque under that one with the words "My Angel". I never went back.

I used the time when everyone else was at her service to go back to my old house and try to save whatever I could. Neal went with me, both to stand lookout and for emotional support. Being a lazy bastard, my dad had never gotten around to changing the locks on the front door after I moved out, so my old key still worked. Unfortunately, when I got up to Gwen's old room, I discovered I was too late; everything, literally everything, including the furniture, was gone. Dad had evicted the remnants of "his angel's" life like a landlord evicts a tenant who is perpetually late with rent. I remember wanting to scream, scream loud enough to rattle the windows, scream loud enough to reach Gwen in whatever plane of existence comes after this one, to tell her that it wasn't fair that she was gone, that the stupidest, most loathsome part of my idiot brain was actually mad at *her* for not being here, and that she needed to come back *right now*.

Instead, I stopped myself, distracted by the open closet door. Neal was saying something--probably apologizing for this having happened, and calling my dad an asshole--but I didn't hear him. I drifted like a ghost over to the empty closet, and saw the hatch to the old laundry chute still sitting closed. Hoping against hope, I dug my fingernails into the seams and pulled, popping the hatch open. Sitting there, on top of the board we had used to block the chute so many years prior, was Snooty Crow.

"Five minutes!" Lore yelled across the Dirt Mall, snapping me back to the present. I did *not* want to have to buy lunch again! The last time we'd gone on a Monstrosity Hunt, I thought I'd had her with an old toilet seat cover designed to make your toilet look like a human mouth, but she had coasted to an easy victory with a custom-made teddy bear that had a photograph of some unfortunate child's face printed onto it. My eyes darted around the upper floor. There was no shortage of ugly, but nothing really 'popped'. A commemorative plaque bragging that the owner was "proud and sober" was depressing, and an old wedding album where someone had gone through all the pictures and used an Xacto to cut out the bride's eyes in every photo was depressing *and* concerning, but nothing really seemed like it was going to be a sure victory.

Until I saw Felix.

"You worry me sometimes, Miss Abra," Olivia said, sitting at her desk while I entered grades into the computer.

"Not surprising, I guess," I shrugged. "Why?"

"I was rereading the story you wrote for Fiction Writing," she said, sipping her coffee. "The one about girl in the woods."

"That one?" I asked. "I turned that in at the beginning of last semester. Why were you reading that one?"

"It was good," Olivia smiled. "I wanted to read it again."

"You gave it a B," I said, with an eyebrow raised.

"You could have done better," Olivia shrugged. "But your 'good' is still a lot better than most students' 'best.' Don't let that leave this office; I'm not supposed to have favorites."

I brushed my finger against the side of my nose and nodded.

"Anyway," continued Olivia, "it worries me. Why are you so afraid of happy endings?"

"I'm not afraid *of them," I said. "It's not like I'm scared one is going to jump out at me. I just...don't really believe in them."*

"Why not?"

"You moonlighting as a shrink now?" I laughed.

"No," Olivia smiled. "And I'm not asking as your professor, either."

"Okay," I said, feeling my face pinken. "It's just not the way life works out."

"You're, what, 21?" Olivia asked, not unkindly. "I know you've seen a lot more than a lot of people already, but--"

"I know," I groaned. "I'm 21. But it's like, what really ends happy? You fall in love with the person of your dreams, they love you, too, and then one day, best case scenario, one of you has to watch the other one die. Or you have kids and you love them and they make you happy, but then one day they leave and never call. Or--"

"I understand," Olivia put up a hand. "Abra, I'm 48 this July. I'll pause to let you tell me how I don't look it."

She really didn't. I had previously heard how old she was, but I would have put her at 35, tops. Of course, being 21, I was a terrible judge of age back then. I opened my mouth to agree with her, but she just started laughing.

"I was kidding!" she blurted. "Anyway, my point is, here's my 48 years: Abusive mother, absent father, bullied in school, fell in love with a jackass at eighteen, married at nineteen, widowed at twenty-eight, diagnosed with cancer at 34, celebrating twenty years in a career I hate next September. Not as catchy as Solomon Grundy, I guess. But here's the thing: I've had a very happy life. Everyone thinks I should be moping around or, since I'm not, that I must be deluded or naive about my own circumstance. 'How could Professor Paulson be pleased with a sunset when her husband died, and she had cancer? She must just be fooling herself.' But I'm not. My life isn't the tragedies, it's the spaces around them. My point, which I'm feeling I'm not being very articulate in expressing, is that you should consider updating your definition of a happy ending."

"You...hate your job?" I asked, in a hushed tone.

Olivia grimaced. "I guess I don't hate it. I just...never wanted it. But I got a degree in English, and the Great American Feminist Novel didn't come pouring out of me the way I thought it should, so I went to grad school. Got my Masters, didn't know what to do. Got my PhD. Somehow, eventually, ended up here. But there's beauty in a snowball rolling down a hill, I guess."

"Kinda left all of that out when we had our first advising meeting back when I was a freshman," I laughed.

"Well," she reddened, "I guess that's two things that won't leave this room. I've got a question for you. I've been pretty honest today--probably too honest, I was always bad at professionalism--so I'll ask you to do the same."

"Shoot," I said.

"What's your stupidest dream?" she asked, her startling green eyes looking back

into mine.

"My...stupidest dream?"

"The one that you have that you'd never tell anyone about, because they'd laugh at you," she clarified. "The one you love to play with in your head, but then feel stupid because it's so outlandish. G-rated, I mean, of course."

I looked down, pretending to ponder for a moment. But I didn't really need to, I just needed to build up the courage to say it out loud.

"I want to own a store," I blurted, realizing instantly how much I sounded like a small child. "I want to sell things you can't get anywhere else; vintage toys, music, books, just random crap that is still...fun. I want to decide what we sell, do everything based on my whims. A place where my friends and I can all work together and just...make our own rules."

My face was burning as I finished. I sounded so stupid. It had been one of those things you say, where every word coming out of your mouth sounds more idiotic than the last, but you can't stop yourself from talking. I felt like crying. Olivia reached across her desk, putting one hand gently on top of mine.

"Mine was to write a novel that was both wise and witty, full of strong female characters who broke through stereotypes and held a mirror up to society, engaging the reader while simultaneously putting them on trial."

"What? That's not a stupid dream!" I objected, feeling even more foolish.

Olivia muttered something under her breath.

"What?"

"Also there were aliens!" she blurted. "Aliens who looked like incredibly attractive humans, but purple, who came from a more enlightened society to breed with us and usher in a true era of human unity! There, are you happy?"

I tried in vain to stop, but couldn't. I burst out laughing. Thankfully, Olivia joined me. By the time we finally stopped, we both had tears in our eyes.

"The stupid dreams are the best ones, Abra," Olivia said, still chuckling. "There, I'm done being wise for today. Go on, you have a class to get to!"

She was right, I did. But damned if I could remember which one.

"So," Lore said between bites of the bacon cheeseburger she had paid for, "Drew told me this morning that he finalized the bands for Thursday. We've got Old Bones, Rattler, and Wild Weasel."

"Old Bones is still playing?" I chuckled, taking a bite of my free-to-me burger. "Don't that beat all."

"That was her band, right?" Lore asked.

"Her favorite," I nodded. "They're this weird bluegrass/hip-hop fusion thing. They used to be the house band at Bernard's out by the highway. She took me to one of their shows once. They were...not great."

"So…do you ever wonder if she, like, had feelings for you?" Lore asked. "I mean, I know you never did anything, but you didn't really have a usual professor/student relationship."

"We didn't," I shrugged. "But no, she didn't have feelings for me."

"How do you know?"

"Because *I* was in love with *her*." I stated, out loud for the first time.

"Oh," Lore said. "Did...did you ever tell her?"

I thought about it for a moment.

"It's a hard question to answer," I finally responded.

"Okay," Lore nodded. "Hey, none of my business. All I know is that I loved the one class I took with her."

Intro to Fantasy Literature was the class where I met Lore. Being a business major, she didn't make it over to our shadowy corner of the campus very often, but her program had a three credit English requirement, and she had decided learning about Tolkien and Lewis was more fun than taking Intro to Essay Writing. Fantasy literature was a passion Lore and Olivia shared, and (since Lore was unencumbered by English major cynicism) Olivia quickly became one of Lore's favorite professors. Unfortunately, Olivia was unable to convince her to switch majors.

"So, as long as you're fessing up to things," Lore said, "did you used to have a thing for me?"

I turned as red as the blob of ketchup on my plate.

"Just, like, right at the beginning," I stammered, leaving out my brief relapse. "Before you and Drew…."

"Oh, sweetie," Lore cooed. "I'm sorry! I always kind of worried, after that night when you invited me to your dorm to study. When I met Drew."

"Yes, I remember that night," I grumbled. "I had to sleep in the student lounge. You two move fast."

"Guilty," Lore chirped. "But I remember lying there in his bed, and all of the sudden thinking, 'wait, was Abra inviting me over here as, like, a date'?"

"Little bit," I said, holding up two fingers with a small space between them.

"Oh, sweetie," Lore repeated. "I'm sorry!"

"It was a long, long time ago," I laughed. "I lived. And you and

Drew were so instantly awesome together, I never really minded."

"Well good," Lore said, her face now red. "So... for some reason I didn't think that conversation was going to be awkward, but it sure was! So...."

"Never speak of it again?" I offered.

"Never speak of it again," she nodded.

"So, what else do we have for Ides of December?" I asked, changing the subject as gracefully as I could.

"What we *need* is a catchier name," Lore grumbled. "But to answer your question, I'm going to be doing a live feed to my channel, doing people's makeup for free as long as they're okay being a part of it. Also, half-off white chocolate mochas, of course."

They were Olivia's favorite; she was seldom seen without one in her hand. It only seemed right to discount them on her night.

"What about you? What's going on in Cadabra's Corner?" Lore wondered, taking another bite.

"All books are buy-one-get-one," I said, and then smiled. "I'll also be offering a 20% discount to anyone who can show school ID proving that they teach kindergarten."

"Nice," Lore laughed. "What a shitty group of people, complaining that someone was *too* happy and nice."

"Well," I said, "if it makes you feel any better, their ring leader never did set the literary world on fire like he always swore he was 'just about' to do. Last I heard, he was selling insurance."

"So it goes," Lore snickered, and then grew quiet, staring down at her food, like it was a puzzle she was trying to solve.

"Fuck, I have to be really bad friend right now," she whispered.

"Why? What do you mean?"

"Not to you. To Neal," she sighed. "Look. I need to tell you something, and it's something he asked me not to tell you, but you need to know."

"Lore, if he doesn't want me to know...," I started. She silenced me with a gesture.

"You need to know," she repeated. 'Serious' was an odd look on Lore's spritely face. I think I'd only seen it a handful of times, and it was always unsettling.

"Okay," I said slowly. I had a feeling I knew what this was about. Same thing I had been putting off addressing for years.

"There's a reason his comic is stalled, and it's not because he can't think of what to write next," Lore started. Okay, that's *not* what I thought the discussion was going to be about.

"What's the reason?" I asked.

"About a month and a half ago, Dan emailed him," Lore said, as if every word was having to be forced out of her mouth. "They've been talking back and forth ever since."

"That's great!" I exclaimed. "Why wouldn't he want to share that?"

"There's more," Lore continued. "Dan's living in New York now, working for one of the larger comic companies. He contacted Neal initially because a friend of his at another comics company--not one of a huge ones, but not a small one, either--knew that he had a connection to Neal and was interested in publishing *And All the Rest* and maybe bringing Neal on as onc of their illustrators."

"I'm confused, this news continues to be amazing," I beamed. "What's the problem?"

"Abra," Lore whispered. "He'd have to move to New York."

And suddenly, it felt like I'd taken a tank-round to the chest. Neal had been my magnetic north since grade school. He was there at every important moment in my life, and all of the unimportant ones, too. To not have him around would be like having a limb fall off. My mouth hung open, no words ready to come out.

"He's not going to do it!" Lore blurted.

"What?" I asked, ashamed of the relief that washed over me in that moment. "But it's his dream."

"Yeah, I know," Lore said. "But he's not going to do it because he doesn't want to leave."

"Why not?" I asked. Lore stared at me like I was the stupidest, most infuriating person on earth.

"Well, it's not because he's going to miss Drew and me so much!" she snapped. "Don't get me wrong, he'll miss us, but it's not the thought of not having us in his life that is keeping him here. Hmm, Abra the Smart, Abra the Wise, let's see if we can suss out what might be making him throw away his chance at achieving his ultimate life goal. Let's just see."

Lore was fuming now, red faced and exasperated. I would have been, too.

"I know," I whispered.

"Then do something about it!" Lore begged. "You have to talk to him. You have to get him to reconsider. You have to--"

"I have to break my best friend's heart," I finished.

"Yeah," Lore slumped, the fire going out of her. "Yeah, you do. I'm sorry."

"Me, too," I whispered. We at the rest of our meal in silence, right up to the end, when it became too much for Lore.

"I still can't believe you found something that beat 'half-made jackalope taxidermy holding a beer can." She said, ending the quiet.

"Hey, you know what they say: Nothing beats clowns." I said, remembering my winning find, an old circus poster advertising a ghoulish harlequin named 'Famous Felix' and '99 other clowns.' It seemed more like a threat than an advertisement.

"I'm sorry I yelled at you," Lore whispered. "I know this isn't easy."

"I'm glad you did," I sighed. "I needed it."

"I can yell at you more, if you want," Lore shrugged. "Louder maybe? With more swearing?"

"No, that's okay," I laughed. "I'm good."

Lore smiled at me and set her debit card down on the check that the waitress had brought over sometime during our conversation. A free lunch had never cost me so much.

Garrnet Hall was one of the older buildings on campus, and as such held numerous secrets that got passed around the student body yet, somehow, slid right under the noses of the faculty. One was that the deep storage room (a sort of black hole where the department threw everything they didn't want to dispose of but also didn't want to look at) had a vent in it that, due to just the right twists and turns in the ductwork, allowed you to hear everything going on in the dean's office. Since students didn't usually hang out in deep storage, it wasn't much of a problem. Just one of those little 'fun facts' that gets passed down, year to year.

The week before our annual used book sale, I actually had a legitimate reason to be in the storage room. Olivia had volunteered me ("it's nice to be nice, Abra") to move boxes of old, musty paperbacks out into the common area where the sale would be held. I was in there, trying to figure out how to unearth one last box of books without sending a giant pillar of crap collapsing on my head, when I heard the dean's voice.

"Have a seat, Olivia," he said, with a grave tone. But then again, everything Professor Campbell said had a grave tone to it. He was a stone-faced, balding man with a meticulously trimmed beard and distinctly not trimmed eyebrows. He was one of the college's minor celebrities, having years before published a dreary book about a white guy coming to terms with things in a New England fishing town

("Who cares?" raved Publisher's Weekly). I didn't hear Olivia say anything, but I heard one of the antique chairs across from Campbell's desk squeak.

"We've had some concerns raised, Olivia," Professor Campbell stated. "Both from students and other faculty members. There are some who feel that you may have issues staying professional."

"How so?" Olivia asked. Her voice was steady, but I had a feeling she was biting the inside of her lip.

"Well, it's a number of things," Campbell continued. "One concern is how you present yourself in your classes. Your students have expressed that you are not--How shall I put this?--the most academic *in your teaching style. They've cited numerous asides to tell stories from your life that only loosely connect to the readings at hand, a lack of familiarity with critical theory, and a failure to promote meaningful discussion."*

"I feel that I--" Olivia started.

"Our feelings are really irrelevant to this discussion," Professor Campbell spoke, right over the top of her. "What matters is how the students *feel. They are the ones paying for a thorough, academic education. We serve them."*

"I understand," Olivia said, her voice losing some of its cool. "My teaching--"

"I'm honestly not all that interested in going ten rounds with you, Olivia," Professor Campbell sighed. He sounded about ten seconds away from asking her if she was on her period. I seethed in the storage room. I wanted to yell through the vent that the complaining students were nothing but small minded, arrogant jackasses who didn't like Professor Paulson because she made them think instead of spoon-feeding them the answers or telling them that all answers were correct as long as you used enough words. I wanted to yell that she was the only professor at that college-shaped toilet who ever taught me anything. I wanted to talk over him in the same condescending way he was talking over her.

"Then why am I here?" Olivia asked, irritation creeping into her voice.

"We'll deal with the issues regarding your teaching," Campbell said, still cold and calm. "I think next year we'll pair you with another professor to serve as a mentor to--"

"I've been teaching for twenty years!" Olivia snapped.

"Please don't interrupt," Campbell said, again without even trace emotion. "You've been teaching here *for five. Private institutions have...different standards than state colleges. But we'll deal with that. The real reason why you're here is to discuss the other concern that has been brought to my attention."*

"Which is?" Olivia asked, trying to get herself back down to a calm level.

"There have been questions regarding the appropriateness of your relationship with the boy who TA's for you in several of your classes."

My heart thudded into my stomach.

"Then I'm confused, Ted," Olivia stated. "I don't have a boy who TA's for me."

"I would prefer you address me as Professor Campbell, or Dean Campbell," Chief Douche-nozzle Campbell said. The irritation was creeping into his *voice now. "But fine. The 'girl.'"*

"Woman," Olivia said. "She's not wearing pigtails and playing with dollies."

"Is this really the hill you wish to die on, Olivia?" Captain Dickwad asked.

"Seems I'm here to die, anyway," Olivia retorted. "May as well be for this."

"What is *the nature of your relationship with...Miss... Collins?"*

I wanted to burst through the wall and just start screaming. Maybe not even words. Just something to shut Campbell's sanctimonious mouth.

"She is my student," Olivia stated. "And my TA. She's very good at both. She's one of the most intelligent, insightful--"

"Olivia," Campbell snapped. "Don't play coy; you know what I mean."

"There is not now, nor has there ever been, any kind of inappropriate relationship between Abra and me," Olivia declared.

"That's not the perception," Campbell said.

"I honestly don't care," Olivia replied. "I gained the right to not care about gossip when I earned my PhD. I think it's insulting both to me and to Abra to--"

"Okay," Campbell said, as if dealing with a tantruming child. "We'll return to this conversation later, when you're less emotional. But we will return to it, Olivia. I met with you today as a courtesy. Fair warning, our next meeting won't be so casual. Until then, I would strongly suggest you begin to care about how you and your actions are perceived."

"I--"

"That's all for now," Campbell dismissed. "You may go."

Olivia started to speak again, but then all I heard was the door to the dean's office clicking closed as she left. When I saw her next, she was her usual bright, exuberant self. I never told her what I'd heard in the storage room. I never would have done that to her.

"I have many questions," Drew said when we were all back together at Cluster. "Like, what makes Famous Felix so special that he gets a call out and the 99 other clowns don't?"

"Well, obviously, he's famous," Neal said as I helped him hang up a new drawing he was offering for sale, his first in a long time.

"Yeah, but, like, why?" Drew asked. "How do you become a famous clown?"

"I think you have to kill the famous clown that came before you," I offered. "Then absorb his essence. Like *Highlander*."

"So, at one point there were 101 clowns?" Lore called from behind the coffee counter, the customer she was serving looking somewhat bemused.

"It would stand to reason," I nodded.

"Okay, but the 99 clowns," Drew continued. "How do you fit that all into one circus? Is it, like, a four hour show and they each come out one at a time?"

"I think they're all out at once," I mused.

"They just charge at you," Neal added. "In one giant ball of clown."

"That's horrifying," Lore laughed. Her customer seemed to agree, and hurried toward the door.

"Well, how do you think new clowns are made?" Drew asked.

"Aaanyway," I interjected, "Drew, I wanted to thank you. Lore told me you managed to book Old Bones for Ides of December"

"Yeah," Drew chuckled. "The weirdest part was convincing them that they didn't have to pay *us*. I don't think they get a lot of gigs these days."

"Still," I said, "thank you. They were Olivia's favorite."

"No problem, Abby," Drew shrugged.

"No, seriously," I insisted. "I'm feeling weirdly thankful today, and I want you to know that I appreciate all the work you do around here. All of you. I don't know how I'd do it without you."

Neal thanked me, but Drew and Lore stayed oddly silent.

"We have to tell them," Lore moaned, finally.

"Fuck," Drew sighed. "Yeah. Go grab the folder out of the truck."

Lore nodded as Drew tossed her the keys. We all watched her tear off toward the parking lot.

"Wait...what's going on?" I asked, like someone driving down the road who suddenly notices that they are looking at the backs of all the street signs. I looked to Neal, who shook his head and gave an "I don't know" gesture.

"I'll wait until Lore gets back," Drew muttered, looking down at his boots. Lore rejoined us moments later, a plastic accordion folder tucked under her arm.

"So," Drew said, gesturing for us to sit down at one of the tables, "we haven't been completely honest with you."

"Andrew," I mock-scolded. "What happened to the circle of trust?"

"Only about half the trips we've been making to see my mom have actually been visits. The other times we've been going to Spokane." Drew admitted.

"Why in God's name would anyone do that?" I asked.

"There's a property up there we want to buy," Lore said, sounding ashamed.

"Wait, like, a house?" Neal asked.

"No," Drew shook his head. "A restaurant. My mom heard about it through a friend of hers and passed it on to me. It's a great location, great setup.... It's a great opportunity to finally give my dream a shot."

My chest cavity felt suddenly hollow as the implications settled in. I looked to Lore, who wouldn't meet my eyes.

"I have news, too," Lore muttered. "There's a production company in Spokane that has been looking for a makeup artist. They mainly do local and regional stuff, but sometimes work on actual movies that film there. I interviewed with them on our last trip, and they said the job is mine if I want it."

"O-oh," I finally said, the word drifting out of me a ghost.

"Abra, we're sorry," Drew said, putting a hand on my shoulder. "We were going to wait until after the Ides to tell you, but...."

"Yeah," I absently nodded.

"Hey, this is good news," Neal piped in. "I'm happy for the two of you!"

"Me, too," I declared, gathering myself up and putting on a pretty unconvincing brave face. "Congratulations, you two. So, when...?"

"Start of the New Year," Lore said. "It'll take at least that long to finalize paperwork on the restaurant, and my new job has agreed to let me settle things here until the beginning of January. Which brings us to this folder."

"We didn't want to leave you high and dry," Drew said, as Lore opened up the accordion file and began pulling out stapled bundles of paper. "For the last month or so, we've been quietly collecting resumes of people we think would be good replacements for us."

I looked down at the cover letter Lore was trying to hand me, my brain feeling like it was going to start oozing out my ears.

"We're not trying to torpedo your dream, Abra," Lore assured me. "We just need to follow our own now."

Nodding, I took the application packet from her hands.

"Are...are we okay?" Drew asked, trying to lean in to see my face.

"It's...a lot to take in," I swallowed. "Yeah, we're okay. I'm happy for you."

I didn't feel guilty for lying to them, but I did feel guilty that I had to lie to them. Turned out this was just the outer edge of a storm that was headed my way at that very moment. I just didn't know it yet.

"So what are you doing with your Summer, Miss Abra?" Olivia asked as I sat across the desk from her in her office, the last of the students' papers graded and entered into the computer for the year.

"Not really sure," I admitted. "Maybe get a job as a barista or something?"

"Not making as much as you used to on Ebay?" she questioned, tilting her head a little to the side.

"No, still doing great," I said. "Making more than enough, actually. Just...probably should have something *to do this Summer."*

"Why not take a trip or something?" Olivia asked, putting her feet up on the desk, her purple running shoes resting on top of a beat up copy of The Golden Bowl.

"I'm doing college-great," I laughed. "Not trip great. I'll probably just hang out with my friends whenever they're in town. Drew and Lore are going to be spending some time visiting her parents in Seattle, and I think Neal is being a counselor at an art camp for kids, so I don't know how much I'll see of them."

"Neal is the one who…?" Olivia asked, with a knowing look.

"Yeah," I blushed.

"Well, Abra," Olivia said, though a yawn, "I suppose this is the part where I, as a responsible, free-spirited, wise, hopefully-not-old-yet-but-not-necessarily-young mentor am supposed to give you a speech about making the most of your youth, gather ye rosebuds and all that. But honestly, if a quiet summer around Comstock hanging out with your friends is what you want, don't let anyone make you feel bad about it."

"So what are your plans, Professor?" I asked, getting a hearty eye roll as a response.

"Miss Abra," she said, prim and proper, "how long and how well do we have to know each other before you realize how much being called that by you annoys me?"

"Oh, I know," I laughed, getting a look shot back at me.

"I'm going to be leaving for my usual bookstore jaunt right after commencement," Olivia said. "Heading east this time, through Idaho and Montana. And who knows how much farther after that."

"Sounds amazing," I affirmed. "Any idea when you'll be back?"

"Sometime before the start of the next school year," Olivia shrugged. "Other than that, nope. One of the benefits of being a lonely old spinster."

Olivia had married young, and, by all accounts, not well. She didn't talk much at all about her husband. I knew he had been pretty well off, I knew he had owned several properties around town which were now in Olivia's possession. I knew that one time, over coffee in her office on the first day of winter break, Olivia referred to the day he died in a car accident as the best day of her life. They had no kids, and she never remarried, which left her free and clear to do as she pleased. Unfortunately, even in the 'progressive' halls of academia, it opened her up to a great deal of gossip and rumors as well. No one was sure if she was a slut, a lesbian, or both, but it had to be something *they found untoward. Of course, there were also the ones who thought we were sleeping together, too.*

"Good to know there are some," I sighed.

"Now, it would be unprofessional for me to ask while you're still a student," Olivia said, looking down at the top of her desk, "but after you graduate next year, would you want to join me on my Summer trip?"

"Really?"

"You're the best company I've had in years," Olivia admitted, "and, if I'm going to be honest, there are times during the trip that can get kind of lonely. It would be nice to have someone to talk to. I mean, I know you'll probably have other things to do, having just graduated and all. It was probably a stupid thing to ask. I'm sorry."

In that weird moment, we seemed to unintentionally have switched roles. I reached across her desk, setting my hand next to, but not touching, hers.

"That sounds amazing," I said, again. "I'll make it work."

Olivia smiled and thanked me. We never got to make that trip, and it's one of the biggest regrets of my life. The next time I saw her, everything had changed.

"I was somewhat surprised to hear from you," said Calli, as we sat in the back room of her tattoo parlor. "Is everything okay? You usually don't call...well, at all. We just have our standing appointment."

"I think I just needed someone outside of my core-group to talk to," I sighed, leaning up against a wall with one of Calli's paintings hanging over me, a skull with butterflies coming out of its mouth.

"You four do kind of live right on top of each other," Calli said, taking a seat in a split open red-vinyl chair. "I was always kind of surprised that your house hadn't turned into either an orgy or a crime scene."

I was not necessarily convinced that my decision to come to Calli with my problems was a smart one. But I was in a bad place, and Calli was a good tour guide for those.

"Well, it's not going to be like that for long," I grumbled, tapping my fingers on the wall behind me. "Drew and Lore just announced that they're moving at the end of the year. To Spokane."

"Ugh," Calli stuck out her tongue. "Why?"

"He's starting a restaurant," I muttered. "She's doing makeup for some production company."

"Shit. How are you holding up?" Calli asked, tilting her head and letting her ice blue eyes give me a soft look.

"I'm okay," I said, as a reflex, before correcting myself. "No, I'm not. I'm not doing okay at all. I mean, it's stupid: I knew, deep down, that it was unrealistic that we were all going to live and work together forever. It's pretty miraculous that we have for this long. But...."

"You aren't ready to let go," Calli finished.

"Yeah," I sighed. "I'm not. And I know it's not that far, and it's not like we don't have ways of talking. Jesus, I'm being an idiot. Instead of celebrating my friends getting to achieve their dreams, I'm whining that they aren't going prop mine up for a few more years. This is what you get for answering your phone, Calli."

Calli smiled, stood up, and leaned against the wall with me, resting her hand on mine.

"Yesterday I heard a DJ on the radio say that sunny days were the best possible days. It made me angry because I love it when it rains, and I got angry enough that I wrote a five-page letter letting her know that she was wrong and telling her all the reasons why," Calli admitted. "I had it all folded up and in a stamped envelope, ready to send, when I realized how stupid I was being. But it's how I felt, and I'm allowed to feel things, even if they're stupid. You are, too."

"Thanks," I smiled. "So, you didn't send the letter?"

"Of course I sent it," Calli said, perplexed. "Why wouldn't I send it?"

"Because...never mind," I muttered. "I dunno. I think it's just that everything is happening all of a sudden."

"Is it going to be awkward, just you and your fan club sharing that house?" Calli asked.

"Don't call him that," I elbowed her gently. "But no, it's not. That's the even worse part. Neal has been talking to his old boyfriend again, and--"

"Is this the one he was with when we were together?" Calli interrupted. "The one who looked like a sexy Bible salesman?"

"Uh, sure," I muttered. "Dan is his name."

"I'm sure it is," Calli smiled, closing her eyes. "I've never wished more that someone was into girls. Mmm MMM! So they're back together, huh?"

"No," I sighed. "I don't think so, at least. That's the problem. Dan is asking him to move to New York and work for a comic book company there."

"Wow," Calli said. "Did your friends find a genie that hates you? It's not a good time to be Abra, is it?"

"No," I grumbled. "It certainly isn't. But that's the problem; he's not going to go to New York. He's going to stay here, even though it's everything he's ever wanted."

"Abby-Cadaby," Calli said, as gravely as one can say that obnoxious pet name, "you are so, so smart; how could you say such a stupid thing?"

"Excuse me?"

"I knew he wasn't going to go to New York before you even finished your thought," Calli laughed. "And I definitely know why. You do, too. You really think working at a comic book company is 'everything he ever wanted'? Are you that dense?"

"No," I sighed. "I just...wish it was different. I wish he didn't have these feelings for me."

Calli stared at me for a long time before speaking, clicking her acrylic nails on the wall behind us.

"I will never get you, Abra Collins," she shook her head. "How are you not seeing this?"

"Seeing what?" I asked. "I get that he has feelings for me--"

"No!" Calli snapped, spinning away from the wall and grabbing both of my shoulders. "You get that. Fine. How do you not get that you have feelings for him, too?"

"What? No!" I blurted. "I'm not...not like that."

"Ugh!" Calli groaned. "Call it what you want, Abra. Fine; you don't want to fuck him. And you don't like guys. And, and, and. Do you have any idea how jealous I was during our time together?"

I actually hadn't. I always figured I was the perpetually jealous one in the relationship. Calli had hordes of admirers, male and female, everywhere she went, and her habit of encouraging their affections in front of me didn't help, either.

"No, I didn't," I said. "Why?"

"Because I've never seen two people look at each other the way you two do!" she yelled. "And yeah, it's two different ways. He's definitely got feelings for you that aren't the ones you have, but you have some strong-ass feelings, girl! I don't know what to call them, and that's what made it so infuriating when we were together. I've been with people who've lusted after someone else. I've been with people who've been in love with someone else. I've been with people who have weird 'brother/sister' friendships. I don't know what to call your relationship with Neal. Some kind of sexless soulmate? The other half of you as a person? I don't know! All I know is that you can't just write this off as *he* has feelings for *you*. You're both so wrapped up in each other that I doubt anyone has a chance with either of you while the other person is still alive."

I stood there with my head down, Calli's hands still on my shoulders, processing what she had said. Just like Lore, just like Gwen years ago, I knew she was right.

"I know," I whispered. "And I know what I have to do, too."

"Abra," Calli said, appalled, taking a step back from me. "You can't! You can't kill Neal! It's *wrong*."

"Oh for fuck sake!" I yelled. "I'm not going to kill Neal! Why would your brain go there?"

"The last thing I said was that no one had a chance with either of you if the other person was still alive," Calli shrugged, letting go of me. "Seemed like the natural conclusion. But okay, good. What are you going to do?"

"I have to tell him to go," I whispered, feeling my eyes get wet.

"I thought you said you weren't going to kill him," Calli responded, and then embraced me. I had forgotten how well she fit right up against me. And how good her hair smelled, right under my nose. I felt bad that my tears were beginning to soak the top of her head. But the dam had broken, and everything came tumbling out, to maybe the last person I ever thought I'd open up to.

"Everyone I love goes away," I yelled through tears. "Everyone, except Neal. And now I have to do it, I have to *make* the one person who stayed leave. How is that fair? How the fuck is that even a bit fair?"

"It's not," Calli said, stroking my hair. "But nothing is."

"I just don't know why this is all happening all at once," I cried. "It's just...fuck, I don't know."

"You're having a bad day, huh?" She whispered in my ear, nuzzling against me. I nodded.

"You know we were terrible for each other, right?" She asked. Confused, I nodded again.

"And you know that us getting back together would be the worst thing either of us could do?" Another nod.

"Okay," Calli said softly. "As long as you know. Come back home with me, Abra. You've had a bad day, you're tired, you're fried. Come with me."

"Calli," I protested, "I--"

"I care about you, Abra," she whispered, running a hand through my hair, her fingernails tickling my scalp. Goosebumps raised all over my body, along with a tingling that ran head to toe. "I know that our relationship was weird and... weird, but you know I cared about you, right? We're very different people, but you're still in my heart. Now I won't ask again, I'm not trying to add to your stress. But you deserve to take your mind off things for a while, and I'd like to help you. If you want."

She separated from me and took two steps toward the door, pausing to look over her shoulder, her eyes almost glowing blue, biting her lip and giving me a look that could have raised the dead. She extended one soft, slender hand toward me, which I took, without a moment's hesitation, everything melting away the second our fingers touched.

"If it makes you angry, hit me!" Drew yelled, shirtless at the center of our room.

"Drew, I'm not going to hit you," I sighed from my desk. "I'm not mad at you."

"Yeah, but I'm here," Drew barked. "Come on, hit me! I can take it!"

"Why do you want me to hit you so bad?" I asked, leaning back in my chair.

"I have a wrestling gig this weekend and I need to remember how to take a punch," admitted Drew. "It's been awhile."

"So Maul Bunyan rides again, huh?"

"Yeah. What can I say? Textbooks are expensive." Drew chuckled. "But also, you're all twisted up. I don't like seeing you like this, so let some of it out. You're not pissed at me, who are you pissed at?"

"At the school," I growled. "This stupid fucking school."

"And? Come on."

"Dean Campbell," I yelled, standing up from my desk. "And that asshole Brandon who complained. And all the other cowardly assholes in the mob of complainers."

"And?" Drew yelled.

"And the whole fucking world right now!" I shouted.

"Yes! Do it!"

This time, I did. Without thinking, I flung out my fist into Drew's chest. It was like punching cinder block.

"Yes! Ha! Agai--oh, shit, is your hand okay?" Drew asked, noticing me clutching my already reddening fist.

"I think you're ready, Drew," I squeaked.

"Oh, shit, I'm sorry," Drew stuttered.

"I'll be okay," I winced, flexing my fingers. "Nothing broken."

"Good," Drew said, sheepishly. "I am sorry about Professor Paulson, though. What reason are they giving for firing her?"

"They aren't," I growled, sitting back down. "We didn't know anything about it until we all showed up for what was supposed to be her class and Dean Campbell informed us that she 'would not be a member of Freemond faculty this year' and that he would be taking over all of her classes until a suitable replacement could be found. He said there would be an announcement at a later time. Just going to be a bunch of carefully edited bullshit, I'm sure."

"Have you talked to her since?" Drew asked, taking a seat at his desk.

"No," I sighed. "I worry she's avoiding me. She's not answering my emails. Her office is still all set up, but it doesn't look like anyone has been in there all Summer."

"Shit. Sometimes I think the only worthwhile purpose this place serves is matching up friends," Drew huffed, pulling on a shirt and sitting down on his bunk. "I can't hate it, because if not for Freemond, I never would have met Lore, you, or Neal. But it's fucking hard to like."

"I get it," I nodded. "I guess forty-five grand a year to find people who can actually keep you sane isn't too bad. Olivia was one of mine, though."

"You going to say anything?" Drew asked.

"I don't know what to say," I sighed. "Honestly, what I really want to do is just fucking tell off Campbell right to his big, dumb, gargoyle face. Right in the middle of the class he stole from her. I know it would be stupid, and pointless, and probably get me expelled, but--"

A better angel chose that time to ring my phone.

"Hello?" I grumbled, hitting 'accept' without even checking the screen.

"Abra?" Olivia's voice asked from the other end.

"Olivia!" I blurted, way too excited. "Where have you been? I've been trying to--"

"I know," she stopped me.

"What happened?" I asked. "Did...did they fire you?"

There was a hard pause before she spoke again.

"No," she said, finally. There was something wrong, and it didn't sound like anything small. "Can...can you meet me at my office? I want to talk to you."

"Sure," I said. "When did you want to meet? I have class tomorrow until--"

"I'm here now," she interrupted. "Can you come now?"

I glanced at the clock; it was 9pm.

"Sure, I guess," I said, Drew giving me a quizzical look. "I'll be right over."

"Okay," Olivia whispered, and then hung up before I could say anything.

"Everything okay?" Drew asked.

"I... I don't think so."

The run across campus wasn't a long one, but I was still out of breath by the time I reached Garnet Hall. There was only one light visible, the one coming from Olivia's office. Thankfully, the door to the main building wouldn't automatically lock until 10.

"I'm here," I called out, swinging down the hall as I turned to enter her office. "I'm--"

I froze as I opened the door. For the first time since I had met her, Olivia looked her age. Her perpetual youth had seemed to have sloughed off like dead skin. Her eyes were sunken, her skin sallow and tight, her cheeks hollow. She looked like she had lost at least ten pounds that she hadn't had to spare.

"Hello, Abra," she whispered as I tried to recompose myself. "Not so spry anymore, am I?"

"You...what...what's going on?" I asked, feeling like a woman stuck in the middle of train tracks, seeing an oncoming light in the distance.

"Back in July, I stopped in a used book store in Hamilton, Montana," she said, her voice weak. "While trying to reach a copy of The Milagro Beanfield War off of a high shelf, I suddenly lost consciousness and collapsed. The next thing I remember, I was in the hospital."

"God, what happened?" I asked.

"Abra," Olivia said, her face steel but tears escaping her eyes. "My cancer is back. Except this time it's in my brain. And other places, too. It... spread."

We were standing in a black, empty void in that moment. My mouth opened, not to speak or scream, but to yell, yell as loud as I could. But no sound came out.

Sound didn't exist anymore. Neither did time, space, or language. I blinked, hard, surprised that that was still something I could do.

She didn't say another word, not then. She instead took two steps toward me, reached down and took my hands in hers. We stood there, just stood there, inches separating us, no feeling but the warmth of her hands surrounding mine, and the warmth of mine filling hers.

I don't know how long we stood there. I don't know if either of us tried to speak. I'm sure I did; I can't let silence sit. But what I would remember, later, was that feeling, that warm, soft sorrow passing between the two of us. We spoke more truth in that silence than we ever had before.

"Abra," Olivia finally spoke, her voice dry and raw. "I want to ask you something."

"Of course," I croaked, surprised my tongue worked.

"The last time I had to go through this treatment, it was...lonely," she said, looking down to not meet my eyes. "My husband had died, and I didn't have any friends to sit with me during my infusions. I really didn't have friends who would stay with me during the worst times."

"So... there are treatment options?" I asked, unintentionally ignoring everything else she said. Olivia responded by smiling and continuing to look down.

"I don't want to be alone this time, Abra," she said, ignoring my question and answering it at the same time. "This is incredibly unprofessional and hideously pathetic of me to ask, but fuck it, I'm beyond caring. Abra, will you...I don't know...come keep me company? I'm guessing you've already figured out I'm not coming back to teach this year. Officially, I've been given medical leave, but…."

"Of course," I blurted, not wanting her to finish the thought we both knew the end of. "Of course I will."

"It just gets too quiet in my house." Olivia sighed. "It's huge, and creaky, and I just get tangled up in my thoughts. You don't need to be interesting or anything, I would just like someone to talk to."

"Got it," I nodded. "No being interesting."

Olivia burst into a sharp, loud peal of laughter way too exaggerated for my softball joke.

"I know that wasn't that funny," Olivia said, still laughing, "but that's the first joke anyone's even tried to tell me since I got the news. Are you sure, Abra? I know this is senior year for you, you've got to have a ton of work piling up. Not to mention any social life. I feel bad. I'm talking myself out of this. I'm sorry, I--"

"Professor," I said, putting up a palm and getting a narrowed-eye glare from Olivia, "I want to keep you company. I have no social life, and frankly, I only cared about your classes anyway, so no big loss. I want to help you with this. You've

been one of the only people keeping me sane at Freemond, let me return the favor."

"Thank you, Abra," she whispered. Tears were streaming from her eyes.

"You're going to beat this," I blurted, not knowing what else to say and instantly regretting it. Olivia closed her eyes and smiled.

"Abra," she sighed, "I'm not an idiot. And neither are you."

Unfortunately, I remembered too late that "relaxing" was the last thing that sex with Calli was. Enjoyable? Yes. Thrilling? Yes. Like snorting a line of the ground-up bones of a fallen angel off of the third rail? Yeah, probably. It certainly took my mind off things, though. At the end, I crashed, hard, and fell into a deep, dark slumber that I didn't emerge from until early the next morning.

"Well look who has rejoined the living," Calli chirped, reclined on her side of the bed, completely naked and reading a gossip blog on her phone.

"That might be an overstatement," I mumbled, the haze of sheer exhaustion still thick around my brain. I gradually became aware of the world again, realizing after what was probably too much time that I, too, was without clothing. A jolt of adrenaline shooting through me, I snatched one of the blankets that had been discarded off the side of the bed and clutched it to my body.

"Your sudden fits of modesty are never not funny to me, Abby-Cadaby," Calli laughed.

"I don't like it when you call me that," I grumbled, becoming aware that I was somewhat cranky.

"I know, sweetie," Calli cooed, taking one finger and tapping the tip of my nose. "Boop."

I made a grumbling noise and turned away from her.

"This is holding up nice," Calli commented, running her fingers over the crow heart tattoo on my bare shoulder, peeking up out of the blanket wad surrounding me. "I always loved how it came out."

"You did an amazing job," I agreed, trying to shift out of my bad mood. I decided to raise a question that had been nagging at me. "Hey, can I ask you something?"

"Of course," Calli said, putting down her phone and turning toward me. "What is it?"

"Just something I've been thinking about ever since Lore and Drew dropped the bomb on me. Why do you stick around Brahmton?" I asked, propping myself up on my elbows. "You have an amazing talent, you could go have a career anywhere. Hell, you could probably star in one of those tattoo artist reality shows."

"Oh, a super-hot transwoman who does tattoos and is prone to emotional instability? Sweetie, I'd have a primary reality show *and* a second reality show where I judge whether or not people are worthy of being on my first reality show if I wanted to." Calli laughed. "But I don't. I never told you much about my life before Brahmton, did I?"

"Yeah, you told me to 'not worry about it' every time I asked," I said, the blanket slipping down below my meager breasts. For some reason, I didn't feel the need to readjust it.

"Well, one must maintain an air of mystery, Abby," Calli smiled. "But I'm in a sharing mood today. I'm originally from a little town in Louisiana named Excelsior. Ever heard of it?"

I shook my head.

"Exactly," Calli said. "It's this kitschy little dot on the map where the economy is propped up almost entirely by pass-through tourist money and the only time you ever hear about it is on one of those shows where bumpkins talk about all the ghosts they've seen. I saw one, but it didn't get me on TV, so whatever."

I'm a little disappointed in myself that I wondered if she had fucked the ghost she claimed to have seen. Dammit, Drew.

"Anyway," Calli continued, "my point is, it's a little nothing-burg in the middle of swampland. You can imagine how much fun it was growing up there. I was really shitty at pretending to be a guy, so I was a magnet for local bullies. My mom and dad ran the local tattoo parlor, so that's where that comes from. My dad used to let me watch him work. Spent hours and hours teaching me everything he could. A few times, with the client's permission, he even let me ink a pre-drawn line or two. They were really special bonding moments for us. You know, as opposed to all the times he came into my room at night and raped me."

My mouth fell open and I started to say something, reaching out to put a hand on Calli's back. She shrugged me off and made a 'moving on' gesture.

"So the second I graduated high school, I hit the road." Calli said, looking toward the window, purple curtains still drawn over it. "I'm not exaggerating; the actual second. I had thrown everything I could into a backpack and brought it with me to the graduation ceremony, took off right from there. I never told dear old ma and pa I was leaving, and to my knowledge, they never cared to look for me. I had been communicating online with a tattoo artist in Portland who was willing to take me on as an apprentice. She was super chill and okay with me being trans, and most importantly she was in Portland. Portland! Do you know what a paradise that place sounds like to a trans kid growing up in Hicksville? I was going to live in the big, progressive, aggressively liberal Mecca of America! I would be able to walk down the street being me, date whomever I wanted, wear whatever I wanted. The sun would always shine! Birds would always sing! Every morning a glimmering rainbow butterfly would wake me up for the day and tell me how pretty I am!"

Calli's face fell into a 'can you believe this bullshit?' expression and she made a hand gesture that implied vigorous masturbation.

"I'm guessing it didn't play out that way," I ventured.

"Not so much," Calli chuckled. "Parts were great. I was...*less*...conspicuous. There were, like, ten other trans-people in the city, so that was cool. And the woman I apprenticed with *was* super chill and awesome. I owe her a ton. But no. No rainbow butterfly for me. There were still glances and whispers, and also gawks and yells. But I ignored it and convinced myself it was still better than Excelsior. Meanwhile, I was drowning in the city. You can't just go from breadcrumbs to Thanksgiving dinner, you know? I was constantly lost, I didn't know anyone other than my mentor, and she had her own family she was busy with. I always felt out of place. Then, one day, I met a guy at the shop who seemed nice. We hit it off and went on a few dates. He was cute and sweet, and on about our fourth date--because I'm a lady, dammit--I decided to bring him back to my place."

Calli dropped quiet and looked down at the bedsheet.

"I thought he knew what he was getting," she whispered. "I guess he did, too. We were both wrong."

"Calli…," I started.

"He broke two of my ribs and my nose. I had it fixed, the new one looks better, anyway," she struggled to say, trying to force a smile. "I was black and blue for almost a month after. I went to the police, got a lecture about trying to 'trick' men--called 'sir' about a thousand times--and asked if I 'really wanted to drag this all out.' I didn't."

I slid over in the bed toward Calli. Receiving a go-ahead nod, I put my arms around her shoulders.

"It wasn't the broken bones," she said, quietly crying. "I mean, those were pretty fucking bad, too, but.... It was what he said after he was done. 'You're disgusting! You're a freak. What the fuck is wrong with you? Fucking disgusting pervert!' And really, it wasn't even the words, either. It was the look on his face. This person I thought was nice and sweet...he looked at me like I wasn't even human, like I was some monster or some...piece of garbage. Like what he did was just the most natural reaction to seeing something as terrible as me."

Calli nuzzled her face into my neck, and I kissed the top of her head.

"I didn't bolt, though," she said, her tears starting to subside, but not entirely there yet. "I'm pretty proud of myself for that. I finished my apprenticeship the next month. My mentor wanted me to stay; she even offered me a job at the shop, and said she'd kick the ass of anyone who had a problem with me. She would have, too. But I couldn't take Portland anymore. So she gave me my first tattoo machine as a 'graduation' gift and wished me well. I got in my car and drove. This was the first place I stopped where people treated me like a person; I decided to stay. So here I am, Abra. The long answer to your question, I guess. There are shitty people in big cities, there are shitty people in little towns. But at least here I know my way around."

She gave a little laugh that dropped some more tears down my chest.

"See why I don't share more?" She asked, batting at her face. "I'm an ugly-crier."

"Liar," I said, wiping a last tear from under her eye and getting an actual smile.

"I wish we weren't so wrong for each other," Calli said, her head resting on my shoulder. "And I know a lot of it is me. But I'm glad you're in my life, Abra."

"Me, too," I said. I was ashamed of myself for forgetting how much I missed actually talking with Calli. Our relationship had been largely a whirlwind of sex and outlandish behavior, but tucked in there were moments like these, where both of our shields were down, when we could just talk and...be. Unfortunately, back then, they never lasted long.

"We should see each other more than once a month," Calli said, her hair tickling my nose. "I'm sorry about the mug."

"Yeah," I said, "what exactly was that about?"

"I just had this moment, you know," Calli explained, "where I had this uncontrollable curiosity about what it would look like if I smashed it."

"Well, what did it look like?" I asked.

"Like a broken mug, mostly," Calli shrugged, her shoulder bumping into me. I couldn't help but laugh.

"I like you, Calli," I said, still laughing.

"I know," she smiled. "I'm likable. I like you, too."

She turned and kissed me. We spent the rest of the morning sitting there in bed, just watching the sun rise through purple curtains.

I spent a great deal of time with Olivia in her last months, something I'm forever grateful for. She had a nurse who would visit her twice a day to do all the 'heavy lifting' tasks, so my job was just to keep Olivia company. I pitied her the first time I entered her house in Brahmton. It was like a series of vast caves, all interconnected, each one emptier than the last. She told me her husband bought it for the two of them, back when she was working at CWU. Her commute be damned, his work was in Brahmton. She stayed after he died, for reasons she never really shared. It was only after he was gone that she realized how cavernous and empty it was.

By April, the doctors had discontinued most treatments. There were experimental procedures that she was on the waitlists for, but was told that the likelihood of getting accepted in her state was slim. She rarely talked about it, preferring to sit with me and discuss literature, or have me read to her once holding up a hardback became difficult. Our favorite hobby, however, was finding the worst movies possible at the video store and making fun of them together. As her stamina dropped, we were forced to split our viewings into two sessions. Watching her waste away almost literally before my eyes was the second hardest part. The hardest part was that she was still in there. Her mind was intact, her personality was whole, her kindness, her sense of humor, her intelligence, her warmth...all there. It was just her body that was failing her.

"I wonder how that movie really *felt about women," Olivia joked as what would end up being our last film together, a schlocky old monster flick called* The Horror of Spider Island, *wound to a close. "See, I couldn't tell. Sure, they're all in their underwear 90% of the time, but occasionally they also got murdered."*

"I'm more disappointed that Spider Island is apparently home to roughly two moderately-large spiders," I laughed. "I've killed bigger in my dorm room."

Olivia laughed and took a sip from the plastic water cup that had become a fixture on the nightstand next to her adjustable bed.

"I really want to thank you for doing this, Abra," She said, her old self still burning bright behind her faded eyes. "You've made these last few months a lot more bearable. I know this couldn't have been how you imagined spending your free

time your senior year."

"Olivia," I said, turning my chair away from the TV to face her bed. "Last time: This is where I want to be. You're not keeping me from anything, and even if you were, again, this is where I want to be."

She reached a withered arm up and took my hand in hers. It had become our private gesture of sorts, when we couldn't find the words, when we couldn't find the strength to say them. Our hands against each other spoke everything that needed to be said. We sat there, hand in hand, for several minutes.

"I wish we'd met at a different place," Olivia sighed, "Maybe a different time. But definitely a different place."

I nodded, adding my free hand to the two already clasped together.

"Remember me better than this, Abra," Olivia whispered, looking down at our hands. "Remember how I was. I don't want you thinking of me as this...thing...that I've become."

Sweat was starting to bead on her forehead. Taking a soft washcloth from the nightstand, I dabbed it off, and then leaned over and kissed her forehead. Before I drew back, she moved her head up, her lips meeting mine.

"I'm sorry," she said, a pale blush crossing her sunken cheeks. "That was...inappropriate of me. I--"

I leaned in and gave her a second kiss. Her lips were dry and chapped, but still warm against mine.

"Campbell was right," she started to laugh through tears as we parted. "The goddamn son of a bitch was right: I am the worst *at being professional."*

She reached over and picked up her water cup again, and lifted it skyward.

"To different places and different times," she declared. Having no cup of my own, I mimed a 'cheers' as she drank. She fell asleep shortly after, and I sat with her for another hour, until the night-shift nurse arrived. I paused at the door of her room, which would one day be my room, looking back at her thin, wasted body curled under the sheets, knowing that we had just said our goodbyes.

I showed up at Cluster around ten. Calli and I had decided to have breakfast--which consisted of freezer waffles and a side of green olives, pretty much the only food she had on hand--before saying goodbye. I felt odd that morning, like somehow I'd crossed some Rubicon, but I wasn't sure how or what.

"Geez, there you are!" Lore exclaimed as I walked in the door. "We've been trying to reach you all morning. Where were you?"

"Yeah, Abra," Drew said, emerging from the stage section still holding a microphone stand. "We were getting worried."

"I'm fine," I said, my illogical frustration with the two of them still hanging thick around my brain. "Just running late. Where's Neal?"

"He's pitching his ideas to the truck guy," Lore said. "He'll be in later. Seriously, Abra, where were you? You didn't come home last night, and you weren't answering texts."

I made a noise somewhere between a sigh and a growl. They needed to leave me alone. I was cranky and illogical and still pissed at them for stupid reasons, and they needed to leave me alone so I could put my brain back together.

"What's with you this morning?" Lore asked, coming out from behind the coffee counter. "Are you still mad about--?"

"I'm fine!" I snapped. "I was with Calli, okay?"

"Oh, geez," Drew chuckled. "Was she, like, holding you hostage or something?"

"Oh, sweetie," Lore mewed. "Why? Why would you do that to yourself?"

"Leave her alone," I growled, standing in the doorway between the coffee shop and Cadabra's Corner. "I was with her because she was there. I needed someone, and she was there, and she was kind, and she listened. I needed someone, and she dropped everything to be there for me. And I know she's a lot, but she's not a monster, so stop talking about her like she is. We all have our shit."

"I'm sorry," Lore mumbled, taken aback. "I didn't mean to make it sound like--"

"No!" Drew yelled. "No! Enough of this! So you were with Calli because she was there. You used her, but *we're* the bad guys for talking about her in the same way you usually do? Fuck that, I'm tired of this!"

"I was wrong!" I yelled back. "And I didn't use her!"

"Sure you did," Drew shouted. "Sure you did. You were lonely or mad or whatever, and you called her up because you knew you could lean on her, and I bet all the money in my pocket against all the money in yours that by this time tomorrow, you'll be making jokes about what a wide-awake nightmare of a person she is!"

"You don't fucking know what you're talking about," I barked, storming back to my Corner.

"Yeah, I do," Drew yelled at my back.

"Drew!" Lore hissed.

"No, I'm tired of this," Drew continued. "Yeah, I do know what it's like. You use people. You see us all as loyal sidekicks and helpers here to be drawn on as you need. We helped you put together your dream here at the shop, and yeah, we had a ton of fun doing it, but as soon as we decide it's time to move on, you act like we betrayed you!"

"You didn't even tell me you were thinking of leaving!" I screamed back. "If it's so hard to understand why I might be mad at you, why did you hide it for so long?"

"Because we knew you'd do this!" Drew retorted. "It's what you do! And don't even get me started on how you treat Neal!"

"Nah, you go right ahead," I yelled. "Go right the fuck ahead. I need one more person telling me that I'm the devil for not ripping his heart out. Go ahead."

"Oh get off it!" Drew groaned. "You don't want to tell him how it is because you don't want him to leave. You don't want him to leave because he makes you feel good, and fuck whatever it's doing to him."

"Drew!" Lore snapped.

"I'm done," Drew huffed. "I've said what I needed to say. Abra, I love you. I really do, and I know that sounds like bullshit right now. But I can't watch you do this anymore. I don't think you're trying to, I just think you've fallen into this pattern. I know life dealt you a shit hand, but--"

"I don't need your goddamn pity," I snarled, slumping into my chair behind the counter. "You said what you needed to say, and you're probably not wrong. But I don't need your pity. And leave Calli alone. She deserves better than how we talk about her."

"Okay," Drew nodded, and walked back to the stage section. Lore stayed in the doorway and stared at me for another half-beat, then turned and walked away.

"Well, I've saved Christmas *and* the American auto-worker!" Neal declared as he burst through the door about an hour later. We had a few customers at that point, all regulars, though, who barely looked up at such a statement. Drew, Lore, and I didn't react, either.

"I... I got the job designing the truck lot's Christmas brochure," Neal mumbled, the wind knocked out of his sails. "Sorry, I guess I should have made that clearer."

"That's great, Neal," Lore said, trying to muster enthusiasm.

"Yeah, good job, man," Drew called from the stage. I gave a silent thumbs-up from my counter.

"Did...did someone die?" Neal asked, looking back and forth

between his three friends.

"Things got...real while you were gone," Lore said. "And somewhat heated."

"Oh," Neal said. "Okay. Well...get over it? I mean, it's not like we haven't had fights before. Remember the Christmas lights fiasco last year? If we can survive that--"

"Bit bigger, Neal," I grumbled.

"Oh," Neal slumped. "Well, what was it about? I need to know who to go be a grump next to."

"A lot of things, Neal," Lore sighed. "Drew and Abra got into it about some old stuff. It's just...going to take some time."

"Hmm," Neal grunted, thinking to himself for a few seconds. "Nah, screw that. Tomorrow is the Ides of December! It's like our Christmas. I don't know what you two got into, and no one seems to want to tell me, but do you really want to ruin the Ides? Especially since it's probably our last one as a group?"

Drew and I both shook our heads.

"Okay, good," Neal nodded. "So, what do we need to do here to move on?"

"I'm sorry for how I said what I said," Drew spoke, to his feet. "Not for what I said, though."

"Okay," I said, also to my feet.

"Abra?" Neal goaded. "What do *you* need to do?"

I looked up from the ground and across the building, past Neal, meeting Drew's eyes. I gave him a small nod.

"Okay," Drew nodded back.

"Well, I don't understand what just happened, but as long as everyone is satisfied," Neal shrugged. "Come on, everyone over here, bring it in. It's cheesy and stupid, but we're going to do it anyway. Everyone hug it out."

Drew and I reluctantly joined Lore and Neal in the coffee shop, all four of us wrapping our arms around one another. A few of the patrons applauded and gave exaggerated "aw!" calls. I looked over toward Neal, on the other side of the circle, but couldn't meet his eyes.

Neal went with me to Olivia's funeral. She had passed away quietly shortly after our final visit, about three weeks before commencement. It was a good service. Not wonderful, certainly not beautiful, but good. And right. Though we had seldom talked about it, Olivia's faith had been an important thread through her life, and her pastor, a woman who could have only been a few years older than her, gave an appropriately gut-wrenching homily thankfully devoid of "everything happens for a reason" or "God needed a new angel." The overall message was, "This is terrible and it's okay to hate that it happened." It was maybe the first sermon I was ever entirely on board with.

Worse than the funeral itself was commencement. Since her death was so fresh, the school devoted a section of the ceremony to honoring her, inviting several of her students past and present up to share their favorite memories. I was, conspicuously, left off the list, though one of my favorite pictures, a shot of her and me both wearing ugly sweaters and drinking eggnog at the English department Christmas party my sophomore year, was featured in the slideshow. The hardest part, though, was watching Dean Ted Campbell preside over the whole thing, blubbering big crocodile tears and talking about how beloved and central Professor Paulson was to his department, and how sorely she would be missed.

My insides had seethed and I was on the verge of jumping from my seat, tossing down my mortarboard and telling him what a two-faced, pathetic vulture he was. But then I had what may have been my only paranormal experience. As I was about to push myself out of my chair, I felt a soothing, familiar warmth on my right hand. I'm sure it was just some psychosomatic sensation, something akin to a phantom pain brought on by watching so many pictures of Olivia flash by on the screen combined with my surge of emotion. Ghosts, spirits, whatever you want to call them, don't exist, they aren't real, they're the product of deluded, overactive minds. Except, people say that about me, too. I know all the rational explanations, and they make perfect sense. But I also know what I felt that day; the warm, calming glow that filled my body and lowered me back into my seat. Like most things, I don't feel like arguing it.

A week after commencement, there was a knock on the door of the crappy little apartment Neal and I had rented after graduation.

"You want to get that?" I asked Neal as we sat in the living room, him drawing and me reading.

"May as well," he grumbled, putting down his tablet and taking the short walk over to the door.

"Hello," a smooth female voice said from the door as he answered it. "I'm looking for a Ms. Abra Collins."

"And you are...?" Neal asked. I craned my neck around my chair to try to see the front door without being seen myself. A statuesque woman with dark skin and close-cropped hair stood in the doorway, wearing a suit that was nicer than anything I'd ever owned and carrying a briefcase.

"My name is Monica Wilson," the woman said, offering a hand to Neal. "I'm

the attorney in charge of managing the late Dr. Olivia Paulson's estate."

"I'm Abra Collins," I called, pulling myself out of my chair and heading toward the door, suddenly aware that I was wearing baggy jeans and a stained Black Sabbath hoodie.

"Pleased to meet you, Ms. Collins," the lawyer said, extending a hand, which I shook with some trepidation. She was the type of poised and attractive that made it seem weird that we were both humans.

"Is this your husband?" she gestured to Neal, whose eyes grew enormous.

"No," I said, probably too harshly. "No no no."

"Oh, I'm sorry," Monica Wilson said. "Boyfriend?"

"No," I repeated, as Neal began turning shades of red verging on violet.

"How about I just stop guessing?" Monica asked.

"Best friend," I helped. "Roommate. Partner in crime. He can hear anything I can hear."

"Right," she nodded. "Do you have time to talk?"

"Sure," I said, moving to clear space at our refuse-covered kitchen table. "What's this about?"

"Well, Ms. Collins," Monica said, every word sounding like it should be part of the narration of the movie adaptation of a fantasy novel, "as I told your...friend, I'm the attorney in charge of Dr. Olivia Paulson's estate. I understand the two of you were close?"

I nodded.

"Dr. Paulson was very fond of you, Ms. Collins," Olivia continued as the three of us took our seats around the particle board table.

"You can just call me Abra," I interjected.

"Alright," she nodded. "She was *extremely* fond of you. As such, she's left you, well, a great deal in her will."

"What?" I asked, my mouth suddenly dry. "What's 'a great deal'?"

I had never felt entitled to anything, of course, but I will admit that part of me had always hoped she'd leave me some memento of herself, something I could hold onto, like I had with Snooty Crow. A pen, a favorite book, a mug. Just something of no value that I could treasure. 'A great deal' was never a phrase that came up when I was hoping.

"Dr. Paulson modified her will about a month before her death," Monica continued. "She had me make sure everything was squared for you. Ms. Collins--Abra--Dr. Paulson left you her house, as well as another property in Brahmton. A commercial space, a small strip-mall with three stores. Abra?"

My jaw had almost unhinged, my mouth open almost as wide as Neal's eyes. Words were eluding me.

"W-what?" I stammered.

"Like I said," Monica smiled, "she was very *fond of you. I have all the paperwork ready, and she already paid for me to help you with the whole process of taking ownership of the properties. She said you are, of course, free to sell them, and I'd be happy to help you prepare for that process, too, but she hoped you wouldn't."*

"This is incredible," Neal said for me, as I continued to sputter like a clogged sprinkler head.

"She was an incredible person," Monica smiled, her tone dropping to a more conversational level. "I'm sure you knew that, though, Abra."

I nodded, tears coming to my eyes.

"Would you like me to give you a moment?" Monica asked as I tried to hide my face. "Or I can come back tomorrow to do the paperwork. I understand this has to be a lot to take in."

"Just a moment," I nodded. "I can get myself together."

"Alright," Monica said. "I'll go make some calls I need to make in my car. Come get me when you're ready?"

I nodded again.

"Oh, I almost forgot," she said, pausing as she stood, reopening her briefcase. "She wanted me to give this to you, too. She gave it to me about a week before she passed."

Monica handed me a fancy brown envelope, sealed with a blob of wax that had an embellished letter P stamped into it. I muttered a word of thanks and I turned the envelope over in my hands as Monica stepped outside.

"I... think I'll give you a moment, too," Neal said, starting to stand. I grabbed his forearm and shook my head. He nodded and lowered himself back into his seat.

I slid a finger under the flap of the envelope, easing the seal up, trying to preserve as much of it as I could. Inside was piece of faux-aged stationary that I unfolded.

"My dear, dear Abra," the letter started. It was handwritten, the letters all in shaky cursive. "I'm going to say things now that I never could have made myself say in person, and I'm sorry for that. I know that you liked to keep things light, and that's one of the things I love about you, how you can find the humor in anything, but bear with me because I'm dead now anyway, which means you pretty much have to listen."

Here she had drawn a winking smiley face that made me laugh.

"You are easily the most enjoyable person I've ever met." The letter continued. "I am so, so blessed to have met you. You are wonderfully unlike anyone else. I wish we had had more time together. I wish we had gotten to go on the trip we had talked about this June. I wish we had been able to spend so many more years just talking about books and making fun of old movies.

Here the letter dropped down a line.

"I love you. And I'm sorry. I'm sorry because I know that's not appropriate or professional, and I'm sorry because I'm worried that it will make you uncomfortable to hear that, but I needed to say it, if only to a piece of paper. I didn't set out to fall in love with a student, I didn't even consider it a possibility. And I know it puts me in a category with a group of very unlikeable people, but like I said, I'm dead now, so I don't know what can be done about it."

I leaned back so tears wouldn't drop onto the letter. Neal, who was sitting on the other side of the paper, where he couldn't see the text, started to ask what was wrong. I shook my head before he could.

"Maybe one day I would have told you," Olivia's words continued. "And maybe you would have been happy to hear it, and you felt the same way, and since you weren't my student any longer, we could have been together and lived out the rest of our days happily. I know what your face is doing right now."

Another winking smiley face.

"Or maybe you would have been disgusted," she wrote. "Maybe you would have told me that I had completely misread our friendship, and that I was just a sad old lady you felt pity for and you wanted me to leave you alone forever. I've played both possibilities out in my head way too many times for a highly educated woman. Like I said, this was never the career for me. I don't do detached and stoic. Which brings me to my next point."

That was the end of that sheet. Fortunately, there was another tucked into the envelope.

"By now, Monica has told you about what I've left you," the second sheet continued. "I hope it's a gift, not something I'm yoking you with. I'd almost recommend selling the house. It's lovely, but it seems to grow larger and emptier with every passing day. At the very least, fill it. But the strip mall, I would like you to keep. It was one of my husband's properties that I inherited when the miserable bastard died. It's been languishing empty ever since; I never got around to selling it. I think you know what I hope you'll do, but you, of course, are a free woman. Please never forget that. I frequently did. None of your dreams are stupid; There's no such thing."

The letter finished on the back.

"I'll leave you with this, Abra," she concluded. "I'm hoping after reading this you're still fond of me. Because I am so very, very glad to have had you in my life, even briefly. You are the only person I would have wanted with me at the end. Thank you for walking with me.

All of my love, which I hope is okay,

-Olivia"

I folded the pages and quickly tucked them back in the envelope before Neal could see them. Clutching it to my chest, I fully broke down, my head against the table. Neal rubbed my shoulders, letting me sob without asking why.

So I lied to Lore when she asked. But it was a good lie. I've never shown anyone the letter Olivia wrote me. Every year, on her birthday, December 15, after everyone has left for the day, I'd take a seam ripper and gently open the stitches running down Snooty Crow's chest to retrieve the carefully folded pieces of stationery from their hiding place. I'd sit alone, read the letter to myself, toast different times and different places, and then return it to Snooty Crow for safe keeping.

Snooty Crow is not for sale.

Despite our 'resolution,' the rest of the day was spent largely in thick silence with poor Neal caught in the middle, still dreadfully confused and desperate to bring peace to the store. It was not to be, however, and when we arrived home Drew and Lore made a beeline to their room, turning the white-noise machine that sat outside their door to full blast. There were only two reasons they ever did that, and I doubted they were about to have sex. My suspicions were confirmed seconds later when muffled yells began emanating from their side of the hall, obscured by the loud static being blasted by the machine.

"Let's...head downstairs," Neal suggested, gesturing to the basement door. I shrugged and followed him, not knowing what else to do.

"Okay, out with it," he said, turning on the lights, including the hanging Christmas lights that were the subject of what was now our second biggest explosion. "What the hell is going on with you three?"

"It's...stupid," I sighed, flopping myself down at my computer.

"Yes, I figured that much," Neal, getting annoyed, said.

"Just...can we do something else instead?" I asked. "I'm not trying to be a pain in the ass, I just spent my whole day thinking about it, and I need a break."

"Okay," Neal sighed, lowering himself into the chair next to me. "Tomorrow's the Ides...how are you doing?"

"As far as that?" I asked. "I'm okay. I miss her, though. I always do, but I've been thinking about her a lot, lately. I don't know how she did it, living in this house all alone. I know she was lonely. But she put on not just a brave face but a joyful face every day and tried to make sure everyone she met felt better because of it. Drew told me he 'knew I'd been dealt a shit hand by life,' but fuck that. I don't feel that way.

Olivia, she--"

"Probably didn't feel that way either," Neal said.

"Yeah," I said. "I really miss her. Fuck, I'm a downer tonight. You want to give the maze another shot?"

"Well, if constant defeat and consternation are going to make you feel better, sure!" Neal laughed. I laughed, too, and switched on my computer, loading up *Unwelcome.* I looked over at my friend--my best friend, who would have been my best friend even if Gwen and Olivia were both still alive--and watched his face light up as the opening title of the stupid game we'd been beating our heads against for almost two decades loaded up. This wasn't going to make me feel better.

"The tapestry room!" I yelled an hour later, pointing wildly at the screen we could both clearly see. "We're back at the tapestry room!"

"Fuck yeah!" Neal yelled. We had been unable to relocate the room with the hanging tapestry that we had first discovered on our last maze session. This time, though, we had a few minutes to spare.

"Okay, 'hit' the tapestry," I suggested. Neal selected 'hit' from the menu and then clicked the tapestry.

"*You have hit the tapestry. Your hand is sore, but nothing else happens.*" The game declared.

"Fuck, okay," Neal muttered. "We'll try 'take.'"

"*You cannot take the tapestry*," said the text at the bottom of the game's menu.

"Fine," I grumbled. "I don't want your ugly-ass tapestry anyway. 'Move'?"

Neal started to click 'move,' then stopped.

"Wait," he said, moving the cursor over to our inventory menu, a list of items we had already found on our quest. He selected "torch."

"Neal, you beautiful bastard," I said, tapping him repeatedly on the shoulder. "Do it! Do it!"

Neal's next click was on the tapestry. Crudely animated flames ignited the digital wall hanging, consuming it and leaving an almost bare wall.

"*You have destroyed the tapestry*," the game informed us.

"What the hell is that?" I asked, pointing at the small, round dot in the wall that had been behind the tapestry. Neal clicked 'look' and then the dot.

"*It seems to be a key hole of some sort*," the game said.

"Holy shit!" I yelled. "Holy shit! Inventory! Inventory!"

Neal quickly scrolled through our inventory screen, past amulets, swords, gold chalices and other items we had discovered. But no key.

"Dammit!" We both yelled. Suddenly, the screen turned red, and the familiar face of the elder demon appeared in all its unholy glory, declaring that our souls were delicious.

"Fuck!" I screamed.

"I am so sick of seeing that guy!" yelled Neal, highlighting his point by shoving both middle fingers at the screen.

"We were so close," I moaned. "I think. It feels like we're close, right?"

"Yeah," Neal agreed. "Now we just need a key. Could it be back in an earlier section?"

"I don't think so, we scoured the rest of the mansion pretty well," I grumbled.

"We'll get this," Neal said. "That asshole won't win."

I looked back at the screen, back at the fanged grin of the horned devil staring back at us. It occurred to me that he had been giving me that same 'fuck you' grin ever since childhood. When I realized I was trans, he gave me that grin. When my sister was murdered, he gave me that grin. When I met Olivia, there was that grin. When she died, he was there, too. He grinned the same when my father died, and he was still grinning at me now.

"He's my last villain," I said, out loud.

"What?" Neal asked.

"Nothing, I…," I started. "All of my villains are dead except that one, and he's a fucking bundle of pixels. My father, the asshole who killed Gwen...hell, even Ted Campbell had a massive stroke about a year ago. He's not dead, but last I heard he has to have a nurse help him eat Jell-O, so…. it's just this demonic asshole and--"

I stopped, realizing mid-sentence what Gwen, Calli, Lore, Drew, and even my dickbag father had all tried to tell me in assorted ways. There was one more villain in my life, and it was time to stop hiding from her.

"Why haven't you told me about the job in New York?" I asked, turning away from the monitor and facing Neal. "Or about Dan?"

"I…," Neal gaped, his eyes wide and face drained of blood. "How…? Did Lore tell you?"

"Neal," I asked again, keeping my voice as steady as I could. "Tell me about the job."

"I'm not going to take it!" Neal blurted.

"Why not?"

"Because I don't want to!" He replied. "Do I need more of a reason than that?"

"Kinda, yeah," I said, losing some of my calm. "Neal, you've talked about drawing comics professionally your whole life! Suddenly you don't want to? What, you want to draw truck advertisements for all eternity now?"

"Excuse me? I'm fine with what I'm doing!" Neal snapped back. It was then that I noticed his eyes were getting shiny.

"You need to do it!" I begged him. "Neal, I know it's big, but you need to do it! You'll regret it forever if you don't. And you and Dan were--."

"It's not like that," Neal grumbled, getting out of his chair and pacing the room. "He has a boyfriend. Or something. He just reached out because--"

"Come on, Neal," I rolled my eyes. "You know how Dan felt about you. I don't know what happened between the two of you, but--"

"He asked me to marry him," Neal admitted, for the first time.

"W-what?" I stuttered. I had known that something big had transpired between Neal and Dan, something Neal had never wanted to talk about. My wildest guess was that one of them had cheated on the other. My worst fear was that Dan had gotten tired of having Neal's affections split between him and me. This, I had not seen coming.

"It was our anniversary," Neal mumbled into his chest as he stopped his pacing. "He took me up to the lookout at Thorton Park. It was this...just beautiful day. We had the whole place to ourselves, so we ate our lunch and then just sat and looked out over the town."

My heart was sinking. Tears were flowing in two marked paths down Neal's face.

"Then he asked me to stand, and he told me that he loved me, and that his life hadn't been complete until he met me. Then he said he never wanted to be without me and got on one knee. I said no." Neal finished.

"Neal," I whispered. "Why?"

"It just...wasn't right," he said, looking down and to the side.

"Neal…."

"I wasn't in that place yet."

"Neal."

"I didn't feel the same way, it wasn't fair to him!"

"Neal!"

"Because I was in love with you, okay?" Neal yelled, loud enough to rattle the basement windows. My heart pounded in my chest as he looked back up.

"Because I still am, okay?" he said, back in a gentler tone. "Fuck, I'm sorry, Abra. Look, I'm not an idiot; I know you don't feel the same way. And I wish I could turn it off, but I can't. I've tried for so long. I know that this is all we'll be, but that's okay. I just need you in my life. I always have."

Ashamed, he slumped down onto the floor, his back against the side of my desk. My joints feeling almost fused, I slid myself down next to him, my shoulder up against his.

"I love you, too," I said, causing him to turn away from me.

"Abra, don't," he objected.

"I love you, too," I repeated. "Maybe not like you love me, but I love you, Neal. You're my best, dearest friend. I--"

"Don't," Neal said again. "I don't need you to do that. I let go of the delusion that you'd feel the same way a long time ago."

"How...long?" I asked.

"I honestly don't remember," Neal shrugged, still crying. "Forever, I think. Before you were Abra."

He looked down and gave a burst of sad, quiet laughter.

"You were my first crush," he said, into his lap. "I've been in love with you so long that I don't know how it feels to not be in love with you. You've made everything so much better just by being there with me. I don't need you to love me like I love you. I don't. I just...need you. I'm sorry, I never planned on telling you this. Can we just pretend--?"

"No," I cut him off. "We can't, and I don't want to. I love you too, Neal. I'm not saying that to make you feel better, I'm not saying it to make me feel better. I love you, probably more than I've ever loved anyone. And no, it's not like you love me, but it's also not like I love Drew or Lore or even Olivia or Gwen. I don't know what to call it, but it's real, and it's strong, and I can't imagine my life without you, either."

I leaned my head over onto Neal's shoulder, tears flowing from my eyes. This week was dehydrating. He gently wiped my cheek and looked down at me. I'd never looked into his eyes from that angle. I leaned up, and ever-so-slightly, for the first time ever, our lips touched.

In that moment, I saw a life with him. So what if it wasn't the typical life two people have together? We could live together and do everything together, be there for one another in the bad times and celebrate the good times. We could grow old, but our love wouldn't fade. It hadn't in all these years. Being loved by someone the way he loved me felt warm and amazing. It made me feel like I could do anything. It felt wonderful in ways I had always been afraid to admit. To have someone who lives only for you.

And that's when the fantasy stopped, and the cold blade of reality slipped between my ribs. I looked down, pulling my lips away from his.

"Neal, I'm sorry," I whispered.

"Me, too," he stammered. "I shouldn't have--"

"No," I stopped him. "Not about that. I love you, Neal. And I could live the rest of my life happily with you. But because I love you, I can't do that to you. I can't be the reason that you don't get to have someone who looks at you the way you look at me. I can't be what holds back your dreams. I can't let you trade everything you deserve for the stupid thing you want."

"Abra, it's not--" Neal started, standing up while I stayed on the floor.

"You have to go, Neal," I said, through tears. "I'm sorry. You have to go."

"Abra..."

"If you don't want to be with Dan, or don't want to go to New York, that's fine," I stammered. "But you have to go. I can't be the anchor that holds you back. I can't do this to you anymore."

"Abra! You're not--" he started to object.

"If you love me," I sobbed, "then please don't make me do this to you."

Neal's mouth hung open, but instead of saying anything, he slid back to the ground next to me. We sat like that for a long, long time.

"I'm sorry," I whispered, finally. "I'm sorry for keeping you so long. You weren't mine to have."

"I'll never, ever, regret a single moment we spent together," Neal said, his eyes red and his face wet.

"Me, either," I said. "Jesus, we never finished the maze."

"Maybe it's time to admit that we're just shit at video games," Neal suggested.

We both laughed, or at least made the approximate noise.

"To best friends," Neal whispered, lifting an invisible glass.

"To first crushes," I replied, lifting an imaginary glass of my own. We sat there for the rest of the night, in a cold silence that was anything but empty. At some point, we both fell asleep against each other.

In the morning, I woke up alone. His art tablet was gone, as were most of his clothes and the smattering of sentimental items he kept in his room. His car wasn't in the driveway. I went to Drew and Lore's room, to see if they had been there when he left, but they were gone, too, already headed to Cluster for the day. It was just me in the house.

Alone.

3 A DEPRESSED BUTTERFLY

When I was nine, my father took me fishing at some local lake whose name I don't even think I knew then. It was one of the few times I remember him being excited to spend time with me, and the whole week prior he had bragged to everyone who would listen that he and "his boy" were going to go on their first fishing trip together. Even at nine, I knew this was a rite of passage in my dad's mind, so I spent the week before psyching myself up for it. I asked Neal a million questions about the fishing trip that he had taken with his dad, being told that, mainly, they sat in a little boat with lines in the water until his dad declared it was time to go home. I could do that.

Our fishing spot wasn't a boat, it was a dock that stretched out over the edge of the grimy lake. It was also a pretty popular spot that day, with at least three other families gathered with lines in the water. According to a large, bald man in hip-waders, the fish just weren't biting, though. Dad shrugged, surprisingly unperturbed, and said that we'd just have a nice day by the water, then.

And we did, for a while. It was a warm day, but not too hot, the sun out but with enough clouds passing by it to keep it from being oppressive. Dad taught me how to cast a line, and I got praise from him and two of the other fathers for how well my first attempt went. He drank a beer from the cooler he brought along with us and gave me a soda, something that was prohibited by my mother except on special occasions (and, in all fairness to mom, I still have all my teeth). We actually talked a bit, too. Mainly about the lake, but he did ask me how school was going, which happened so infrequently that I felt the need to fill him in on everything from first grade on.

Unfortunately, about the time I was explaining my book report from earlier in the year, my line jerked.

"Hey, look!" Dad whispered as I grabbed my pole. "Okay...okay...careful now. Here's what you do…."

He proceeded to tell me the steps of reeling in a fish, steps I had already memorized from a book on fishing I got at the library when I found out we'd be making this trip. My hands moved as if I had done it a million times before, putting back with enough pressure to secure the hook without snapping the line, waiting for just the right time to start reeling, bringing it up, up, up until it flapped out of the water, a glistening silver rainbow trout on the end of my line.

"You got him!" Dad yelled, exploding with pride. "He got it!"

Several members of the other families cheered, my catch being the first of the day. Dad swung our net under the struggling trout and scooped it up, bringing it back onto the dock. It was a big one, according to the compliments I was receiving from the other families, and I began to feel the unusual sensation of pride swelling inside my chest.

Then, I looked down at the fish, writhing on the dock amid the net. I'm not a vegan, or a PETA member, and I love animals, but I also understand life. I knew that fish didn't have brains like we do, I knew they didn't have thoughts and complex emotions. I knew that they didn't sing whimsical songs under the water, and they didn't have little fish families who loved them and would miss them if they were gone.

Still.

I watched the trout flail back and forth, its lidless eye staring at me in what looked for all purposes to be panic, its mouth gaping open and closed as if gasping, my hook, now bloody, still embedded in its lip.

"So," I asked, trying to hide my anxiety as I watched the fish struggled. "We're going to throw it back now?"

"What?" Dad replied, as if I had just asked him if I could fly by flapping my arms. "Why would we do that?"

"Well, it's just…." I stammered. My dad stared at me, and I watched all the patience and goodwill drain out of him.

"For fuck sake, boy," he hissed. "Don't go all pussy on me. You knew why we came out here!"

"I just--" I stammered.

"You want to throw this fish back?" He snapped, picking the fish up and tearing the hook from it, taking a large chunk of its lip at the same time. "You see this hook? You see it?"

He held the hook an inch from my face. I could feel the tears building behind my eyes, but I did everything I could to keep them back.

"DO YOU SEE IT?" he screamed. Now the other families were staring

again, but none of them said anything.

"Yes!" I blurted.

"Do you think that that fish really survives having this thing put into him and then pulled out?" He snarled. "Do you? Are you that dumb?"

"N-no." I muttered, trying to keep it together.

"But let me guess," he sneered, "you'd be fine if we threw it back and it just went off and died under the water, right? Because then you wouldn't have to see it. Right?"

I didn't say anything, too busy staring at the fish, still twisting and writhing, now bloodied.

"This is the problem with people these days," Dad ranted. "They want the sausage, but they don't want to see how it was made. You know how many fish just like this you've eaten because I worked to catch them and I brought them home? But you didn't shed any tears for them, right? Because someone did it for you! Goddammit."

Dad reached into his tackle box and drew out a small, dirty hammer. The other families were now pretending to ignore us.

"Let me explain something to you," Dad hissed. "That fish you suddenly love so much is dying right there on the dock. And fish don't feel much, but I guaran-damn-tee you that they do feel the two things all living creatures feel: fear and pain. Now you got a choice to make, boy: Either let that fish suffer and suffocate there, or take responsibility for it and use this hammer to make its pain stop. What's it going to be, princess?"

He shoved the hammer into my hand and stepped out from between the trout and me. I stood there with the hammer, watching the fish flop around, watching its eyes lull around and around, its mouth still making that awful gasping movement. My heart pounding and the tears in my eyes threatening to break free, I lifted the hammer. The fish twisted in the net, seeming to be trying to move away from me. I held the hammer aloft, trying to make myself bring it down, trying to make my hand stop listening to my brain and just act on impulse, trying to--

"For fuck sake," Dad hissed, snatching the hammer away from me. "You can't live your life letting people do everything for you!"

He brought the rusted metal head of the hammer down onto the trout's skull, connecting with a hard, wet crunch. The fish stopped moving after that.

We never went fishing again.

"Incoming," Callie muttered to me from across the table, as a formidable woman with magenta hair emerged from the music section.

"Okay, come on, let's see it," Crystal said, approaching the table

Calli and I were sharing in the coffee section. She gestured at my upper shoulder.

"Fine," I grumbled, easing my arm out of the oversized cotton button-up I was wearing over a tank-top emblazoned with Old Bones' logo. Crystal leaned in and examined my shoulder like it was a Dead Sea scroll. Around my Sacred Heart with crow heads was a new circle of impeccably inked script. "To other places, other times," on the bottom, "To best friends, first crushes," on the top.

"Okay, but, like, what does it mean?" Crystal, who had about 80% of her body covered in ink of incredibly varied quality, asked.

"They're things two friends said to her," Calli answered for me as I put my over-shirt back on. "So she can carry them with her even though they're gone."

"Jesus," Crystal groaned. "See, this is the problem with your generation: You're too 'touchy-feely.' Carry your friends with you? Shit, here's a newsflash: Sometimes friends go away. Saying you're someone's BFF isn't a binding contract, girls. Shrug, make new friends, and get the fuck on with your life. Don't go get some weird quote of theirs tattooed on your arm. Christ."

"Crystal," I said, holding my coffee mug and trying my damndest to not throw it at my employee. "You have a picture on your back of the Grim Reaper sodomizing an angel while the devil jerks off next to them."

"Yeah," Crystal shrugged. "It means death fucks us all in the end, so you may as well have fun. It means *something.* Don't give me that look.... It's not like I haven't had friends. I just don't get my panties in a wad every time one leaves. You can make new friends."

"It's fun that you've managed to make being emotionally stunted noble," I smiled as I took a drink.

"I was thinking the same thing about you and being developmentally arrested, sweetie," Crystal smiled back, tossing her hair over her shoulder and trailing her fingers across the table as she left before pausing to address Calli.

"Stupid tattoo or no, you're not half-bad," she said. "You should talk to Stan at Squid Eye; maybe they'd take you on as an apprentice."

I put my hand on Calli's shoulder to keep her in her seat as Crystal went back into the music section. Squid Eye was Calli's only competitor in Brahmton, and Crystal's shop of choice. It was also doing considerably better than Black Needles, financially.

"I. Don't. Like. Her," Callie sing-songed through her teeth.

"She's...different," I sighed. "Unfortunately, she's also good at what she does."

Boy howdy was she. Crystal was the top pick Drew had left me to take over the music section, but I had heard of her long before he brought her to my attention. She was legendary in the fledgling local music scene, having once run her own venue until it burned down and she became a free-floating force of nature. Any band in the area that was worth anything knew Crystal, and she knew them. There were at least five different songs written about her. Her connections alone made her invaluable, but it was her eye for potential that made her basically a sorceress. Bands lived and died in Brahmton based on her whims.

When news spread that she was back in the venue game, Cluster went from being a fun hangout to *the* place to be. We were bringing in money hand over fist, especially with Crystal's outlandishly popular metal group, which had the classy name War Bitch, essentially being our house band. Unfortunately, Crystal had all the charm and people skills of a possessed bulldozer, and we were perpetually locked in a shadow war for power, me owning the business but her bringing in the most money.

"Here's your drink, ma'am," a mousey little voice squeaked from beside us. Lindsee, Cluster's only barista, stood there holding Calli's drink in a paper cup. I had long since forgiven her for the mug incident, but she wasn't getting anything other than to-go cups anymore. She found subtle ways to protest this policy.

"Thank you, coffee-pixie," Calli said smiling as Lindsee went back to the counter. She then wordlessly reached into her purse and grabbed a black marker, which she used to draw a large picture of a phallus on the side of her cup. "Now *her* I like."

I liked Lindsee, too, though often it felt like I was corrupting her by just being in her presence. She was a local kid who, despite looking about fourteen, had graduated from a Christian university with a degree in business. In theory, she was back in Brahmton just until she could find better work elsewhere, but we'd kept her hooked for two years, doing our books and running our coffee shop. She was further down Lore's pile, but she was the only one of the potential candidates that didn't make me want to drink lye.

"So, what do you want to do for Thanksgiving?" Calli asked as I sipped my coffee. "I was thinking we could get a pizza and eat it in the parking lot of the outlet mall, so we can watch all the Black Friday shoppers fight. Sound good?"

"In that I seriously can't think of anything else to do, sure," I shrugged. Calli and I had attempted a more traditional Thanksgiving the year before, unfortunately realizing too late that neither of us knew how to cook. Ever since then, holidays had been somewhat bizarre affairs, usually centering around whatever kind of takeout we could find still open.

"Great. Now," Calli said, putting down her cup and tenting her narrow fingers, "are we ever going to talk about it?"

"Talk about what?" I asked.

"Sweetie." her mouth said, but her look said, "are you fucking kidding me?"

"Fine," I sighed. "It's no big deal. I'm happy for him. I'm really, really happy for him. I'm glad he moved on."

"That's a great party-line, Abby," Calli said, reaching over and patting my hand. "What a wonderful answer to give everyone else. But this is me."

"I *am* happy," I protested. Calli's face fell, and she stared a hole into the table top.

"When we got back together," she said, slowly, refusing to look at me, "for whatever it is we are, we agreed to one thing: no masks, not with each other. That's was *your* request, Abra."

"I'm sorry," I said, reaching across the table to touch her hand, but having it drawn back. "I am happy for him, but...I don't know what I feel beyond that. It's not fun, I know *that.*"

"You're allowed to hate this," Calli said, putting her hand back and setting it on mine.

"I... don't," I shook my head. "I really don't. It just drives home how much everything has changed the last two years. I don't know, maybe Crystal's right and I do just need to grow up and move on. But there's always going to be this part of me that wishes that everything was back the way it used to be."

"Well, I hope not *everything,*" Calli said, trying to play it off as a joke but her face flashing actual trepidation.

"You know what I mean," I smiled, bringing her hand up to my lips and kissing it. That was the one thing that had improved in two years. Calli and I had kind of stumbled into a relationship after Drew, Lore, and Neal left. It started as a friends-with-benefits thing, and then accidentally took a left turn into *actual* friends, and then ran us both off the unexpected real emotional connection cliff. We'd only been really 'together' for a few months, but we had spent most of our time before that with each other, so it wasn't much of a jump. It wasn't like when we had been together before. I had always known that I had been working overtime to impress Calli during the first iteration of our relationship; I just never realized she had been doing the same. Without all the pressure, we were free to be...well, not *normal* by any means, but comfortable, at least. She started seeing a therapist, too, which didn't hurt. I didn't think I'd ever stop feeling guilty for all the years I'd poked fun at Calli's issues. The more she opened up to me, the more I realized what hell it was to be inside her brain. If she wanted to draw a dick on her cup, the girl could draw a dick on her cup.

"I know," Calli smiled. "I just like making you nervous. Are you going to respond to him?"

"Nothing to respond to," I shrugged, slumping in my chair. "I don't even officially know, remember? Lore and Drew just told me. This is where we are, I guess. We're friends our entire life, and then I have to find out about his engagement second-hand."

I put my head on top of my crossed arms. Calli slid her chair over and rubbed a small circle on my back.

"My poor little depressed butterfly," she cooed. One of these days she'd find a pet name for me that I didn't loathe. "You wanna smash something? I've got a bunch of stuff at my apartment that I wouldn't mind smashing."

"Nah," I smiled, bringing my head up again, "but I kinda want pizza ever since you mentioned it. War Bitch isn't playing tonight, so Crystal can shut down for me. You free for an early dinner? Your place?"

"Sure," Calli smiled, "but you know you have to go home eventually, right?"

"Yeah," I said, blushing. "It would be a lot easier to go home if you were there, too, though."

"Oh sweetie," Calli said, standing up and running her silky hand against the side of my face. "The second you ask me for the right reasons, I'll start packing."

"How do you know I'm not asking for the right reasons now?" I asked.

Calli just smiled and winked.

"I'll see you tonight, Abby-Cadaby," she said. "Fair warning, I'm going to get weird toppings. Like, Canadian bacon and tofu weird."

"Why? Why would you do that?" I laughed as she stepped closer to me.

"Because I can," she said, kissing me and then twirling away. "See you tonight!"

I gave her a little wave as she left, and then turned back toward Cadabra's Corner, pausing as I entered to look up at the bare spot where Snooty Crow had once sat.

Fresh snow was falling the day Drew and Lore left for Spokane. Our relationship had recovered, mostly, since the blow-up over Neal. The morning after Neal left, Drew had greeted me at Cluster with a gigantic, sobbing bear-hug, blubbering about how sorry he was for what he'd said and how he realized he was an asshole. I told him I appreciated it, but didn't think that crushing my ribcage was going to make the situation better. Lore explained, while Drew composed himself, that they had been able to hear my discussion with Neal even over their own fight. They had built up me confronting Neal as a necessary, good and right thing; they never pictured how ugly the reality would be. I told them it was fine, and that they had been right about pretty much everything. We had moved on and had an enjoyable Ides of December, which was good, as it turned out to be the last one ever.

"You promise you'll call as soon as you get in?" I asked, feeling like an overprotective mother. "Snow is really coming down."

"Of course we will," Lore nodded as she dropped the last bag into Drew's Suburban and walked back to the house with me for the final time. "We'll be okay; this thing has snow tires on it that would let it climb a tree."

She put her arm through my elbow and pulled herself close to me.

"You'll be okay, too," she said, leaning against me, her teal hair a stark contrast against my black coat. "You know that, right?"

"We'll be back a ton to visit," Drew said as Lore and I entered the foyer, where he was trying to fit a beanie over his increasingly large head of hair. He was growing it out like Lore had always wanted him to. "And you can visit, too. You'll have to see this space we have, Abra, it's perfect."

"Of course I'll visit," I said, reaching over and helping him ease the back corner of the beanie down. "I have no idea where I'm going to get good breakfast food otherwise."

Drew laughed and then sighed before wrapping me in another gigantic hug.

"I wasn't right about you," he said, into my shoulder. "I didn't even believe it

back then. I was just mad and stupid. Part of me didn't want to leave, and I was looking for someone to lash out at instead of admitting that. I'm so, so sorry."

"Drew," I said kissing him on his bristly cheek, "we had this talk already. I forgive you, and you weren't as wrong as you think. We're okay. You know I love you, right?"

"You too," Drew nodded, releasing me. "We'll call you as soon as we get to our new apartment. You call us any time...any time."

"Same," I said, holding back tears. "Joan of Arc, by the way."

Drew looked puzzled in the doorway.

"Just answering a question from a while back," I said. "Goodbye, Drew."

He waved, wiped at his eyes, and headed out to start the Suburban. Lore lingered in the foyer.

"Hey," she said, wrapping me in a much gentler hug. "Is it too late for me to yell 'KIDDING'?"

"Not at all," I laughed. "It would be one of your better pranks. Go unpack, I'll put on coffee."

Lore laughed with me, nuzzling her head into my shoulder.

"You're going to be okay," she assured me again. "I promise."

"Eventually," I said, as the tears finally spilled from my eyes.

"You never give yourself enough credit, Abra," Lore said. Then, before I could respond, she leaned up and kissed me. Not the glancing peck on the cheek I had given Drew, but a full, deep kiss that lit up every cell in my body. When her lips finally parted from mine and she took a step back, I thought I would either drift away on the wind or pass out.

"I--" I stammered, before being stopped with a wink.

"I've owed you that for a while. Thanks for inviting me up to study," she said with a smile. "It was the best thing anyone has ever done for me. Goodbye, Abra. I love you."

"You, too," I muttered, still tasting her lips on mine as she waved and walked out the door.

Everyone but Red had died. That was how Neal worked himself out of the corner in *And All the Rest.* Instead of writing around his decision at the end of the previous arc to have the team get caught in the destruction of the Space Needle while fighting their arch nemesis, a sinister CEO with a battle-mech, he wrote *through* it. Lore confirmed later that it had been what she had suggested to him, and she was right: it freed him. He was no longer writing a story tethered to the four of us. When Red woke up in the rubble to find his three teammates dead, he set off on a quest to build a new squad to take on the city's villains. I had no idea who Neal spent his time with since moving to New York, so I didn't know if any of his new characters were based on new friends, but I had my suspicions.

Still, the gamble had worked, after a large amount of grumbling from his fan-base. But like those things always go, first they hated it and talked about how the comic was ruined forever, then they begrudgingly started admitting aspects of the new characters they liked, then they started writing erotic fan-fiction about them. The circle of fandom. *And All the Rest* was still mainly an online comic, though now it had a publisher backing it and advertising it, which had expanded Neal's popularity. Collections of the first two arcs had been released in print. Both sat on my shelf, picked up from a display at the comic book shop that had bragged "LOCAL ARTIST" even though Neal hadn't been local for two years. Both were unopened, though I did occasionally go online and binge through the whole series. I told Calli that it was because I couldn't let a story go halfway through, but we both knew the truth.

"When are you going to come and visit finally?" Drew asked from my computer screen, a burst of distortion in our video call obscuring his face momentarily. "We named a dish after you and everything. It's eggs benedict with cream sauce instead of hollandaise, like you always used to order."

"I appreciate it," I said, my mouth almost starting to water. I missed Drew's cooking like a fourth roommate. "When are you going to make it over here?"

"Sometime, I hope," Drew sighed. "It's tough; we're finally starting to get established as a restaurant, but we're still pretty much the only ones running it. We have a waiter and a dishwasher, but I wouldn't trust those two to run the place while we're away. Plus, there's--"

"Meeeee!" Lore called, springing into the frame. I had lost track of how many months pregnant she was, but she was beginning to look like one of those Fisher Price Weeble toys. "Hey sweetie!"

"Hey Lore and Fetus," I waved to my webcam. "What's on your shirt?"

"Spokane Farmer's Market," Lore said, stretching out her grey t-shirt so I could read it and admire the picture of a basket of fresh produce. "We have a booth. I do makeup, Drew sells baked goods. It's fun, you should see it when you come up. Steve and Laurel run it."

"Steve and…?" I asked.

"Friends of ours," Drew said. "She's pregnant, too. We met shopping for cribs. They're big in the hipster circles of Spokane, so they've been a great help getting word out about Cassandra's."

Drew had named his eatery after his mom, which was incredibly sweet, but Lore once confided to me that she was sick of customers asking if she was Cassandra.

"How's Cluster doing?" Lore asked, pulling up a chair next to her husband and leaning into the frame.

"Still exploding," I said. "We're actually mulling the idea of expanding into the empty lot behind us. Crystal is amazing at this."

"But still kind of a…," Lore trailed off, "that word I'm not supposed to say as an enlightened, feminist woman?"

"Oh yes," I rolled my eyes. "She is a *raging* that word that we're not supposed to say as enlightened, feminist women."

"I'm sorry, sweetie," Lore said, her face falling. "But at least you can afford a security system now!"

"Oh, we definitely have one of those," I groaned. Top of the line, too. Cameras, motion detectors, door and window sensors; the works.

"Still blows that that happened," Drew said. I nodded in agreement.

"How are you and Calli doing?" Lore asked while Drew caught himself mid-eyeroll.

"We're doing well," I said. "She has good days and bad, but I guess I do, too. We help each other through them. She finished my tattoo a few days ago."

I turned my shoulder to the camera so they could read the ink, receiving an "aw" from Lore and a "nice" from Drew.

"So... Neal's wedding," Lore said, leaving it hanging in the air.

"Yeah," I grunted.

"I'm sorry you had to find out from us," Lore said, sadly. "I really thought you would have received an announcement, too."

"You know," I said, looking down at my keyboard, "it's better this way. It sucks, it hurts, but it's better this way. He made a clean break, and that's what he needed."

"He was your best friend," Drew stated.

"And in a way, he always will be," I said, repeating the speech I had given myself so very many times. "The time we had together was a blessing, and that's not diminished just because it didn't last forever. I'm going to be a best friend to him by staying away. I'm not lying when I say I'm happy for them."

There, that was good; maybe I'd convince myself this time.

"Okay. So, they're going to be coming through Spokane as part of their roving honeymoon tour in a few weeks," Lore said. "I get that you're not ready to see him, but I just wanted to ask...again…?"

"No," I said. "I don't have a message to pass on to him. It's better if he can forget I exist. I have no right to jump back in his life after I pushed him out."

That didn't stop me from thinking about it sometimes, though. I had drafts of at least half a dozen letters saved on my laptop, and a few handwritten copies pressed between book pages, all written in fits at about four in the morning.

"Alright," Lore accepted. "Well, we've got to go. We're opening early for brunch tomorrow, and Cletus the Fetus won't stop jumping on my bladder, so sleep is going to be a precious commodity."

"Okay," I laughed. "Take care, you two. Hope to see you in person again soon."

"We do to!" They said in tandem. "Bye!"

I said goodbye as well, but the call had already been ended.

And then I was alone, the glare from the laptop screen the only illumination in my room. I thought about going downstairs and getting a midnight snack, but I was still pretty full from the pepperoni and sausage pizza Calli and I had shared for dinner ("What's weird about those toppings?" I had asked. "I told you they were going to be weird. What's weirder than ordinary when you're expecting weird?" Calli replied). She had had some tattoo designs to work on for clients, though, so I didn't stay over, instead coming back to my incredibly cavernous house.

I flipped the top of my laptop closed and sunk the room back into darkness. I was far enough out on the edge of town that no traffic noise ever made it out to me. The silence made sleep peaceful, but being awake oppressive. After sitting in it for a long ten minutes, I spoke.

"I don't know if you're there or not," I said, to the darkness. "In fact, I'm pretty sure I *do* know that you're not, but there's no one around to call me crazy, so I'll just keep talking."

I paused for laughter that didn't come.

"How did you do it?" I whispered, figuring that volume didn't matter in the hereafter. "I thought I knew, but I didn't."

The silence didn't answer.

"I miss you," I said, into the void, sighing and setting my laptop on my nightstand, then pulling the covers up over me. "Goodnight, Olivia."

A stupid part of me waited for a warmth in my hand, but it didn't come. It never did.

"You two crazy kids got Thanksgiving plans?" Crystal asked as I cleaned up and Calli waited for me at one of the tables.

"Nothing big," I shrugged. "You?"

"Going to my in-laws' dinner," Crystal rolled her eyes. "They *hate* me. Last year I let it slip that I had stripped in my twenties and they shoved all the children out of the room. Not like I started demonstrating or anything."

"I'm bringing my boyfriend home to meet my parents for the first time," Lindsee chirped from behind the counter. "He's so nervous."

"Well sure," Crystal said, wiping down a table. "He probably knows they'll hate him."

"What? Why?" Lindsee asked, her eyes getting almost impossibly huge. Calli started laughing.

"Because they probably will," Crystal shrugged. "I've met him; he's boring. Well, I guess if your parents are boring, too...."

Lindsee's shoulders slumped, giving her the appearance of a cartoon character who just found out that the true meaning of Christmas is consumerism.

"It'll be fine, Linds," I assured her as I tidied up my shop. "If they hate him, they'll probably just be passive aggressive about it, right?"

"Yeah," Lindsee squeaked.

"You'll live," Crystal waved off. "So, who wants to set the alarm tonight?"

Crystal, Lindsee, and I all raced to see whose finger could touch the bridge of their nose fastest. Unfortunately, I had been holding an old cassette player at the time.

"Dammit," I hissed.

"Sorry, kid," Crystal said. "I hate that thing. What I wouldn't give to get my hands on that asshole who broke in. Though I guess you would probably enjoy it more, huh Abra?"

"Yeah," I grumbled. "Get him to give me my goddamn crow back. Tell him where he can shove his little message, too."

"Yeah, but you wouldn't," Crystal said, leaning against the coffee counter as Lindsee cleaned.

"Excuse me?" Calli said for me, getting up from her chair, a rage-aura almost visibly radiating off of her.

"Calm down, eye-candy," Crystal chided. "I'm not taking a shot at her, I'm just saying I know how people work."

"And how do people work?" Calli asked, her voice a honed blade.

"We build up these big revenge scenarios in our head, but when it comes time to enact them, we pussy out and just take the path of least resistance," Crystal explained. "It's what I did."

"When?" Lindsee asked.

"My ex-husband," Crystal started. "Piece of shit. Verbally abusive, drunk, manipulative. Worked at the motorcycle shop out by the highway. I think he still does. Anyway, after I finally left him, after all the nasty divorce proceedings, I had to go give him the last box of his stuff from our house. It was the last thing of his left around, but I had specific orders from my lawyer not to destroy it. Asshole wouldn't pick it up, so it just sat there, reminding me, keeping me from moving on.

So I decided to take it into his shop and give it to him then. By then I was so pissed I planned on telling him off in front of all his little butt-buddies, tell him what a pathetic piece of shit he is, tell him I was just starting to remember what orgasms felt like since I left him, tell him he was a worthless user who was probably going to die alone and on the toilet."

Crystal sighed and shook her head.

"I got to the shop, head of steam built up," Crystal continued. "Saw him in the back, fixing someone's Harley. The guy at the front counter, who had known me for years, asked if I wanted him to go get the asshole. I said no and left the box with him. I didn't even intend to say the words, they just came out of me. It's just the way people work. Sorry if it sounded like I was talking shit. Good on you for standing up for your girl, though, Calli."

"Thanks," Calli muttered, sitting back down. Crystal, Lindsee and I finished cleaning the shop shortly thereafter, the two of them leaving first while I set the alarm and Calli waited in her car.

"So," Calli said as I slid into the passenger seat of her little hatchback, "what *would* you say to the asshole who robbed you if you could? I think Crystal is full of shit, as usual."

"Nah," I shook my head as I put on my seatbelt. "This time she's right."

"How do you know?" Calli asked.

"Past experience."

I showed up to the hospice center alone. Neal had offered to go with me, but I didn't want anyone else to see me like this. I was wearing the last outfit of male clothing I had kept since transitioning, a polo shirt and slacks that I had held onto almost exclusively for this occasion. They felt sharp against my skin, hard. Like they were bonding with me, like if I didn't get them off soon, they'd become a part of me, and I would be back to where I had been.

"Down the hall and to the left, sir. Room 195." the older woman at the front desk said, her 'sir' stinging. I had my hair pulled back in a tight ponytail, my earrings out and my face free of any makeup. It was chilling, the thought of how easy it would be to slip back. I had started thinking of my time presenting male as a dead era, gone, buried, and decomposed. But now I caught a glimpse of how it could so easily slither back from the grave.

Father Merton, the young priest who had been with my father the night Gwen was killed, stood outside my father's door, as if keeping watch.

"I'm so glad you could make it," he said, rushing over and clasping my hands. "I... I'm sorry, I can never remember what you like to be called."

"Anything is fine," I waved him off.

"Your father is...very near to the end," Merton said, stopping me as I moved toward the door. "The disease has been hard on him. I know it's been a long time since you last saw him…"

Shortly after Gwen died. Five years prior.

"I want you to prepare yourself for how he looks now," the priest continued. "He's still sharp as a tack, though, so if you need to say anything…."

"Do it now, got it," I nodded, moving past the priest and into my father's room.

Maybe I would have been shocked by my father's appearance if I hadn't watched Olivia wither away. All I could think was that he looked in better shape than she did, thinner, gaunter, balder, but not desiccated. The TV, mounted up by the ceiling, was blaring baseball calls.

"Hi, Dad," I muttered from the doorway. He turned his head and bulged his eyes so hard I feared they would pop out of their sunken sockets.

He called me by my dead name, which I don't repeat; it was his name, too.

"Father Merton called me," I explained taking a tentative step into the room.

"I asked him to," my father said. He looked better than Olivia had, but he sounded like death. With Dad, it was his liver that finally decided it had had enough of him. Surprise. "You look good, son. Have a seat."

I pulled out the chair next to his bed and lowered myself into it.

"I know things have been bad between us, ever since Gwen died," he said. "God, I miss her. She was an amazing girl."

I nodded in agreement, though I knew what Gwen would think of this declaration, coming from him.

"Anyway, I think I'm...I'm coming to the end of the road," he groaned. "I didn't want us to end like that. I think we've both made our fair share of mistakes."

Deep inside, a tiny little ember began to ignite as I clenched my teeth and nodded.

"You weren't the easiest kid to raise, you know?" Dad continued. "But I know I could have done some things differently. There was...there was that time I walked in on you and Gwen in her room, and she was putting makeup on you, and I told you you looked like a retard. Do you remember that?"

I started to give a very honest answer when I noticed that tears were flowing down my father's face.

"I just wanted to say I'm sorry," He said, voice shaking. "I shouldn't have called you that."

And if he'd just left it there….

"...That's a shitty word and I shouldn't have used it," he continued, obliterating what little hope I had that my father might actually accept me for who I was. "I'm smarter now. With all the hospitals I've been in, I've met lots of re--developmentally disabled people, and that's a hurtful, awful word, and I shouldn't have taught you that it's okay to use. So I'm sorry."

"Okay," I muttered, the ember growing into a decent little fire. He looked at me expectantly, like he was waiting for me to apologize for something.

"Well, anyway," he said with a dismissive wave, giving up. "I know it's been tough. We had good times, though, right? Remember when I took you fishing?"

Sure I did. My therapists over the years were pretty familiar with it, too.

"Boy that was fun," Dad said, tears still in his eyes. "You caught that huge trout, remember? I was so proud of you. You were so happy with yourself, too. You don't need to lie, you can be proud. Tasted pretty good when we cooked it up later, too, huh? God, what a great day."

"Dad…" I started. There was now nuclear fission happening within me. I opened my mouth to give him my opinion of his 'great day,' to tell him how helpless and afraid I had felt, how desperate I had been for his approval and how much I felt like a failure afterward. I was going to tell him that he had made Gwen and me, and probably Mom, too, live in constant fear and shame, that he had browbeaten me into doubting everything I ever did, and primed Gwen to fall into the arms of another abusive asshole. I was going to tell him that her blood was on his hands, too, and that one of the greatest tragedies is that she never truly got to

live life without him in it. I was going to tell him that anything I am that is good or right, even if all that was good and right about me was just a tiny mote in a sea of crap, happened despite, not because of, him.

Dad took a deep, wheezing breath and turned on his side, curling in pain.

"Yeah?" he asked.

I watched him writhe, sighed and looked up at the TV.

"How are the Rangers doing this year?" I asked, the fire going out of me.

"Fucking awful," Dad said, looking up at the screen. "Never should have signed Sosa; way past his prime. Fuck it, there's always next year, right?"

I nodded, and we talked about nothing for another half hour before he fell asleep and I left. When I got home, I gathered up the male clothes I had worn, threw them into a trash bag and deposited them in a Goodwill drop box the next morning.

"This is not pizza," I said, taking a bite of the odd bread-circle that Calli had brought for our Thanksgiving dinner. "What are you doing to us?"

"I can't be normal all the time," she shrugged, taking a bite of her own piece. Onions, pineapple, white sauce, no cheese. "But yeah, this is horrible. Oh well. You don't know until you try."

I started to object on the basis that anyone who had ever eaten food could have told her that her pizza creation counted as a crime against humanity, but instead I just started laughing.

"Hey, look at the guy in the red and blue beanie. He's going to do something, I just know it," she said, gesturing out our increasingly foggy windshield toward the line of customers wrapped around the outlet mall, waiting for the midnight Black Friday sale to start.

"My money is on the lady in the teal coat," I wagered, pointing toward a large woman who was already barking at the person in line behind her. "She came ready for war."

"Speaking of war, I didn't mean to jump into the conversation yesterday," Calli said, looking down at her atrocity pizza. "When Crystal was being a bitch. I know you can take care of yourself."

"Hey, you were just 'defending your girl'," I laughed.

"So...is that what you are?" Calli said with a nervous half-laugh. I looked at her, sitting in the driver's seat, horrible pizza in hand, bundled up for the cold in a knit hat and wool scarf. This wasn't the same person I had known back when we had first met. Or maybe it was, and I had never taken the time to notice.

"Yeah," I said. "Of course."

Calli blushed, leaned over the center console and kissed me.

"Okay, my girl," she said, "so what do you want for Christmas? We never really bought each other presents in our last relationship, but I want to do things better this time."

"Maybe we should stop calling what we had before a 'relationship,'" I suggested. "It was more, just...I don't know...."

"Unbridled lust and mutual self-deception?" Calli offered.

"That'll do, yeah," I chuckled. "And I don't know what I want for Christmas. What do *you* want?"

"I'll forward you the link to my wishlist," Calli said. "But c'mon, I want to get you something. I can be a real girlfriend, I swear!"

"You already did such a good job on my ink," I said, "How about that's my gift?"

"I do like how it turned out," Calli said. "Meanwhile, fuck Crystal for what she said about it. Like she's so enlightened because she's basically a robot."

"One that's programmed to lock onto insecurities and open fire," I nodded.

"I know she brings in a lot of money," Calli said, "but seriously, why don't you replace her? The cash can't be worth the headache."

I sighed and looked down at my lap.

"Yeah," I huffed, "but I know this headache. I could replace her, sure, with another person who might be lovely, or who might be another pain in the ass. But it wouldn't be...."

"It wouldn't be Neal, Drew, and/or Lore?" Calli asked.

"Yeah," I grunted. "I don't know. I still enjoy Cluster, but so much of why I loved it was wrapped up in the people. I just wanted to hold onto them a little longer, I guess."

Calli got quiet and set down her pizza.

"I need to ask you something, Abra," she said, quietly. "Actually, first I need to say something. And I need you to take me seriously, okay? Not just dismiss me because it's uncomfortable."

"Okay," I agreed, setting my own slice down and turning to face her as much as the seats would allow.

"I've never had a real relationship, Abra," Calli admitted. "I've had dates, and flings, and affairs, and romances, and hookups, but I've never had a real relationship-relationship. What we had before was as close as I came, and you're right, that wasn't a relationship. It was just the two of us fucking and trying to impress one another."

She took a deep breath and exhaled, a tiny vapor-ghost expelling from her mouth into the cold air.

"I didn't have a relationship because I was scared," she continued. "Not of getting beaten up again. Bones heal. I was scared of putting myself out there, opening myself up. You know I'm fucked up. I know it, too. It's why I ended it last time. I was starting to catch feelings, and I didn't want to make you deal with me. We were terrible for each other then, but...it can't be just me, right? Something changed."

I reached out and put a hand on her arm. She covered it with her hand and continued.

"I want this relationship, Abra," she stated. "I... honestly want it so much it scares me. I've never been in love before, but if this isn't it, I don't know what is. I'm all in, Abra. But I'm scared, and I need to ask you something."

"What? What is it?" I asked, as she turned away and looked out her window.

"Am I just a memento?" she whispered.

"What?" I asked, trying to see her face.

"A memento," she repeated. "Are we just together because I'm the last scrap of the time of your life that you're trying to hold onto? Because if I am, I get it, and I understand, and we can go back to being friends because I really do love having you in my life. But I can't be someone's trinket, Abra. I can't be a collectible on your shelf that you can look at and say, 'remember when...?'."

I looked at her sitting there, twisted away from me, trying not to let me see her cry by shoving her face almost against the window of her door. Worse, I caught a glimpse of myself in the rearview mirror.

"Calliope," I said, putting a hand on her back. She pulled away at first but then leaned back toward me. "I am so, so sorry. I never, ever wanted you to feel like you're just here to help me remember. I hate that my friends left, but I love that them leaving let me have more time with you, because every time we're together I learn something new that I wish I had known all along. I'm in this, too. I know neither of us went in thinking this was what was going to happen, but I'm so glad it did."

"Me, too," she said, turning back toward me with tears in her eyes but trying to smile. "I'm sorry, I'm just a fucking mess. My mind does dumb shit and I get all twisted up inside myself. I warned you I was fucked up."

"No, you're not," I responded. "You're passionate, you're caring, you're strong. And fuck anyone who doesn't see that. Fuck me for not seeing it for so long. Fuck me for making you feel like I was just using you to prop me up. There's nothing fucked up about you, Calli; you're just too interesting to be known by boring people."

"I love you," Calli blurted, her face noticeably red even in the darkened car. "I love you, and you don't have to say it back, I just want you to know, because there's something else we're going to have to talk about, but later. But I wanted you to know I love you *now* so it doesn't sound like I'm just saying it *then* because of what else I'll be saying *then*? Does that make any sense?"

"The part about talking later or the part about you loving me?" I smiled at her. "Not a lick, either one. But I love you, too."

She leaned over and kissed me, and then again, and again, at first gently and then harder, fiercer, both of us moving on raw instinct and hunger, our hands trying to feel around for each other through layers of winter gear.

"Dammit," she hissed, parting from me as her hand got caught in my coat, trying to slide under it. "I really, really want to fuck you right now, but it's so fucking cold!"

"Agreed," I nodded. "And agreed. Also, there's that line of people over there."

"That actually works for me," she shrugged. "But we should probably wait until we get home. There are parts of me I really don't want frost-bitten."

"Fair enough," I said. "Wait, where are you going?"

Calli stopped in the middle of opening her door.

"To get in line, silly," she said. "This pizza is terrible, and they're going to open the doors soon."

"Wait...we're going in?" I asked in disbelief. "You said we were just here to watch the chaos."

"I may or may not have tricked you," Calli admitted. "But I need socks and we're finally going to get you some decent outfits, Abby-Cadaby. Don't worry, I'm still planning on severely dehydrating you when we get home."

"What's wrong with my outfits?" I asked, getting out of my side of the car.

"Nothing, in 2003," Calli replied. "Sweetie, you're pretty as hell, and you have a super cute little figure to you, but you dress with the fashion sense of...well, a transgender woman from central Washington. You deserve better, and since we've established that you're 'my girl,' it's up to me to save you. Now come on; we're going to at least buy you a new dress. The brown one is cute, but getting so threadbare it's almost indecent. Not that I'm complaining. By the way, I've decided what I'm going to get you for Christmas, so don't worry about coming up with ideas."

She winked at me and gestured for me to follow. Confused but with little other choice, I went after her into the maw of consumerism.

"We hope you realize, Neal, how long we have tried to understand you and what you choose to be," I read from the letter Neal had handed me as he walked in the door late one November before wordlessly throwing himself onto our living room couch. "We hope you understand how difficult it has been for us, how embarrassing for our family. How do you think it feels when one of our neighbors tells your father and me that they saw you walking down the street holding hands with another man? How do we explain to our friends that our son lives with a man who dresses as a woman?"

I paused and noticed how much of the letter was still left.

"Is it too early for me to tell your parents to fuck off?" I asked, looking over the folded paper to Neal, who was massaging his temples. He made a 'keep going' hand gesture.

"We wanted so many good things for you, Neal," the letter continued. "We tried to give you a good foundation and point you in the right directions. I'm sure there are things we could have done differently. I know you fell in with a bad crowd and we should have stepped in earlier."

I stopped again.

"That's me, right?" I muttered. Neal nodded. My mind flashed to Neal's mom putting a bandage on my knee after I fell while playing at their house when I was seven. It was amazing how quickly someone could overwrite your good memories of them.

"We've tried for years to get through to you," I kept reading. "I've wanted desperately to believe that my sweet little boy is still in there somewhere, but I just can't see him anymore. Asking to bring your 'boyfriend' to Thanksgiving dinner was just the last straw in a big pile, Neal. We cannot condone this lifestyle you have chosen for yourself. We've consulted with our friends and with Pastor Stevens, and everyone agrees that the best, most loving thing we can do is to cut ties with you until you see the light."

The letter almost dropped out of my hands as I rushed across the room toward

Neal. He waved me off and then gestured for me to keep going.

"We do love you, Neal," his mother's loopy script said. "Our love for you is why we have to do this. We love you too much to let you do these things to yourself. I hope and I pray, every night, that you will understand how hurtful and harmful you have been not just to yourself but to our whole family. I long for the day that you will come back to us, and we will eagerly receive you once you turn from this destructive lifestyle. Love always, Mom and Dad."

I threw the letter on the floor and slid next to Neal on the couch, putting my arm around him.

"It's not like this is unexpected," he said, into my shoulder. "I just...didn't think I'd see it laid out like that."

"That's the most fucking awful thing I've ever read," I said, stroking the back of his head. "I'm so sorry, Neal."

"Oh, it's not so bad," Neal said with a forced chuckle. "They still love me. See? It says right there."

"I'm so sorry," I repeated. "And... I'm sorry for whatever part I played in it."

Neal shook his head.

"You didn't make me bi, Abra," he said. "And you're not a 'man dressed as a woman.' You're just collateral in all of this. They haven't known what to do with me ever since I told them I didn't like sports in second grade. This just gives them an out."

"You know you still have a family, right?" I said, grabbing him a tissue from the box on the coffee table. "I know it's not the same, but--"

"It's way better," Neal interrupted. "You, and Drew, and Lore…."

"And Dan?" I offered.

"We'll see," Neal smiled.

"Oh, come on," I said, elbowing him. "You were going to take him to meet The Grand Inquisitors, and more than that, he *was willing to go with you. That's not nothing."*

"No, I guess it isn't," Neal nodded. "So, can I ask you something?"

"Sure."

"What do you think of him?" Neal asked. "I mean, honestly. Free pass here."

"I like him," I said without hesitation. "I like his goofy sense of humor, I like how he likes to watch us all play video games, I like how he just goes with the flow and never makes us feel bad for being a big cluster of weirdos. I mean, I guess I could stand hearing a little less about his home brewing operation…."

"You'd understand if you drank!" Neal laughed, wiping away some tears. "It's really quite good. He made a cherry and dark chocolate stout last week."

"I'll take your word for it," I laughed. "I like him. And what I really like is

how he looks at you."

"How does he look at me?" Neal asked. There was an easy way to answer that, but I wouldn't address that *issue for about two more years.*

"Like you're the only person on earth, Neal," I answered. "Like nothing else matters."

It was about eight in the morning when I got back home, having stayed at the Outlet Mall for three hours and Calli's apartment for another five. She was in an upswing, and therefore a fount of endless energy, bouncing off to work with only thirty minutes rest. She offered to let me crash at her place while she was away, but I decided to venture home instead, having her drop me off on the way to Black Needles.

Unfortunately, I had stumbled into the odd, terrifying world that came after exhaustion, where the body is running on pure adrenaline and emotion and therefore feels it has evolved beyond the need for sleep. I tossed and turned in my bed without success, very grateful that we had decided to keep Cluster closed for Black Friday to protest consumerism...and us having to get up early on the day after Thanksgiving. But mostly consumerism.

When I finally gave up on sleep, I stumbled downstairs into our old lair. The Christmas lights still hung from the ceiling, but I seldom turned them on. Mine was the only computer left, the cluster of desks gone, leaving a conspicuous void in the center of the room. Neal's chair, where he drew so many comic pages, still sat where it always had, like it was waiting for him to follow me down and settle back into it. It was the only thing of his still left in the house. In the weeks after he left, Drew and Lore quietly shipped everything he wanted to keep to his new address in New York, carting everything else off to Goodwill. I didn't go in his old room. It didn't feel right.

I used some of the space in the basement to set up an old TV with a VCR connected to it. I had been working my way through the tapes with the two crows in the heart in short bursts on days when I needed to see her again, watching just a few moments at a time, trying to savor them. I can't describe how it was, seeing Gwen again, happy, full of life, being goofy and laughing until she cried. All at once I felt the most soaring happiness and the darkest sorrow, soft, warm love and blood red anger. It was like ordering the emotional sampler platter. I never watched the tape with the crow skull.

I hit play on the tape that I already had in the VCR. I had only watched about ten minutes of it, enjoying seeing Gwen and me on an adventure through the jungle (our backyard) to find a lost Incan city (the half-assed fort that our mother had guilted our father into building for us). As the tape restarted, Gwen was dominating the screen, her hair pulled up under an old costume cowboy hat, one of mom's old leather jackets slung over her shoulder, looking like a gender-swapped Indiana Jones. I, much less on theme, hobbled after her with the camera, occasionally turning it back to myself to show off the knight costume I was, for some reason, wearing.

"Step carefully, kid," Gwen said, sounding extra cocky. "This place is full of traps. We don't want to end up falling into a snake pit."

"How do you feel about snakes, Gwendy?" I asked, my name for her getting a peal of laughter in response.

"I'm not very fond of them," Gwen replied, regaining her composure. A length of extension cord hung on her waist (we didn't have a whip).

"Well, we're almost there," Gwen said, putting one foot up on a landscaping rock. "This has been quite an adventure, my good, valiant knight. I'm glad to have had you with me. I--"

An all-too familiar burst of static covered the screen and my blood pressure hit numbers that are only theoretical. I silently swore to myself that if the goddamn Rangers appeared on my screen, I'd have my father's ashes taken out of the niche where they were stored and scattered all over Safeco Field in Seattle. But instead of baseball, my sister appeared again, but this time in her room, and several years older. She was wearing her Shepard Fairey tank-top.

"Ugh," she said on the screen. "Just realized I was accidentally using one of Dad's old Rangers tapes. He never watches them, but God help me if he loses a minute of one of their boring-ass games. Anyway...Abra. I worry about her."

My heart was pounding. He didn't tape over her, she taped over him! I pounded the volume button on the remote, leaning in as if, could I get close enough, I could fall through the screen and be back with her, there in her old room.

"I think I've messed her up," Gwen said, shoulders slumped. "I've always wanted to protect her from...fuck, everything. Dad, bullies, heartbreak. It's not like I think she's too sheltered. She's a little badass when she wants to be, always has been. But I worry that she thinks she can't do anything on her own. I worry that I, like, made her lean on me. I don't know how to tell her that she was keeping me afloat as much as I was her. She gave me this little pocket-universe where I could just be silly and dumb and have fun. I've tried to tell her, but it just comes off sounding like typical big sister inspirational bullshit. 'You can do it! You're special!'"

I actually reached out and touched the screen of the little CRT TV. Gwen was looking down at her bedspread.

"I wish I could tell her," she said, so low that I don't know I would have heard it if I didn't have the volume cranked up. "But tell her what? 'Hey, you're *not* going to be an aunt'? Fuck. I can't put this on her. She's just starting to figure her own life out, I can't make her the dumping ground for my dumb shit. I really miss her, but I worry the only way she's going to understand that she can do things on her own is for me to step back and just...let her be. College is good for that. She'll figure things out and then we can start spending more time together again. I gotta let her go and grow up. I don't want to, though."

She leaned her head down toward her abdomen.

"You hear that, clump of cells?" She asked. "I'm pretty fucked up, and I definitely don't know how to be a parent. You're not missing out on shit!"

Gwen sat there in silence for another minute as I watched, tears streaming down my face, wishing like nothing else that I could reach back into the past for just one moment, one split second, the time of one heartbeat, to put my arms around her.

"Fuck it," Gwen said, her head snapping up. "Fuck it, I'm calling her. I can start letting her grow up later. I'm not going to tell her about...the thing. We'll just...I want to call her. Yeah, fuck it."

Gwen grabbed her phone with one hand and started dialing, reaching over with the other and switching the camera off, the screen turning black.

A sliver of my mind, a small, dumb part of me, honestly expected the phone in my pocket to start ringing. All of me, every cold, rational part, was sad when it didn't.

"If I ever find this piece of shit, I'll shove my boot so far up his ass that he'll have scuff marks on the backs of his teeth," Crystal growled as she swept up glass from the shattered baked goods case. Lindsee was mopping up the puddles of coffee syrup congealing behind the counter, and Calli had stopped by to help me sort through the wreckage of Cadabra's Corner, which had suffered the brunt of the

damage. There was a tarp thrown down over the floor, a rare act of kindness from Crystal, that would have to do until we had time to look up how to remove spray paint from linoleum.

"I'm just glad he didn't get into the music section," I grumbled, creating another pile of old toys swept from their shelves and then stomped on, these too far gone to be saved.

"He sure tried," Crystal said, glancing back over at the pry-marks all around the door between the coffee shop and the stage. We'd installed the door for a situation just like this one, knowing that most of our expensive equipment was in the music section. It had been a good investment. Unfortunately, our front door had, apparently, been much lower quality, chunks of its frame hanging splintered, a chair blocking it closed.

"Insurance will cover most of this," I sighed, gesturing to Calli to help hold the other end of my 'Cadabra's Corner' sign while I reattached the side that had been ripped from the ceiling. "Though not…."

I trailed off, glancing at a conspicuously empty section of shelf behind my counter, one of the few that had not been dumped during the rampage.

"Yeah, that's fucking weird," Crystal said. "You're sure that's the only *thing missing?"*

"Far as I can tell," I said.

"Why would someone break in to steal a stuffed crow?" Lindsee asked, slopping another load of mop water onto the sticky mess at her feet.

"It was...valuable," I muttered, as I started sorting through the contents of another dumped shelf.

"But not for sale," Crystal added. "What was so special about that crow, anyway?"

"It belonged to her sister," Calli answered for me as she held up the cracked remains of a cup topper for me to inspect. I shook my head and gestured to the trash can.

"Oh, is she going to be pissed?" Crystal asked.

"She's dead," I said, flatly.

"Oh, shit, I'm sorry," Crystal said as she dumped a dustpan full of glass into the trash. "That's fucked up. So... why did you have the crow here if you weren't selling it and it was special to you?"

"Just...reasons," I said. Crystal was being more human than usual that day, but I didn't feel like getting into it with her. I didn't even really want to discuss it with Calli. I'd told Neal once, but he was probably the only person I didn't have to tell. Snooty Crow had been Gwen's avatar. I wanted it to be there with me, in my shop, so in a way she--and Olivia, whose letter was still sewn inside--could be

with me, too. It was top-shelf stupid and pathetic, which was why I didn't feel like explaining it out loud.

"Fair enough," Crystal shrugged. "And you think you know who did this?"

"I absolutely know who did this," I said, through my teeth. "I don't know his name, but I know exactly who did this."

"How?" Crystal asked.

"This," I said, standing up and throwing back the corner of the tarp on the floor, revealing a line of two-foot-tall letters in orange spray paint that spelled out the word "Tranny."

Snooty Crow had been gone for a year. I made a police report right away, putting up with the sneers and the sideways glances shared between the two officers sent out, who seemed to believe that the real crime committed was me being allowed to exist. They eventually did write down my description of the man who had been kicked out of our store, though since it had been a year past at that point, my memory had grown hazy and I had trouble convincing the officers that someone would hold a grudge for that long. But I knew better. Still, most of their questions focused on the breaking-in and the vandalism; grand theft stuffed animal was yet to be recognized as a serious crime.

"I love the view up here," Calli said as we walked up to the lookout at Thorton Park, both of us bundled up in winter gear. Snow had, surprisingly, not yet fallen, but frost was still hanging heavy over every surface, making the whole town look crystalline. Calli and I stepped up to the edge of the lookout, each of us with coffee in hand, our free arms locked together.

"I can't believe you've never been up here before," I said, pulling her closer to me.

"It's not exactly advertised in the welcome brochure they hand out when you move here," Calli laughed. "I guess it's just one of the benefits of dating a local. So, you've been coming up here since you were a kid?"

"Yeah," I nodded, looking out over the town. "Neal and me. It was our...I dunno...spot. We played up here all the time. Other stuff, too."

"Oh?" Calli's eyebrows went up.

"Not like that, gutter-brain," I elbowed her. "No, just...we came up here after my mom died."

"Oh, so *really* not like that," Calli blushed. "Sorry."

"'It's okay," I said.

"You miss him, don't you?" Calli whispered.

"I--"

"No canned speeches," Calli smiled, thinly.

"Yeah," I sighed. "I do."

"Of course you do," Calli said. "He was your best friend. How long do you think you'll keep this up before you reach out to him?"

"I'm not going to," I replied without having to think about it.

"Sweetie," Calli said, tilting her head down and her eyes up.

I started to protest, but was interrupted by a notification ding coming from her pocket.

"One sec," She said, holding up a finger and checking her phone.

"What B-list celebrity is cheating on what third-string athlete now?" I grumbled.

"All of them," Calli shrugged. "But that's not what that was about. Anyway…."

Calli plopped her phone back into her coat pocket, which I stared at as if expecting a rabbit to jump out.

"So... what was it?" I asked.

"I'm working on your Christmas present," she winked. "Top secret. You'll definitely know if I manage to pull it off. If not, pretend to enjoy the slippers."

"Okay," I said, slowly, remembering our conversation in the parking lot. "Hey, what did you want to talk to me about the other night? Or not talk to me about?"

"Nothing," Calli shook her head. "We kinda already had the conversation."

"Calli, come on," I said.

"Fine," Calli sighed, looking down at the ground. "But it isn't happening. I've decided. Like, fully decided, okay? So this isn't one of those things where you need to tell me it's okay and half-heartedly try to talk me into it."

"Okay," I agreed, nervously.

"I got a message from my old mentor in Portland, Sera," She said. "She's moving to Seattle and opening up a new shop. She wanted me to come with her and be one of her artists."

"That's...huge," I said, feeling a way too familiar sense of dread settling over me. "Why...why aren't you going?"

"Abra," Calli smiled. "I have a tattoo parlor. And yeah, we're hitting a rough patch, but we always pull through. Once people realize that quantity doesn't trump quality."

She made a little snarling noise that was, frankly, adorable. Squid Eye had hired several new artists in the last few years, whereas Calli was the only one working at Black Needles. Her reputation kept her in business, but Squid Eye could push through more clients, so there was seldom a wait list.

"What I also have, what I just found, is you," she said, pecking me on the cheek. "I know that was really cheesy, but I don't care."

"Calli, I…," I started, but could only think of one thing to say. "Thank you."

"Well, you know, now you pretty much *have* to stay with me," she laughed. "Hey, you think you could talk Crystal into letting me perform sometime?"

"Really?" I asked, overjoyed but confused. "You know we still have the same crappy piano, right?"

"I can make it work," Calli winked. "I want to play for you again. It's been too long."

"I'll tell her to put you on the schedule," I said, leaning against her. "I do still own the place, after all."

"Another perk of you being 'my girl.'" Calli laughed. "Okay, so, I love this view, but I'm getting cold as hell. Walk me home?"

"Of course," I said, locking my arm in hers and walking with her down to the edge of the park, where we gave each other one last kiss before having to separate and walk at least a foot apart. On the streets, we were just two female friends, out for a 'girl's day.' It was safer that way.

I could pinpoint the moment I knew I was starting to feel something real for Calli. It was a year and a half prior, May fifth, the day I first caught myself worried about her.

During our first stint together, Calli would disappear for days or sometimes even a week at a time and I never thought twice about it. That was just crazy, flaky Calli, I thought, like an asshole. Drew and Lore took to calling her the Phantom based on how she would drift in and out of my life, though Neal never joined in. We all figured she was off at some weird, borderline terrifying party or recovering from some weird, borderline terrifying party. She'd done nothing to dissuade us from our conclusions; she had her shields fully up at that point. But I will always wonder what would have happened if we had actually taken the time to give a damn.

May fifth was the day that Calli didn't show up for our usual coffee. Ever since just before my trio of friends departed, she and I had switched our standing date from monthly to daily, and she had shown up like clockwork. She'd often hang out in the shop until after we closed, and we often ended up at either my house or her apartment. We were using each other back then. We'd even discussed it; how wrong we would be for each other if we were foolish enough to try for anything more than being fuck-buddies. But slowly our time together became something else. We were still ending up in bed more than a fair amount, but we weren't retreating to our own dwellings afterward. We started by just watching TV together, her trying to convince me that there was such a thing as a good reality show and me making her watch Hunter's Moon, *a mid-budget werewolf show that shot in Spokane, one of the productions Lore worked on. Soon, we were turning the TV off and just talking, often until the earlier hours of morning.*

But May fifth was the first day I knew something was up. Calli hadn't shown up for coffee, and she also wasn't answering her phone. When I went on her Facebook and Twitter accounts and realized she hadn't had any activity that day, I started to get nervous. When I called Black Needles and got her after-hours message, I began to worry. And that's when I knew our relationship had changed. I could no longer write off a day-long disappearance as "crazy Calli" because I didn't know "crazy Calli" anymore; I knew Calli, my friend.

Still, I was trying not to freak out. After all, it hadn't even been a full day yet. What kind of crazy, clingy stalker was I if I lost my mind because she took a sick day or decided to spend some time at the Outlet Mall instead of in Brahmton? I tried to go about my day, selling action figures and bickering with Crystal, but my mind kept drifting back to her, and my eye to my phone, which I must have checked a million times. I'd stop by her place after work, I told myself. Just calm the fuck down. But something wasn't right, and I couldn't ignore it, no matter how hard I tried.

Around six o'clock, my phone finally rang, the ringtone I set for her, Social Distortion's When She Begins, *blaring out of it.*

"Calli, hi!" I blurted into the phone, probably too loud.

"Abra," Calli gurgled on the other end of the phone. At first, I thought she was sick, but then I realized she was crying. "Abra I... I need help."

"Why, what's going on?" I asked, heart pounding, already moving toward the door. "Are you hurt?"

"No, I... I just need help," she cried over the phone. "Can... can you please come over? Please?"

"I'm on my way," I said, gesturing for Crystal to take over and running for the door. In the months since Drew left and took my means of transportation with him, I had renewed my driver's license and purchased a shitty little Nissan. Throwing

myself behind the wheel, I tossed my phone, still on, into the passenger's seat.

"Calli, are you still there?" I asked, switching the phone to speaker.

"Y-yeah," she said.

"Okay," I exhaled. "Just stay on the line, okay. You don't have to say anything, just stay on. I'll be right over."

I think that that measurably may have been the worst I've ever driven. I lost track of the number of times I was honked at on the way to Calli's apartment, faint whimpers still coming from the phone next to me. After a terrible parking job, I rushed up to her door and began pounding.

"It's open," Calli called from within. I opened the door and my eyes bulged as I took in the chaos.

"Calli, what...what the hell happened," I asked in disbelief. She was huddled on the floor at the back of her kitchen, surrounded by a sea of jagged, porcelain and glass shards that stretched all over the linoleum. Her hands, held in front of her, were wrapped in red-soaked paper towels.

"I...I dropped a teacup," Calli said through tears as I tiptoed through the razor sharp minefield and slid down to the floor next to her.

"It... looks like you may have dropped more than one," I said, putting my arm around her trembling shoulders. She gave me a rictus smile.

"I was putting away the dishes, and a teacup slipped out of my hand and broke. It's that one, there," she gestured to the remains of a blue and white teacup that looked like it once had a picture of a cat on it, actually fairly intact compared to everything else on the kitchen floor. "It was my favorite. I just...just stared at it, and the longer I stared at it, the stupider I felt. Just stupid and worthless and I just started picking up the other dishes and smashing them and every time I smashed one it just made me realize what a fucking piece of shit I am, but I couldn't stop and just...kept...going. Now they're all...broken...and I don't fucking know what to do. I'm just stupid and crazy and a fucking nightmare!"

"Calliope," I said, pulling her close to me, her body shaking against mine. "Calli...you're not a nightmare. You're not worthless. You're not--"

"Look at this shit!" Calli screamed, gesturing at the smashed dishes. "This is my life, Abra: A fucking disaster that I caused. I ruin every damn thing I touch, Abra."

"No, you don't," I tried to argue as she pushed away from me.

"Please get out of here," she cried. "I was wrong to call you, I'm sorry. I'll get my shit together at least enough to pretend to be a fucking normal human being. It's fine. I'm fine. Please go!"

I started to stand up, then looked around the kitchen, and then back at her, and the paper towels wrapped around her hands.

"I... I can't, Calli," I said, sitting back down. "We don't have to talk, but...I need to stay."

"Fuck it," Calli said, dropping her head toward her lap. "Abra, I'm a fucking disaster. Don't let me drag you down with me. Don't let me ruin you, too."

"What happened to your hands, Calli?" I asked.

"I tried to pick up some of the shards," she said, through shallow, gasping breaths, unwrapping one hand and exposing a wicked cut. "Fucked that up, too. I didn't try to kill myself, if that's what you're thinking. Too much of a fucking coward to do that."

"Calli, can you take some deep breaths with me?" I asked, keeping my voice as calm as I could, gently putting my arm around her again. "Breathe with me, sweetie. Come on."

I took a deep, exaggerated breath to illustrated.

"In," I inhaled. "And out."

Calli copied me, filling her lungs for what I feared was the first time all day, and blowing it out in a long, sustained stream.

"In," I repeated. "And out."

She complied again, and again, and again.

"Okay," I nodded. "Okay. Let's just…sit for a second, okay?"

She nodded back, continuing to take deep breaths. Sadly, that was my only trick; Gwen used to make me take deep breaths whenever I got too upset as a kid. I didn't exactly have crisis training.

"I get like this sometimes," Calli finally said, between breaths. "Usually not this bad, but...it happens. Don't worry, I can pull it together, eventually. Or at least pretend. It's okay. You don't have to stay here and watch me be pathetic."

"I know I don't have to," I said, pulling her toward me. "And you're not pathetic. You're not worthless, or stupid, or a piece of shit, either."

"Please," Calli said. "I know how you and your friends talked about me."

"That's because we were assholes, Calli," I said. "I'm sorry that we said those things. That we made you feel like that."

"You were right," Calli shrugged. "Look at me."

"We were more wrong than we've been about anything else," I said. "I am *looking at you. This…these things...how long has this been happening to you?"*

"Most of my life," Calli said. "Just on and off. Sometimes it's bad, sometimes I'll go a few years without getting...like this."

"Jesus, Calli," I muttered.

"See? A fucking disaster."

"No," I insisted. "No. Fuck no. You've made it this long going through this? Calli, you're not a disaster, you're a fucking badass."

"Abra...," she started to protest.

"I'm serious," I said. "You've lived with this your whole life? Shit, Calli, I wouldn't have been able to do it. Or I'd have been some recluse or just fucking terrible human being. But you...."

"Am also a fucking terrible human being," she interrupted.

"No," I shook my head. "Calli, I... look, I know how we started and why we started but...I really like you. You were there for me when I felt at my most alone and afraid. I'm glad you're in my life. And I'm kind of a disaster already, so it's okay."

Calli actually laughed at that, and then nuzzled her face into my shoulder.

"I don't know about a disaster, but you may not be that bright," she said, both of us laughing. "Thank you for staying with me."

"Of course," I said, hugging her and then standing up. I tiptoed back through the debris field to the pantry, grabbing a broom and a dustpan.

"Abra, I can get that," Calli said, still from the floor.

"I know you could," I said, starting to sweep the shards into a pile. "Like I said...."

"I'm a fucking badass," Calli finished, starting to smile.

I was able to convince Calli to start seeing a therapist shortly after the incident. We couldn't find anyone local who was even remotely trans-friendly (the one I had gone to having packed up and moved East years before), so she saw a therapist in Spokane via video chat once a week. It wasn't a cure, but it was a help. Her episodes still came around, but not as frequently and not nearly as severe. She had become better at predicting them, and I had become better at helping her deal with them.

And yet, she didn't show up for our usual coffee date on my lunch break.

But I wasn't going to panic. Part of trusting that Calli was taking care of herself now was letting Calli take care of herself. If she decided she needed a mental health day away from everyone or, hell, if an appointment had just run long or she hadn't looked at the clock, that was her business. Not every missed coffee meant she was sitting huddled among a dishware massacre. I'd try to touch base with her later if she didn't get to me first. No big deal.

And yet.

Fortunately for my brain, Crystal was not having a day where she was willing to let me sit and stew. It was hard to maintain a train of obsessive thought with a middle-aged sentient tattoo ranting at you.

"I'm just asking you to consider it!" She yelled, gesturing for effect at my shelves of vintage merchandise.

"Okay," I yelled back. "Hmm. Mmm? Hmm! No!"

"For fuck sake, Abra," she groaned, stomping around in a circle. "Lindsee has shown you the same books she's shown me; this is the only part of the store that isn't turning a profit!"

"Why the hell is Lindsee showing *you* the books?" I asked, ignoring the more salient point for the time being.

"Because I asked!" Crystal replied. "And I'm glad I did. Abra, you brought me on for a reason. This is a great venue, and you've got to know I'm completely onboard here. I've bought in; Cluster is great. Rah-rah Cluster. Let me do my job and move it forward. It's not like I'm asking you to turn your corner into a housewares section or anything!"

"You may as well be!" I retorted. "This was the original function of Cluster! The music section came about on Drew's suggestion, and the coffee shop exists only because there was a fucking coffee shop already there!"

"We'll sell vintage music here, and memorabilia!" Crystal argued. "We can move all of that out of the far end and expand the performance space. We'll have enough room to let the bands who play here sell their stuff even on nights they aren't playing! Abra, this makes sense!"

It did. I hated that it did. It would have been easier to reject a stupid idea. The books Lindsee had shown me were pretty damn clear, though; Cadabra's Corner was no longer profitable. She theorized that it was due to the change in clientele. When Drew, Lore, and I were still running it, we were primarily a vintage shop that served coffee and occasionally hosted bands. With Crystal onboard, the momentum had shifted. We were now a music venue that served coffee and also had a crappy little shop in the back. Crystal's idea was a good one, but that didn't stop me from hating it.

"I said no, Crystal," I growled.

"Jesus Christ, Abra!" she yelled, slamming both hands on my counter. "Why are you so attached to this being an old crap store?"

"Because that was my dream!" I blurted, feeling like an idiot but not knowing what else to say.

"Well, that's neat and all, but maybe it was a stupid dream!" Crystal retorted. "Or maybe it was a great dream, but you know what the thing is about dreams, Abra? Eventually, you have to wake up and get some work done."

I couldn't think of any more words. She was too right. Turning Cadabra's Corner into a music shop made a ton of sense. But it would mean the end of the last vestiges of what Cluster had been. It would mean admitting that I didn't recognize it anymore. I felt lost in the stage and coffee shop areas. Crystal had done an amazing job with a new set up, but it wasn't the way Drew had had it. Lindsee had a knack for running the coffee shop, but she didn't do it the way Lore had. There were still paintings on the walls, but none of them were Neal's. Cadabra's Corner was the last holdout. Everyone else had moved on, but what about me? What happened when I became obsolete in my own dream?

My phone rang, interrupting my thought train. I glanced down at it, not recognizing the number. But I was eager to end my conversation with Crystal, who was still seething on the other side of my counter, so I answered it anyway.

"Hello?" I said politely into the phone while glaring at Crystal.

"Hello, is this Abra Collins?" a woman's voice asked on the other end.

"Yes."

"Ms. Collins, are you familiar with a Ms. Calliope Watson?"

"Yes," I said, feeling my insides start to clench.

"Ms. Collins, my name is Nancy Johnson, I'm a nurse at Brahmton General," she said, in what I'm sure was supposed to be a calming voice. Crystal, seeing my face, mouthed a concerned "what?" at me, which I waved off.

"What's going on?" I asked, my voice shaking.

"There's been an incident," Nurse Johnson said. "I really can't give you much more information than that. But Ms. Watson has you listed as an emergency contact...."

I'm sure she said more, and maybe I did, too, but I was already a blur of movement, running toward the door, and the rest of the world was less than that.

4 AS THE CROW FLIES

"Thanks for coming out here with me," I told Neal as we walked through the cemetery. It was a crisp, late fall day, though the sun was out. The ground crunched gently under our feet as we clomped off the walking path into section A3. Steam was coming off of the coffees in our hands, regular drip for Neal, a pumpkin spice latte for me because, well, I'm rather basic. Clutched in my other hand was a small bouquet of marigolds clipped from the garden Lore maintained.

"Of course," Neal nodded, putting both hands on his cup to warm them. "I'm sorry I missed last month."

"No worries," I shrugged. "It's not like I can't do this on my own. It's just nice to have some company. Drew came with me last month."

We crested a small hill, and came to the grave that I no longer needed a grid-map to find. I looked down at the polished granite surface and chuckled once again at the inscription.

"You don't think she left that specifically *for you, right?" Neal laughed.*

"Probably not," I said. "But I'm guessing she's pissed that I'm not listening."

The inscription read:

Olivia Evelyn Paulson
"In case no one told you, I died. So you can probably go do something else."

"Every time I read that, I kick myself for not taking one of her classes," Neal said as I knelt beside the grave and laid down the marigolds. The grounds crew had removed the previous month's already.

"She was hilarious," I smiled. "Fuck everyone who complained that she wasn't teaching us anything. I learned more from her jokes than if she had stuck to lecturing

us about fucking Chaucer."

I knelt there in silence for several minutes, Neal patiently standing watch.

"I'll always regret that we didn't get to make that trip," I said, to Neal, Olivia, myself, and no one. "I regret I never said all the things I wanted to say."

"She knew," Neal assured me, crouching down beside me and putting a hand on my back.

"I don't think she did," I sighed. "It fucking tears me up inside that she always worried on some level that I was just taking pity on her."

"Why do you think that?" Neal asked. I reminded myself he hadn't seen the letter she left for me.

"Just...things she said," I dismissed. "Is it stupid of me to say that I fucking hate death?"

"What?" Neal asked.

"I hate death," I repeated. "And I get that that's not exactly a revolutionary stance, but goddamn. There's just...you can't argue with it. You can't tell it 'hey, no, that's not right' or 'you can't take her, our story was just getting started.' It's just…."

"It's chaos," Neal finished.

"I wish I thought so," I said, exhaling through my teeth. "But it doesn't feel that way. Maybe it is, maybe it's just some grand universal random number generator. But it feels like there's a meanness to it, an intent. I don't know, after Gwen died, people kept saying things like, 'it's God's plan' or 'everything happens for a reason,' like that was supposed to be comforting."

"People say dickish things when they don't know what else to say," Neal nodded.

"But here's the thing," I said, down toward Olivia's headstone, "I think they're right. I'm not...religious…but I think they're right. I just don't understand why that would comfort anyone. I'd much rather think of it all as just random chaos, but…."

A cold breeze whipped through the cemetery, and I pulled my coat tight around my body.

"Nah, fuck it," I grumbled, standing up. "I used up all of my half-cooked philosophy in the dorm lounge back in college. Come on; let's go home."

"Do...do you want to visit Gwen's niche?" Neal asked as I started walking.

I shook my head. I felt vaguely guilty when I visited Olivia. I felt convicted whenever I even thought about visiting Gwen.

I tore through the hospital so fast it took a nurse physically putting himself in my path to stop me. Unfortunately, I was wearing the wrong shoes for running on polished linoleum and went sliding directly into him, thumping against his scrub-wearing chest. Even then, one cheery train of thought chugged through my head:

"Death. Pain. Tragedy. Disfigurement. Death. Suicide. Assault. Rape. Death. Beating. Hate crime. Bleeding. Death. Death. Death. She's dead. Dead like Olivia. Dead like Gwen. Dead dead dead. It's your fault; you know what happens when you care about someone. Dead dead dead. You should have called earlier. She's dead now."

"Excuse me," the nurse, a towering man with a shaved head and grim face, said, catching his balance and pushing me back from him. "Please do not run in here."

Dead dead. Dead dead dead. You've really fucked it up this time.

"I'm--I'm looking for--," I gasped, so out of breath that the world was starting to get hazy around the edges. "I'm--looking--Calliope Watson's room. Please."

Cut her wrists. Ran her car in a closed garage. Drank poison. You were supposed to help. How could you think trash like you could help anyone?

"Oh, you're Calli's friend," the man said, his stern face melting. "Come on, she's right this way."

Why was this man being so calm when Calli was clearly dead or dying? I followed after him, my brain feeling like a thousand spider egg sacks had just burst open on its surface.

"Knock-knock, you have a visitor," the nurse said, while tapping on the room door.

"Hi Abby," Calli, sitting up in her hospital bed, said, with a cautious wave. My brain honestly had trouble figuring out how Calli--who was clearly dead--could be sitting up and waving at me with a cup of Jell-O in her other hand.

"Thank you, DeMarius," Calli blew a kiss to the nurse as he smiled and left. "That's DeMarius. He found me blue Jell-O, so he's basically my hero."

"What--why...Calli...," I sputtered. Alive though she was, something had clearly happened. An angry, swollen purple ring encircled her left eye. She had a wrapping around her right food and her lip was split on the bottom, held together with a few tiny stitches. I forgot my question and rushed toward her, throwing my arms around her.

"Ow. Ow ow ow," Calli said, trying to give me some semblance of a hug back. "Sweetie, I love you, but I'm pretty much ninety-percent bruise right now. Can't really kiss you, either."

"Calli I was so scared!" I blurted, forcing myself to part from her, the dam breaking and tears streaming from my eyes. "I was so fucking scared! What happened? Are--are you…?"

"I'm okay, Abra," she said, putting down her Jell-O cup and reaching out to grab my hand with one of hers. Her knuckles were covered in abrasions. "Sweetheart, I'm okay. Split lip, broken ankle, ugly eye, bruises. Nothing that won't heal. Abby, sweetie. It's okay."

"I thought I'd lost you," I whispered. "Jesus, I thought…."

"Knock-knock," a new voice called from the door, this one female. Calli and I turned, seeing a familiar face from long ago standing in the doorway.

"Detective Martinez?" I asked in disbelief as the woman who had been there in our kitchen the night Gwen had died entered the hospital room. The same one who had given me the news of Brock's death personally.

"Abra Collins," she said, warmly, as we both reached out and hugged. "It's been a long time, kid. I was down the hall. I asked Nurse DeMarius to call me when you got here. Your girl tell you what happened?"

"Not yet," Calli said, through a bite of Jell-O.

"Well, I hate to ruin a surprise," Detective Martinez chuckled. It was then I noticed she was holding a brown paper bag, folded over. "Your girlfriend got into a little incident up at the college. You want to tell her why?"

"It's...part of your Christmas present," Calli said, blushing.

"Part of my Christmas present is you getting into a fight at the college?" I asked.

"I've been putting out feelers for something online for a while now," Calli confessed. "Something I wanted to get for you. I got a bite yesterday, and went out to meet the guy who had it. We...had a little disagreement."

"What kind of disagreement?" I asked. "Calli, what were you trying to get?"

"Snooty Crow," Calli grumbled. "There. Surprise ruined."

"Oh, Calli," I said, going back over to her and trying to find a patch of her it was okay to make physical contact with. "I really, really appreciate the thought, but those things go for like $3000 now. But, how is that related to--"

"Actually," Calli said, musing with a piece of her hair, "the market kinda dropped out on Snooty Crow. It's theorized to be because Spinwheel was so short-lived and the generation that remembers it is aging out of the nostalgia sweet-spot. So Snooty Crow only goes for about $500 these days. I've done my homework. So, if someone, say, went online and posted in the local area that they were offering $2500 for one, why, it might even flush out a collector who otherwise wouldn't be interested in selling."

She shot me a sly smile, and Detective Martinez just laughed.

"Wait…," I said, finally putting the pieces together. "You weren't getting me *a* Snooty Crow, you were getting me--"

"*The* Snooty Crow," Calli finished for me. "Asshole took the bait hook, line, and sinker. I told him to meet me by the fountain at the college, so he wouldn't get suspicious. Plus, it was a public place. When he showed up, I made sure he had the crow, then I told him what I knew and that we could do it the easy way or the hard way. He chose the hard way."

My stomach sank.

"Calliope," I said, a wave of guilt washing over me. "This is...amazing what you did for me, but no stuffed animal is worth...this!"

I gestured at her battered body. She shrugged.

"The eye is his," Calli said, "I'll give him that. But that's all I gave him."

"But...what about…?"

Calli reddened and looked down at the blankets. Detective Martinez laughed again.

"Do you want to tell her, or should I?" the detective asked.

Calli mumbled a series of words that I couldn't possibly have understood.

"Wait, what?" I asked, leaning in.

Another string of mumbles, louder but no clearer.

"Calli, I can't--"

"I fell down a fucking set of stairs!" She yelled. "There, is everyone happy now?"

Martinez started laughing even louder.

"You...what?"

"Ms. Collins," Detective Martinez said, regaining some of her composure, "you've got quite the little scrapper here. She's leaving out a small piece of the story. After dumbass took a swing at her, she came back at him like a damn jaguar. The moron is here, too, recovering from, among *many* other things, having surgery to reattach his eyelid. I just got done having a little visit with him. Or at least what's left of him. Unfortunately, badass or not, Ms. Watson, next time you decide to do something like this--which, as an officer of the law, I must stress was a terrible idea--wear a shoe without a heel."

I looked back to Calli for an explanation.

"I didn't think he was going to be stupid enough to try to fight. He sounded like a pathetic little prick, I thought he'd just cave. But after he was down, I got scared and took off running," Calli said, still red-faced. "But there's this stupid little set of stairs that leads down from the fountain area, and my heel caught in a seam in the concrete and... well...."

My mouth hung open as I stared at Calli, so much of her blue and red, her embarrassment palpable. I wanted to put my arms around her again, but didn't know how to without hurting her. Instead, I just took her hand back and held it, trying to avoid the abrasions.

"See, detective?" Calli said, "This is how I know. Tell ninety-nine people that story, they're going to start laughing. And I'd be one of them, because, objectively, it's fucking funny. But."

"Point made, Ms. Watson," Martinez smiled. "Now, Ms. Collins, if I can borrow you for a second, I have some pictures I'd like you to look at. I pulled the report from the break-in at your store, and everything seems to be as Ms. Watson says it is. First, I need you to see if anyone looks familiar in this photo line-up...."

Martinez took out a sheet with several pictures of unpleasant looking men on it. There, second row, third from the right, was the man who we had to kick out of Cluster. The man who looked like the Blue Fairy granted a bottle of Rohypnol's wish to be a real boy. The man Calli had gone to confront for me.

"That one," I said, pointing at the photo without hesitation.

"And circle gets the square," Martinez said. "His name is Shaun Callen. He's a non-trad student at Freemond. No priors, but some sexual harassment complaints at the college, I guess."

Surprise.

"He throws a shitty punch," Calli chimed in. "Seriously, I'm disappointed in my eye for looking like this. It felt like a butterfly crashing into me."

"Well, you're a badass, Ms. Watson. I thought we established that,"

Martinez chuckled. "We're still processing his prints, but I have a feeling they're going to be a pretty good match for the ones taken during the robbery investigation. We'll be in touch with some other questions and some paperwork, but right now, the only thing left is this."

Martinez picked up the brown paper bag she had brought in, unrolled the top, reached in and brought forth Snooty Crow.

"Is this the crow in question, Ms. Collins?" she asked, handing it to me. I snatched it from her hand and began feeling around Snooty Crow's chest seam. Inside, a piece of paper crinkled.

"It's him," I said, a wave of elation that brought tears to my eyes washing over me. "One hundred percent sure."

"Well then, merry Christmas, Abra," Martinez said. "We already took photos at the station that can be used for evidence, so enjoy your crow. And you, Ms. Watson…."

Calli, who had gone back to eating her blue Jell-O, looked up, her eyes wide.

"Again, I have to stress that this was a terrible, dangerous idea that could have gone much worse than it did," Martinez declared, her voice suddenly grave. "This is central Washington; you don't know who has a gun on them. This could have been a much different reunion for Abra and me. Leave law enforcement to the police, do you understand?"

"Yes," Calli muttered, with a little nod.

"Okay," Martinez said, her voice softening. "Now, unofficially: that was amazing, and you two are adorable. Have a good Christmas, Calliope. Abra, can I see you in the hall for just a minute?"

"Merry Christmas!" Calli called as I followed Martinez out into the hall.

"I just wanted to ask you how you've been," she asked once we were outside Calli's room. "Your sister's case has always been one that stuck with me."

"I'm...okay," I finally decided. "I have my own store. Dad died a few years back. My girlfriend might secretly be Batgirl. Usual stuff. The crow was Gwen's, you know."

"Calli told me that, yes," Martinez smiled. "Abra, I know we don't know each other very well, but can I give you some advice by way of a story?"

"Sure," I shrugged.

"My husband loves me," she said. "I mean *really* loves me. We don't have one of those marriages where the love and passion died out two years in. But last Christmas, I asked him for a specific coffee maker in a specific shade of blue that would go with our kitchen."

She stopped and snickered to herself.

"He bought me a very nice coffee maker," she continued. "In black. Because the one in blue was only sold at the Outlet Mall, but the black one he could get at the Walmart in town. Do you feel me?"

"Yeah," I smiled. "I feel you."

"Good," Martinez nodded. "Merry Christmas, Abra."

"Merry Christmas, Detective," I replied.

"It's Nadine," she smiled as she walked away. I glanced back toward Calli's room, watching her scroll through her phone, pausing to wince as she moved her arm the wrong way. Then I looked down at the plush crow in my hand.

"I say, my good lady," Snooty Crow said in my mind, as I stared into his black plastic eyes, his stuffy British accent still intact, "I don't believe either of us was worth all that."

I looked back up at Calli, who saw me and waved from her bed, wincing again. Suddenly, all the pieces clicked into place, and for maybe the first time in my life, I knew exactly what I needed to do. More than that, I knew exactly what I *wanted* to do.

My friend group had attempted exactly one triple-date in its entire existence. In the brief window during which Neal was with Dan, Lore was (of course) with Drew, and I was with Calli (the first go-around), we all decided to have a dinner out at Char, Brahmton's only 'nice' restaurant.

The evening started smoothly, lots of pleasant small-talk which turned into Neal, Lore, Drew, and me reminiscing about our adventures in college, which, as usual, turned into Neal and me reminiscing about our adventures before *college, almost to the exclusion of anyone else, one of our worst habits. Shortly after our food arrived, Calli, who had been uncharacteristically quiet during the meal, stood up, grabbed her purse, and walked out without a word.*

It would be so easy for me to put every failing of our first relationship on Calli. Comforting, too. She was unhinged, mentally ill, unmedicated, and trying too hard to be some sort of stereotypical trans party-girl. But that wasn't the reason our relationship wasn't a relationship. It was me. All I wanted to see her as was an unhinged, mentally ill, unmedicated trans party-girl. That's how it was comfortable for me to think of her. Treating her like an actual person would have meant realizing how many cries for help I just wrote off as 'Crazy Calli.' If I could go back in time, I'd disembowel the dumb bitch who was past-me. Time paradox be damned.

"Is...is Calli coming back?" Dan asked, leaning across the table to me as I finished my pasta.

"Probably not," I shrugged, like a piece of shit.

"Should you go after her?" He asked.

"She does this," I dismissed.

"Oh...okay," he nodded, still looking concerned. The rest of us finished our meal and headed out. By the time we got back to the house, Calli was already there, sitting on our front porch. She greeted us like nothing had happened, and we all went inside, dispersing to our respective rooms.

I woke up that night around three. The pasta dish I had ordered had been about ninety-percent salt, and I was painfully thirsty. Irritatingly, the water bottle I kept for my meds was empty, and the faucet in my bathroom didn't have a filter, so, leaving Calli dead asleep, I ventured downstairs.

"Hey, Abra," a low voice whispered as I entered the kitchen, the light over the stove illuminating the room.

"Dan?" I said, eyes adjusting to the light.

"That fish was not filling," he said, gesturing to the sandwich he was making himself. "You hungry too?"

"No, just thirsty," I said, suddenly very aware that I was only wearing a flimsy pair of sleep shorts and an even less concealing cami. Reddening, I slid past him and grabbed a glass, taking it to the sink.

"So, is Calli okay?" Dan asked, spreading mayonnaise on his sandwich.

"She's fine," I shrugged, again, like an ice-hearted viper. "She's just Calli."

"Hmm," Dan nodded. "You know you and Neal are pretty intimidating, right?"

"What do you mean?" I asked, after taking a long drink.

"There's so much shared story there," he said. "It's like breaking into someone's marriage, almost."

"Dan," I sighed, "I can assure you, Neal and I--"

"Oh, I know," Dan stopped me. "And I think Calli knows, too. It's just something to be aware of."

"Dan, Neal loves you," I said to him, leaning against the counter. "You have to know it."

"I do," Dan smiled. "He shows me all the time. It's how I learned to not feel drowned in your shadow. But when he and I first started dating, I couldn't decide

if he was in love with you, you were in love with him, both, or neither. No matter what the answer, I worried I was always going to be relegated to the roll of 'boyfriend.' Like, 'Hi, this is Dan the Boyfriend. He's my boyfriend, and he serves the function of a boyfriend. Stop trying to talk to me about other things, Dan the Boyfriend! I already have someone for that!'"

"You really should have done that in a robot voice," I muttered. Dan laughed.

"Look, the two of you talk like you share a mind, and I think that when two people are that close, it's easy to turn everyone else into add-ons."

"Dan, you're not and 'add-on,'" I assured him, my dumb brain not able to see why he seemed suddenly so paranoid. "Don't worry."

"I don't," Dan said, looking me in the eye. "Like I said, Neal shows me that he loves me. I've never felt like an accessory. He treats me like a person, not an idea. I don't worry."

I stood there, water glass in hand, staring at Dan, who gathered up his sandwich and walked back toward the living room.

"Goodnight, Abra," he said.

It took me way too long to figure out what he was trying to tell me. When I did, my reaction was, of course, irritation and dismissal. My brain has always been very good at self-preservation.

Due to Calli's broken ankle and the three flights of stairs that led up to her apartment, we decided that she would stay at my house during her recovery. After the declaration that the storage room that had once been Drew and Lore's quarters still "smelled like sex, and not in the good way," we decided to crack the seal on Neal's old room for the first time since he moved out.

The bare furniture was still in there, an old bed with mattress, stripped of bedding, a thrift store dresser, and the desk where he had sat. Little doodles covered sections of the walls next to the bed and desk, remains of one of his nervous habits, drawing little scenes on whatever was nearby whenever his ideas weren't flowing. No matter how many pocket sketch pads Lore, Drew and I tried to supply him with, he always seemed to prefer the walls of his room.

"These are cute," Calli said, using her little knee-scooter to wheel herself over to Neal's old desk on the third day she resided there. "Did you ever see all these?"

"Just in passing," I said, coming up behind her and looking at what she was pointing at. It was a line of cartoon caricature of Drew, Lore, Neal, and me. Mine looked similar to the drawing he'd done for my sign in Cadabra's Corner, though minus the hat and cloak. Drew's cartoon towered over the rest of us, beard in full glory, face radiating confidence. Lore seemed to be floating next to Drew, looking every bit the moon-pixie that Neal had once compared her to. Neal's figure was the oddity. While it was recognizable, it lacked the detail given to the other three, all of which seemed to almost pop off the wall with lives of their own. Neal's caricature, standing with Drew on one side and me on the other, looked rough. Crude. Lifeless.

"I've been reading his comic strip," Calli said as I pondered Neal's drawing. "Comics aren't my thing but...it's fun. Shade is definitely you, right?"

"Afraid so," I sighed, stepping back from the wall.

"The girl with the power to create and destroy with her words," Calli mused. "This is one of those, 'the less said about that, the better' things, isn't it?"

"Probably," I nodded. "It took me way too long to realize those implications."

"Yeah. Yikes. So... changing the subject…I need your help with something," Calli said, biting her lower lip. "And I need you to not make fun of me."

"Of course," I responded. "Anything. What do you need?"

Calli scooted out the chair at the desk that had once belonged to Neal. I had moved my old gaming computer upstairs, so she would have something to read her blogs on while her phone charged. I hadn't been playing as many games in the last two years. I'd love to say it was because I had matured and 'left behind childish things,' but it was more that I didn't have anyone to play with anymore. Online gaming wasn't the same. If someone calls me an asshole, I want to be able to throw something at their head.

Calli reached over and clicked on the monitor. The computer, popping out of sleep-mode, grinded to life, displaying the title screen of *Unwelcome.*

"How the fuck do I get past the ghost lady in the foyer?" She yelled, pointing at the screen. I instantly broke my promise about not laughing.

"Hey!" Calli snapped, flipping a section of my hair. "Not everyone spent their whole youth on these things!"

"I get it, I get it," I laughed. "It's not that…why are you playing *Unwelcome*?"

"I got bored," Calli grumbled. "I can't believe I'm going to say this, but I actually got tired of watching TV. But I can't exactly go for my usual morning jog. So, I started puttering around on your old computer--"

"You were hoping to find porn, weren't you?" I groaned.

"No! Well," Calli blushed, "I wouldn't have been opposed to discovering that maybe, like, Lore sent you a nude or something one time and you had it saved. Lore or Neal. Or Drew. Really, your friends are all pretty hot."

"Why the hell would my friends send me nudes?" I groaned, louder.

"Hope springs eternal," Calli shrugged. "But, alas, this was the most interesting thing I could find. I got past the main gate and into the mansion, and I know that you're supposed to use the stupid locket that 'radiates an ethereal energy' to kill the ghost lady, but every time I try--"

"She secretes a caustic fluid that melts the skin off your body," I finished for her.

"Yeah," Calli rolled her eyes. "Speaking of things the less said about, the better."

"The game likes to dick with you," I laughed. "Here, start it up. I'll go get the dinner I picked up for us. If we're doing this, we're doing it right."

"What'd you get?" Calli called as I headed toward the kitchen.

"I went to Lotus Garden," I called back. "And yes, I got you pot stickers."

"I love you so fucking much," Calli yelled from Neal's old room as I prepared our plates. By the time I got back in, she had *Unwelcome* started and was already clicking 'open' on the skull of the stone gargoyle next to the mansion's main gate. The jawbone unhinged, revealing a key inside that would unlock the mansion's entrance. We made it through the main gate as Calli ate a pot sticker, pausing to examine the bush next to the front door to collect the ethereal locket.

"Okay," I said, putting my hand on Calli's as she was about to click open and enter the mansion. "Before you do that…like I said, the game likes to dick with you. The locket doesn't do anything until you open it."

"Wait...I have to 'open' the locket?" Calli grumbled. "Do I have to wipe my feet before I go in, too? What kind of game is this?"

"One made by vindictive designers," I laughed. "And you have to open the locket out here, too, or the ghost lady will realize what you're doing and--"

"Jizz acid all over me, right." Calli finished, clicking 'open' and then the locket.

"The locket clicks open. Inside is a picture of a dour woman. It glows a faint green color." The game declared.

"Now?" Calli asked. I nodded, and she clicked 'open' again and then the main door, taking us into the mansion's foyer. A phantasm in a dress appeared in front of us, staring at the screen with glowing green eyes.

"Eat locket and die!" Calli yelled, clicking 'use' on the locket and then on the ghost. A crude animation of the ghost woman screaming and her form dissipating played on the screen, eliciting a loud "Woo!" from Calli.

"There you go!" I declared, gesturing at the screen.

"That felt strangely good," Calli said. "Why did that feel like such an accomplishment?"

"It's called a dopamine jolt," I said. "You want to keep going?"

"You bet!" Calli cheered, popping the last bite of a pot sticker in her mouth. I smiled and gestured for her to click on the next door, preparing to go on my first journey through *Unwelcome's* mansion with someone other than Neal.

"Pass me the gouda we shredded," Drew requested, standing on the other side of the kitchen by a partially assembled pie. Obediently, I handed him the bowl of shredded cheese.

"Great," Drew said, examining the apple slices he'd just dumped into the scratch-made pie crust. "This is going to be good. You're a pretty decent kitchen assistant."

"Thanks," I said, tightening the apron he let me borrow, which was a good three sizes too large. "I'm still not sure about this, though. Cheese in a pie?"

"Cheese on *a pie. You have to trust me on this one, Abra," Drew said, placing on the top crust and sprinkling it with cheese shreds. "Gouda apple pie. Delicious as fuck. Lore and Neal will love it."*

"If you say so," I shrugged. Lore and Neal's birthdays fell within a week of each other, so Drew and I always set up a joint party. This was the first time I was allowed to help with meal prep. Typically, I was just stuck on decorations.

"When are they getting here?" Drew asked, setting the pie in the oven.

"About an hour," I said, looking at my watch.

"Okay," Drew nodded. "I think everything is ready. So... can I ask you something?"

"Sure," I said. "What?"

"Do you have a thing for Lore?"

I felt every drop of blood drain out of my face and my heart stop. This was, unfortunately, during the year where my feelings for Lore had inexplicably swelled up and bubbled back to the surface. But I thought I was being discrete!

"Uh…." I finally managed to say.

"It's okay," Drew burst out laughing. "I'm not going to, like, beat you up, Abra. Oh my God, your face. It's cool, I get it."

"I'd never act on it!" I blurted, the blood returning in full force, my face burning red.

"I know," Drew said, still laughing. "Oh geez, Abby; it's okay. You know you could, *right? We have an open--"*

"Oh, yeah, that'd go great!" I rolled my eyes. "Like you could deal with looking me in the eye for the rest of our lives knowing that Lore and I had…."

"You can't even say it!" Drew laughed louder.

"Of course I can't!" I yelled. "It's Lore!"

"I know," Drew nodded. "It's too real."

"What do you mean 'too real'?" I asked, leaning against the counter.

"You have actual feelings for Lore," Drew said as he wiped flour from his hands. "You do this, Abra; if you feel nothing for someone, you go after them like a shark after a piece of bloody meat…."

"Can we find a less problematic comparison, maybe?" I grumbled, not knowing how I'd stumbled into a psych evaluation.

"But if you have real feelings for someone," Drew continued, ignoring me, "then you pull the e-brake and leap out the window."

"I do not!" I protested. "I pull the e-brake because she's married to you and you're my friend. My increasingly annoying *friend, but still…."*

"You need someone who can call you on your bullshit, Abra," Drew stated. "We all do. I have Lore. Lore has you. Neal doesn't bullshit, so I guess he's the exception. Be honest, and you don't have to answer--not to me, at least: If I were to drop dead right this very minute, and my last words were to give you my solemn, unequivocal blessing to be in whatever kind of relationship you choose with Lore, can you honestly say you'd pursue her, in any way? Or would you come up with a thousand excuses as to why it would be 'weird' or 'inappropriate' or whatever?"

"Are you honestly trying to convince me to fuck your wife?" I yelled, digging my fingers into the countertop.

"No," Drew smiled. "I'm trying to convince you to start calling yourself *on*

your own bullshit, so that you don't end up being your own biggest obstacle to happiness. That's all. Now come on, we've got to set the table."

I was still fuming in the kitchen while Drew started setting up the dining room.

"Lore thinks you're cute, by the way," he called back to me.

"So, what the hell is the point of all of this, again?" Calli grumbled as we reloaded a save game, restarting us outside the desecrated chapel, which was the last stop before the maze.

"Are you being philosophical, or....?" I asked, snickering at her. I was letting her make most of the choices in the game, though I had everything up to the maze pretty much memorized. It was fun watching *Unwelcome* unfold before fresh eyes.

"In the game! What's our goal in the game?" Calli snapped.

"Oh, right," I said. "We're trying to rescue our girlfriend."

"So, like, it's a poly situation, or…?" Calli asked.

"Well, it's designed to be played single-player," I answered.

"Oh," Calli said. "I like my way better. But wait, how did she get into the mansion?"

"Didn't you read the story at the beginning?" I asked, shifting in my chair next to her. "You both got lost in the woods, and she ran ahead of you and into the mansion to get help."

"Wait." Calli said, setting aside the mouse. "No, wait. So, she's already been through all of this? She didn't get dragged in, she came in the same way we did? Have we not considered the possibility that she is, like, way smarter than we are and that she should be saving *our* sorry butts?"

"Calli, that's....," I paused, looking at the screen in front of us, which was waiting for our input. "...Not a bad point, actually. But here we are."

"Okay, so, what haven't we tried on this goblin-thing blocking our path?" Calli asked, going back into battle-mode. "We tried hitting it with an axe, we tried setting it on fire, we tried all of our spells…."

I grunted an unintelligible word of three syllables.

"What?" Calli asked, studying my face. "I know you know what to do! Be helpful!"

I didn't want to just tell her. So I made my hands into pincer shapes and began opening and closing them.

"Okay, well, that's adorable, but I don't see how it helps," Calli grumbled. "Wait…!"

Calli's eureka moment hit, and she opened our 'inventory' window, displaying all the items we'd collected up until that point. She scrolled through until she came to the scorpion in a jar we had found in the haunted laboratory.

"Okay, let me guess," Calli muttered. "I have to open the jar, right? Do I have to do anything else like, open the scorpion or give the scorpion a manicure or something?"

I made a 'lips are sealed' gesture.

"Oh, you are so lucky you're cute," Calli growled. "Okay, scorpion out of the jar, here goes…."

Calli used the scorpion on the goblin.

"The goblin has fled in terror from the scorpion you have thrown." The game declared. *"The path is now clear."*

"Ha!" Calli cheered. "Fuck you, goblin! You came from hell, so I don't know why you're scared of a scorpion, but fuck you! Onward!"

"Okay," I laughed, "so this next section is the maze…."

"Wait, *the* maze?" Calli asked. "Like, the one you and Neal beat your head against for years? That maze?"

"The same," I nodded.

Calli paused the game and took her hand off the mouse.

"You know I'm okay if you contact him, right?" she said. "I know I said I was jealous of him the last time we were together, but...it's different now."

"Well, *we're* different now," I sighed. "Neal and me...I don't want to derail things for him. And he hasn't contacted me, either. Not that I blame him. I broke his heart and shoved him out of my life. I can't imagine how pathetic I'd feel crawling back after that, if the roles were reversed. I think it's better that he hates me."

"He doesn't hate you," Calli said, giving me her 'no bullshit' eyes. "You don't go from eternal love to hate just because of one shitty conversation. He's probably talking right now with that succulent slab of meat he's marrying about how you probably hate *him,* and he doesn't want to make you feel uncomfortable again. I love you, Abby-Cadaby--oh roll your eyes all you want--and I liked Neal, but both of you have the same habit of getting lost running in circles around your own brains."

"It's not that easy," I grumbled, getting frustrated again. I wanted to contact Neal. More than that, I wanted to wake up and find an email or a text or a letter from him. But how do you re-invite someone into your life knowing that they've just finally started moving on from you? How do you call someone back in after you've shoved them out the door?

"Two years ago, I made a choice," Calli said, stroking my shoulder. "You called me and wanted to talk. That was all I had in mind, too, when I told you to come see me at the shop. But while we stood there talking, I started realizing how much I liked you, and how much it hurt me to see you so sad. So, I took a risk. And I knew it was a risk, but I wanted to make you feel better, and I only knew one way to do that for you back then. I gave you a little speech about us being terrible for each other, but I was giving it to me more than you. If you'd said 'no thanks' that day, or if, afterward, you had just jumped out of bed and headed home, it would have crushed me. But I took a risk and I'm glad I did. I know it's not the same, but it's not different, either."

I leaned over and kissed a non-bruised patch of Calli's cheek.

"Two years ago I made a choice, too," I said, letting her lean her head gently on my shoulder. "I made it for absolutely the wrong reasons, but I'm glad I did, too. Calli, when you were in the hospital...when they called me...I thought I'd lost you, and it felt like someone had torn my insides out. I've lost so, so many people, but...it felt different. I didn't know how I was going to go on. I didn't know how *anything* was going to go on. Jesus, please, never do anything like that again."

"You're hard to shop for," Calli whispered, kissing my neck. As I sat there, feeling her soft, comforting warmth next to me, I knew it was time. I needed to take the leap I'd been preparing for since we sat there in her hospital room.

"Calliope," I said, drawing in as much air as I could, "tell me about Seattle."

"It's...like Portland but with stuff?" Calli shrugged, confused. "They have great seafood and terrible sports teams? What do you want to know?"

"You know what I mean," I replied, giving her my own version of her 'no bullshit' glare.

"Abra, we talked about this," Calli said, taking her head off my shoulder. "I'm not leaving you. This isn't like with Neal or Lore and Drew. I have my shop here, I don't have some burning urge in my loins to travel west and have one there instead. I'm not leaving you."

"Calli, you're miserable here," I sighed. "You're being held back as an artist by your own clientele. You know you'd have more opportunities to stretch your creative wings working with Sera. She's good, right?"

"The best," Calli said. "That's why she's opening a second shop. She's going to split her time between Portland and Seattle and let some hand-picked artists back her up."

"So you'd pretty much be running the place while she was away?" I asked.

"Yeah, along with some other artists," Calli answered. "That's why she was headhunting me so hard, because I have experience running my own shop."

"Calli…," I said, looking her in her excruciatingly blue eyes.

"It's a moot point, Abra!" Calli exclaimed. "I'm not leaving you! It took me my whole life to find...this. This wonderful, weird thing that I had almost come to terms with never having. So my shop goes under because this town is full of yokels who only want tribal designs and Looney Tunes characters. I'll find something else to do."

"Calli," I said, softly. "I'm not asking you to leave me."

There was a brief, yet pregnant silence.

"What...what are you saying?" Calli asked, voice shaking.

"Is this something you want," I asked, feeling my pulse quicken. "If it wasn't for me, would you be going to Seattle to work with Sera?"

"It doesn't matter, it--"

"Calli."

"Yes, probably, okay?" Calli blurted. "But it doesn't matter!"

"Yes, it does. Let's go," I said, finally.

"How's Calli?" Crystal asked as I arrived back at Cluster after bringing Calli home from the hospital.

"Resting," I said, realizing for the first time how exhausted I felt. "But okay."

"What the hell happened?" Crystal asked, as Lindsee sped around the counter to hand me a coffee that she somehow knew I needed.

"Well," I said, reaching into my messenger bag and pulling out Snooty Crow.

"Wait, is that…?" Lindsee asked, pointing at the slightly dusty crow.

"Yeah," I nodded. "The same one. She found the asshole. Kicked the shit out of him, too."

"Ha!" Crystal cheered. "That's fucking awesome! I've always said, it's the little ones you have to watch out for. Damn, I wish I could have seen that."

"But she got hurt, too?" Lindsee asked, still examining Snooty Crow.

"Yeah, but...only tangentially connected," I said. "She'll tell you later if she wants to. She'll be okay. She's back at my place resting. Crystal, I need to talk to you."

"Hey, if it's about the shit we were getting into before you left, don't worry about it," Crystal said, waving me off. "We can duke it out about that later. I just--"

"If it was for sale, would you be able to buy Cluster," I interrupted.

"Huh? What?" She asked, looking truly surprised for the first time since I'd met her. "What are you talking about?"

"Just what I said," I told her. "If I were to sell Cluster, would you be able--or willing--to buy it from me?"

"I... yeah, probably," Crystal said, flabbergasted. "I still have all my insurance money from when my old place burned down. I'd probably have to get a loan, but I have good credit.... Wait, what are we even talking about? You want to sell Cluster?"

"I think so," I nodded. "I have to have a conversation first, but I think so."

"But isn't this place, like, your baby?" Crystal asked.

"It was," I replied. "Which is why I want to make sure it is left in good hands. Is it something you would want?"

"I... yeah, of course!" Crystal exclaimed. "I've been dreaming about having my own venue again for fucking years! But...Abra...are you sure about this? You just got back from seeing your girlfriend in the hospital, are you sure your brain isn't just all fucked up right now?"

"Yes," I said. "And no. But I need to have another conversation first. I just wanted to know if it was something you could do."

"I... I could," Crystal responded. "But, Abra...I'm not going to be, like, a museum curator. If I take over Cluster...."

"You're going to gut it and make it completely unrecognizable to me," I finished for her. "That's what I'm counting on, Crystal; do that exact thing."

An hour of circular talk had passed, *Unwelcome* still paused on the screen between us.

"I can't let you do this, Abra," Calli protested. "I can't take you away from everything you've worked so hard to build!"

"But I haven't!" I countered. "Don't you see? Everything has just been dropped in my lap my entire life by some very kind, very well-meaning people. Gwen did all the heavy lifting when I transitioned. Olivia gave me all of this. And God bless both of them for it! But--"

"You've made it your own, Abra," Calli said. "I'm fine here! I'll make it fine. This is your home. Your history is here."

"I know," I said. "That's why I want to leave."

"Abra?"

I paused and looked down at my hands, trying to get the phrasing right for what I wanted to say.

"My history is here," I repeated. "I can drive by the old house where my mom died in the kitchen, where my father tortured me my entire childhood. Every day on my way to work, I pass the coffee shop where I first met the asshole who murdered my sister. Her grave is here, along with the grave of the only woman besides you that I ever loved, reminding me that they're both gone. I can sit around this house where Olivia died, where I watched my friends leave me, one by one. Where I forced one to. I'm...stuck, Calli. I used to hold on because I didn't want to let go of the people I've lost. But I just keep spinning in circles, living in a life that was built for me instead of one I built. I need to go, Calli. More than that, I *want* to go"

Calli sat in silence for more than a few moments before speaking again.

"I can't save you, Abra," she whispered. "I love you, but I can't save you."

"I don't need a savior," I said, putting my hands on her shoulders. "People have been saving me my whole life. That's how I got here. You can't save me, and I can't save you. But I don't think either of us need saving."

"This is crazy, Abra," said Calli. "What if, like, we get to Seattle and you realize you're sick of me? Or you meet someone else? Or my brain breaks for good and I drive you off? What if we both end up lost and alone in a strange city?"

"I can't tell the future. I don't know what will happen." I admitted. "You're right. This is absolutely crazy. But so is everything else about us. Us being us is crazy. Us finding each other is crazy. I've been crazy all my life. But I never knew how happy I could be until I was crazy with you. I've never met anyone like you, and I know I never will again. I love you, Calli. I know you and I love you. I don't love you *in spite* of what you are."

Calli laughed suddenly. "Abra…."

"Calli?"

"I've got to warn you, my hair gets crazy in the rain," she said, pressing her forehead against mine.

"So…."

"Fuck it," she smiled, almost wickedly. "Let's be crazy. If you're sure."

"I'm sure," I smiled back. And I was. Of that and nothing else.

"Tell me about Calliope," Lore said, right after the waiter brought our lunch. I was paying for this one. Nothing I could find could beat a set of dentures with angry faces engraved on each tooth.

"She's...thrilling," I said, not knowing what other word to use for the girl who had taken me on an almost non-stop ride through the underworld I never knew Brahmton had, punctuated only by increasingly intense sex. "I've never met anyone like her."

"I believe it," Lore nodded. "She seems very...exciting."

"She is," I said, hoping the conversation would be over soon, because I truly didn't have a clue what else to say about her. We'd been together about two months—which made it about two months and one day since we'd met--and we'd yet to have an actual conversation. But she could make my blood feel like it was made of lightning just by looking at me over her shoulder and biting her lip, so, I hate to admit, I didn't really care.

"Abra," Lore said, taking a bite of her reuben, "level with me, okay?"

"What?" I asked, setting down my burger.

"What's this about?" she asked. "Being with Calli, I mean. Is it...is it just the trans thing?"

"I... I like Calli." I protested. It didn't seem becoming to tell Lore that I was horny as hell and Calli looked like every sexual fantasy I had ever had.

"Abra," Lore sighed. "You don't know Calli."

"I know Calli plenty," I insisted, getting testy. I didn't like this conversation, and it was ruining a perfectly good mushroom-swiss burger. The waitress began to approach to ask how we were enjoying our meal, but wisely split off at the last second.

"No, you don't," Lore responded. "Look, it's fine if this is just some fling; I get that. But you're getting that dreamy look about you."

"That dreamy look?" I grumbled.

"Yeah, Abra," Lore said. "The one you get before you start projecting your list of desirable traits onto someone."

"That's not something I do," I lied, mainly to myself. "Can I ask why I'm getting the third-degree here? I finally have someone in my life, and you're acting like I'm mashing my own self-destruct button."

"Abra," Lore said, softly, looking down at the table. "I love you. I love you so much. But I also know you've been lonely, and I know what that can do to

someone's brain."

"Lore, don't do this," I groaned. "Don't become one of those women who has been in a relationship so long that they decide they get to be the expert on everyone else's life."

"I'm not the expert, Abra," Lore snipped back. "But I don't have to be to see what's going on here."

"What do you have against Calli?" I asked, feeling my teeth start to grind of their own accord. "We've been together for two months and you're acting like we're getting married tomorrow. I'm not the lonely spinster you seem to think I am; I've had girlfriends before. Why are you acting this way about this one? I'll ask you what you asked me, Lore: is it a trans thing?"

Lore looked like I had struck her, and I instantly regretted what I'd said.

"No, Abra," Lore said, through her teeth, looking like she was holding back tears. "It's not 'a trans thing.' I'm sorry if I've given you reason to think I would have a problem with someone because they are trans. I would think that years of friendship and support--"

"Lore, I'm sorry," I tried to interrupt. "I--"

"I'm worried about you, okay?" Lore said, over the top of me. "I'm worried because I love you. Because I want you to be happy. Maybe Calli is wonderful. Maybe she's awful. I don't know. But what I do know is that what she's showing you isn't really her."

"We've been together two months, Lore," I groaned. "What should she be showing me? What's wrong with her wanting to put on her best face?"

"I wasn't done," Lore said, putting a hand up. "That's not her best face, Abra; it's a disguise. But that's not what worries me. What worries me is that you're doing it, too. That's what I've never seen from you before. It scares me, Abra. Maybe the two of you could be amazing together, but these two people you've invented are going to drag each other to hell."

"Well," I said, defiant, "then I'll go to hell."

A long, painful silence settled over not only our table, but the whole restaurant, and I realized that we had become the entertainment for all the other diners. I was mad at Lore, but didn't feel like it. I felt closer to sad than anything, and I couldn't put my finger on why. I knew she was right, but that wasn't it. Later, I would realize that it was because I'd never seen Lore look at me like that: like I was so far gone that I could only be mourned.

"I'm sorry," she finally muttered. "I shouldn't have pressed. It's none of my business."

"No, I'm sorry," I muttered back. "I shouldn't have accused you of...that thing I accused you of."

"You...do you...I don't want you to ever think," Lore stammered, tears dripping from her eyes.

"I don't," I said, reaching over and putting my hands on her arms. "I was angry and hurt, and so I lashed out in a way that I knew would hurt back. I'm sorry, Lorelei."

"You haven't called me that in years," Lore gave a thin smile.

"I... I thought it would make me sound more serious," I admitted. "I'm an asshole. You've never done anything but support me. It was an asshole thing to say. I'm sorry."

"It's okay," Lore said, though I could tell she was still smarting. "I didn't mean to make you feel like I thought you were a lonely spinster. I just...I love you, Abra, and I want you to be with someone who can see you for who you are. Someone who you feel comfortable letting see who you are."

The silence came back, thick and murky, but not as painful this time. I almost told her. Almost told her that I had found that, twice before, but neither was meant to be. One because she died, the other because she fell in love with my roommate. Instead, I stayed silent, and made a promise to myself that the next time it came around, I wouldn't let it go.

"Ow," Calli said, rolling off of me and onto her side of the bed. "Ow ow ow. Okay, so, that didn't work. We know that now. Dammit, there has *got* to be an angle where I'm not sore!"

"Calli, it's okay," I laughed. "We can take a raincheck."

"It is so not okay!" Calli snapped, betraying herself with a quick warble of laughter. "When did I become frail?"

"Sometime after the point where you beat the living shit out of a burglar," I said. "If that's frail, I'm made of spun sugar."

"I'm still pissed I let him get off the shot he did," Calli grumbled. "He telegraphed it and everything, and I just stood there and let him punch me in the damn eye."

"Calli, you're not Wonder Woman," I started.

"Take it back!" she demanded.

"Okay, okay," I laughed. "But you pretty much turned that guy inside out. You just...you know...need to look where you're going and stuff."

"Stupid stairs," Calli groaned. "So... what's next?"

"What do you mean?" I asked, leaning up on my elbow next to her on the bed. "If you're suggesting we try again, I really think I need to say no, for your sake."

"No, not that," Calli laughed. "I have to admit defeat on that one. Raincheck, though. I meant, like, what's the next step for us? I know I have to contact Sera and be like, 'hey, remember when I told you for the fifth time that I wasn't going to come work for you? Well….' and then start talking with my landlords about the shop and the apartment."

"I need to call Olivia's old lawyer, Monica," I said, turning onto my back again. "See if her offer to help me sell Cluster and the house is still good years later."

"We'll need to find a place in Seattle," Calli said. "I... I mean, I'm assume we're…."

"Huh, I dunno, Calli," I said, affecting a valley-girl voice and twirling a strand of my hair. "I mean, sharing an apartment? That's kind of a big step, don't you think?"

Calli grabbed the pillow from under her head and whapped me with it.

"I'll need to find a way to dump my inventory," I said, straightening my hair out of my face. "Probably have a blow-out sale the next few weeks and then shove what's left on eBay. Need to pack up all my crap from here, too. I'll probably just dump most of it on Goodwill…."

"I'll need to finish up with a few clients before we can leave," Calli mused, putting the pillow back behind her head. "Jesus, starting a whole new life is *hard*."

"Yeah, I know," I sighed, feeling somewhat overwhelmed by the tasks in front of me, feeling like a kid who decides to run away from home, makes it to the end of the block and then realizes she doesn't know how to make chicken nuggets or do laundry. "But...I'm kinda tired of easy. Does that make any sense?"

"As much sense as anything does," Calli shrugged, turning toward me. "Hey, so...as long as we're saying batshit crazy things and making giant declarations that are probably putting us in way over our heads, can I add one?"

"Of course," I nodded.

Calli shifted under the covers, her cheeks getting pink as she bit her lip. She started to speak several times before the words finally came. I wasn't used to seeing her speechless.

"I... kinda really want to marry you," Calli whispered, closing her eyes and putting her head down into the sheets. I think she thought I'd be stunned, but the only thing that surprised me was that I didn't feel surprised. It didn't seem big or shocking or stupid. It didn't even feel momentous. It just felt warm. And right. And good.

"So do I," I said, not even pausing, realizing it for the first time, but feeling like I'd known it for much longer. I reached down under the covers and took hold of her hands, nudging the sheet down from her face and leaning my forehead gently against hers. "I want that, too."

"This isn't going to win any 'cutest engagement story' contest, is it?" Calli giggled, kissing me around the stitches in her lip. "'Oh, you know...we were lying in bed naked after having spent the last hour trying unsuccessfully to have sex because I was still all roughed-up from the street fight I got into....'"

"We can tell people we were on a hot-air balloon and then I told you to look down and I had had all of our friends on the ground hold up a giant sign asking you to marry me." I suggested, through laughter.

"And then we landed and rode horses over to them, and they scattered rose petals at our feet while I retold the entire story of our relationship to everyone, in the style of a fairytale." Calli offered.

"And then fireworks went off and trained doves flew by," I said, both of us in hysterics.

"And *then* I got into a street fight," Calli said, trying to catch her breath. "But with, like, an army of sexy ninja women, not one slimy loser."

"Are we still naked during all of this?" I asked.

"Of course we are!" Calli laughed. "And then we just start having amazing, mind-blowing sex, right there on the beach--"

"We're on a beach?"

"Of course we're on a beach!" Calli exclaimed, offended. "And the sex is so amazing that when we finish, mermaids jump out of the water and begin applauding us."

We were both laughing too hard to add any more to the increasingly surreal story of our engagement. It took a good ten minutes for us to spin down enough to say anything at all.

"Oh...oh my God I love you," I said, finally catching my breath.

"I love you too, weirdo," Calli replied, gasping for air. "Do you want to make it official?"

"Okay," I said, composing myself as much as I could. "How do we do this?"

"What do you mean?" Calli asked.

"Like...which one of us does what?"

"Shit, there's no guide book for this, is there?" Calli muttered. "Just...on three?"

"'Kay," I nodded. "One. Two. Three."

"Abra will you marry me?"

"Calliope will you marry me?"

"Yes!" We both yelled at the same time, starting to fall into a laughter pit again, before stopping to kiss, once again avoiding Calli's split lip.

"We just got engaged," she whispered to me, close enough that our lips brushed as she spoke.

"We just got engaged," I repeated, carefully kissing her again.

"Well, that's that, then," Calli smiled, nuzzling her head against my chest. I stroked her hair until she fell asleep, with me following close behind her. She was right: that was that.

There were six of us there that day, not including the officiant. Drew's moms had driven in. Lore's parents, an exceedingly well-off couple from the Seattle area who viewed Drew as some sort of bog monster who came from hell to corrupt their daughter elected not to attend. Neal served as Drew's best man, and I was Lore's maid of honor.

"Aw, you look so amazing, Lorelei," Cassandra cooed as she pulled her car into the courthouse parking lot with Lore and me in tow. "My son is so lucky to have found you. You look very cute, too, Abra."

"Thank you," we both said. She was certainly right about Lore, looking like a celestial being even though her dress was an inexpensive white and black purchase from the outlet mall. I'd done her hair that day, with lots of help from her leading me through the steps. It was a simple updo, with two baby's breath sprigs carefully placed, a contrast to the navy her hair was dyed that month. It was her 'something blue.' The bracelet on her wrist was 'something old,' having been her grandmother's. The dress was 'something new.' 'Something borrowed' hung around her neck, the butterfly pendant Gwen had given me, lent to her for the day.

As we got out of Cassandra's car, Drew's truck, being driven by Loretta, pulled up.

"You doing okay?" I whispered to Lore as she locked a bare arm through my elbow. I was wearing my usual brown dress.

"I really am," Lore said, with a serenity I envied. Across the lot, Neal and Drew, both in black suits, got out of the truck, Loretta walking between them.

"Oh, there you are, sweetness," Loretta called, walking toward Lore with open arms and enveloping her in a powerful hug. "Look at you! Drew, I don't know

what you did to deserve a woman like this, but don't screw it up, you hear me, kid?"

"I hear you, Ma," Drew laughed, his voice far away, unable to take his eyes off of his soon-to-be bride. "Lore, you look…wow."

"I know, right?" Lore said, curtsying. "Not so bad yourself, future husband."

"We should get inside," Neal said, looking at his watch. "Your appointment is in like five minutes."

"You ready?" Cassandra asked both Drew and Lore, who nodded with their eyes still glued to one another. The whole ceremony went like that, with the judge, a sullen older woman with jowls like a bulldog mumbling her way through while Lore and Drew stared at each other like the entire rest of the world didn't exist. When the ceremony was over—after one of the most graphic 'first kisses' in history—we all retreated to the house, Loretta and Cassandra commandeering the kitchen for one of the best meals I've ever had. Though there were only six of us, Lore insisted there be music and dancing.

"So," I said, sitting down next to Neal in a lawn chair while Drew and Lore swayed along to, of all things, Whiter Shade of Pale. *Cassandra and Loretta were sharing the yard with them, Cassandra's head resting on her wife's shoulder as they danced.*

"So," Neal repeated.

"You wanna?" I asked, gesturing toward the grass.

"I…I, uh," Neal stammered. I chuckled and stood, holding out a hand, which he timidly took. I pulled him up out of the chair and led him to the lawn, Lore and Cassandra both winking at us as they glided past. Keeping hold of Neal with one hand, I slid my other onto his arm, which was currently dodging around the air near my torso like an excitable bee.

"My waist," I whispered. "You've done this before."

"Not with you!" he blurted, his face beet red. I took pity on him and guided his hand down, putting it into position. I couldn't tell if that relaxed him or put him five seconds away from a stroke, but he started to lead.

"See? We can do this," I said, resting my head on his shoulder as I realized looking him in the eye was making him nervous. "One, two, three, one two three…."

"Jesus, look at them," Neal whispered, gesturing with his chin toward Lore and Drew, who were curled into each other as they moved.

"I know, right?" I said. "Think we're ever going to find something like that?"

"Well, maybe," Neal sighed. "It just seems so…effortless…for them."

"I'm guessing they'd loudly protest that," I laughed.

"Yeah, probably," he responded. "Still…."

"Yeah," I said, swaying with him. "You and me, we're going to have to work for it."

"Maybe," he nodded. "Maybe it's better that way. Or maybe I should just shut up and enjoy the song."

"Probably that last one," I laughed, and we spent the rest of the song swaying in, for me at least, a very soothing silence.

I woke up about two hours after I fell asleep to the sound of Calli swearing.

"Goddammit!" she hissed, probably what she thought was under her breath.

"Problems?" I groggily asked, rolling over in bed and seeing Calli sitting back at the computer.

"Shit, sorry!" Calli blurted with a start. "I couldn't sleep."

"Gee, why?" I asked, getting up and sliding into the chair next to her. "Did something happen that may be on your mind?"

She gave me a playful shove and laughed.

"One or two things," she said. "But good ones. It's 'can't sleep because I'm excited,' not 'holy fuck what have I gotten myself into.' Promise."

"Good to know," I said. "So what are you asking God to damn?"

"This stupid maze!" Calli growled, gesturing at the screen which displayed the section with the worn tombstone.

"Did you find the tapestry room?" I asked, unable to keep a smile off my face.

"Yeah," she nodded. "And I set it on fire and I see the keyhole, but I don't have a fucking key and I went all back through the rest of the mansion and collected everything that wasn't bolted down, but nothing does any damn thing with that stupid fucking keyhole!"

"And now you're officially an *Unwelcome* player," I laughed.

"See, here I thought video games were supposed to be fun," Calli grumbled.

"Yeah, that's how they get you," I nodded. "But the best games are really just mind-stabbing hell-puzzles that slide into your subconscious and torment you until you set yourself free by finishing them."

"Uh huh," Calli said, arching an eyebrow. "Remember when you used to say *my* hobbies were weird?"

"Sure," I said. "But hey, feel free to stop attempting the maze any time."

Calli paused and started to lift her hand from the mouse, glaring at me defiantly.

"Goddammit," she muttered, setting her hand back on the mouse. "You've entrapped me, vile temptress."

"It's what I do," I said, standing behind her and rubbing her shoulders. "Hey, you feel like making a trip with me tomorrow?"

"Sure," Calli said, scowling at the screen as the time-out demon appeared. "Where are we going? Do I need to dress up?"

"Well…not sure how to answer that," I said, inhaling. "I'd…I'd like to take you to meet someone."

"Abra Collins," Calli smirked, looking over her shoulder. "After all this time, are you going to reveal to me that you have a *fifth* friend?"

"Hey!" I yelped. "I…no, I don't."

"Then who am I meeting?" she asked, kissing me on the forehead.

"My sister."

"Oh," Calli whispered, her eyes wide. "Abra, that's…I'm honored. But I thought you hadn't been out there since…."

"I haven't," I sighed. "But…I'm ready. I want to make some changes, too. When daddy dearest died, ownership of her niche transferred to me, so…. But I want you to meet her. If that's not too weird for you."

"No," Calli said. "No, not at all. It's…thank you. Wow."

"Yeah," I smiled. "Wow."

The next morning, we woke up early and drove out to the cemetery. The December air was biting, the two of us wrapped head to toe in winter garb, each carrying a steaming coffee cup in one hand. In my other, I held a brown paper bag.

"It's just up here," I said, gesturing with my coffee-hand to the wall of niches at the top of the hill to our left. We ascended it, the frost encrusted grass crunching under our boots and the wheels of Calli's knee-scooter. It was a grueling climb for her, but she insisted she wanted to make it. A grizzled old man with a beard that looked like a series of barnacles stuck to his face stood next to the niche wall, looking impatient.

"I called ahead," I told Calli. "He's going to open the niche for us. So I can…."

"Sure," Calli nodded. "You know, if I knew this is what you were going to do, I'd have just bought you the slippers."

"Calli, it's just that—"

"I know, I'm teasing you," Calli smiled, elbowing me. "I think it's sweet."

"You Abra?" the man by the wall called.

"That's me," I said. "Jake?"

"Yup," Jake the caretaker nodded. "Okay, I've opened it up for you. Just set the cover back in place and let me know when you leave, I'll get it sealed again. Oh, and we took this off, but your replacement plaque got rejected. Let me know if you have another idea."

Jake handed me the brass "My Angel" plaque and headed down the hill, his footsteps fading as he descended.

"What did you want to replace it with?" Calli asked as I set down my coffee on top of the niche wall and turned the plaque over in my hand.

"'Total Badass.'" I said, getting a laugh from Calli. "Guess that's not appropriate or something. Ah well. I'm just glad this isn't on there anymore. It's just…gross. But…here we are."

"Here we are," Calli repeated, looking at me expectantly.

"Okay," I said, feeling awkward but pushing forward, facing the small brass box in the open niche. "So…hi Gwen. It's your sister, Abra. I'm sorry I haven't visited more but…yeah."

"Abra, if you want some time, I can—" Calli whispered.

"No, it's okay," I said. "Gwen, I needed to come here today because…I'm getting married! Woo, right? This is Calliope."

"Hi, Gwen," Calli said, nervous as if she was meeting her face to face.

"I…I wish you could have met her," I continued. "She's amazing in the weirdest ways. I love her, Gwen. I think you would have, too. I wanted to bring her here because…because I didn't want you to worry about me anymore. I mean, I don't know if there *is* such a thing as worry in the afterlife. Or even if there is an afterlife. If there is one, you're laughing at me right now. But…but I'm okay, sis. I'm okay, and I'm happy, and I miss you so damn much. But I'm okay, because of the things you taught me. I never got to thank you. I don't think I'll ever know everything you did for me, but thank you. Thank you, you amazing, wonderful, badass woman. Thank you. I love you."

We stood there in silence, save for the wind whipping around the tombs, for several minutes.

"May I?" Calli whispered. I nodded.

"Hi Gwen," Calli said, stepping in front of me. "I'm Calli. I…I really wish we could have met. Abra's told me all about you, and you sound awesome. You did a great job with her. It sounds like you raised her more than anyone, so…thank you. Your sister has literally saved my life more than once. She didn't know that until just now, but she has. I hope wherever you are, you approve of me. She has a gift for you. Well, I picked it up. It's a long story."

I turned and faced Calli, the question hanging on my lips.

"Yeah," Calli said. "Twice."

"Calli," I said, with no breath behind it. "Was it…the day in the kitchen?"

"No," she shook her head. "You'd never remember them. I was good at hiding it. Just days when my brain had had enough, and my soul was too tired to argue. You happened to stop by at just the right times. Seeing you pushed me through it, Abra. We can talk about it later if you want. Or not. I just wanted her to know how incredible her sister is. Now let's give the woman her gift and find a fireplace to sit in front of?"

"Sounds good," I said, kissing her forehead. I couldn't wait until her lip healed. I took the bag out from under my arm and unrolled the top of it, gently bringing Snooty Crow out.

"I wanted to give this back to you," I said, tears filling my eyes as I looked at Snooty Crow. "Thank you for letting me hold onto it. I used to think I needed it to keep you around but...you're always with me. I'm sorry it took me so long to realize that. There's something sewn inside of him now, too. Keep it safe for me, okay?"

I slid Snooty Crow next to Gwen's urn, the niches designed large enough to hold two sets of cremains if necessary. I almost grabbed Snooty back out as I looked at him sitting in there, but I stopped myself. It was time to move on. I gestured for Calli, who handed me the slab of marble that served as the cover to the niche. Sliding it back into place, I locked arms with my fiancée, picked up my coffee cup, and looked back one last time.

"Goodbye, Gwen," I said. "Love you."

Exhaling, I nodded to Calli and we meandered down the hill, stopping by the visitor center to let Jake know he could seal the niche again. On our way out, I paused by a brown trash can and unceremoniously tossed the brass "My Angel" plaque in.

"You okay?" Calli asked as we got into my Nissan.

"Yeah," I said. "I am. I really am. Also, I think I had a bit of an epiphany out there."

"Really?" Calli asked. "About what?"

"I'll show you," I winked. "Come on, we're going back to the maze."

"Dear Neal," I typed one night at three-thirty, having slid out of Calli's arms and down to the basement, where my laptop was set up.

"I've been wanting to write to you since the day you left, but I still don't know what to say. I know we needed to talk about our feelings for each other. I know we needed to have some space from one another so that we could discover who we were apart from each other. I know it wasn't fair to let you just keep pining after me, year after year, pretending I didn't notice. But I hate how it ended. I hate that I pushed you out of my life. And I hate that you stayed away. I'm sad and I'm angry, angry at both of us and knowing how stupid that is. You did exactly what I asked you to.

So much has changed, Neal. It changed when you left, and it didn't stop changing. Some of it has been very good. Some hasn't. Most has just been different. I look around my life and I don't recognize it anymore. In many ways, it's better. I'm not sure if Drew and Lore have told you, but Calli and I are together now. They don't approve, but she's different now. I'm different now. But other things aren't better or even worse, it just feels like I've stepped into a mirror universe. Cluster is different now. We have new workers, new regulars…it's not bad, it's just not the way it was. And I know it's stupid to hate something just because it's different. Change happens. I just never thought you and I would change. I never thought I'd be walking through life without you.

I'm so happy to hear about you and Dan, and I understand not wanting to tell me directly. I'm glad we both have people who love us. I couldn't give you what you needed from me, and I'm sorry. If I could have flipped a switch and made it so, I would have. It was unfair to take what I needed from you for so long.

But I can't stand this. I can't stand being apart from you anymore. I can't let you go. I don't want to add you to the list of people I've lost forever. But I'm the one who pushed you out, so I'll leave it up to you to decide if you want to come back. If there's any hope for us. It would be different, too; I know that. But maybe it would be better? I love you, Neal. I didn't lie about that. I wasn't just saying it to make you feel better. I haven't stopped, either.

If you don't want anything to do with me, I understand that. If it's too hard, or you're too angry, or if your life is just better without me in it, I understand that, too. I will always treasure the time we had together. You held me up in ways no one

else did, during times when no one else was there. I miss you with all my heart.
Love forever,
Abra"

I took my hands off of the keyboard and read the letter over. Then I read it again. I had Neal's address, given to me by Lore 'just in case.' My cursor hovered over the 'print' command, then I read it a third time. And a fourth.

Then, with a loud sigh, I selected all the text, hit delete, swung my laptop closed and shuffled back to bed.

"Strangely enough, we were going to go to Seattle," I said, with a sardonic chuckle as I helped Calli pack up her apartment. "Make a weekend of it, really live it up."

"Well, isn't that easier now?" Calli asked, doing what little packing she could from a seated position, mainly directing me which pile to dump things into. "You could just invite him out. Sera says she has a lot of good leads on apartments for us. He could stay over. I'll behave, I promise."

"I don't think so," I sighed. "I feel like I've betrayed him, finishing the maze without him."

"I still can't believe that in all of those years...." Calli started, laughing.

"Hindsight is twenty-twenty, Calliope!" I snapped, getting another roar of laughter. "Laugh it up...wait, is this a library book?"

I held up a copy of *Wuthering Heights*, holding open the cover to show Calli the Brahmton Library stamp.

"Oh, shit, I didn't realize I still had that," Calli said, covering her mouth. "That's, like, years overdue. Can...can you take it back for me? I can't really go back there."

"Wait, why?" I asked, through half-closed eyes.

"Well, it's not like I'm banned or anything, it's just...," she bit her lip. "I kinda had a thing going with the head librarian there. Nothing serious, just, like, weekly hookups. But then you and I started seeing each other again, so I...uh...kinda just stopped answering his texts."

"Oh for the love...the white-haired guy?" I groaned.

"He's actually about our age," Calli shrugged. "Just prematurely grey. Nice guy, just...you know, not you."

"That's weirdly sweet," I said, closing the book cover. "I'll drop it off next time I'm out, and try not to make eye contact with the librarian. A librarian, really?"

"Oh like you've never had a librarian fantasy!" Calli retorted. "It can go both ways!"

"Fair enough," I laughed.

"So…changing the subject, have you told your other friends the news yet?" Calli asked, musing with a lock of her hair. "Lore and Drew?"

I paused, looking down at the book in my hand again.

"Yeah, I did," I said, finally.

"Oh," Calli said, right before her face fell. "Oh."

"It's not…like that," I said, setting down *Wuthering Heights* and sitting next to her. "They're just…."

"They don't like me," Calli said, putting her head in her hands. "I don't blame them. They only knew me…before."

"I don't even think it's that, really," I said, rubbing little circles into her back, through her thick sweater. "Selling Cluster is what really seemed to bother them."

"Why?" Calli asked, lifting her head up. "They're the ones who left!"

"Yeah, I know," I shrugged. "That's why I think it doesn't really have anything to do with Cluster or you or even me, really. It's like…remember when you talked about how you couldn't be my memento?"

"Yeah," Calli blushed.

"Well, I think I was theirs," I sighed, resting my chin in my hands. "I think they liked having me as an anchor for them, so that even if they needed to go live different lives away from here, I'd still be around, tending to the past. I was the big, boring clock that they could set their watches by."

"Oh," Calli said, softly. "That's…that's got to hurt. I mean, if nothing else, I know you had feelings for Lore at one point."

"At one point," I nodded. "But there was nothing there. I'm making it sound harsher than it is; I'm not angry at them. I don't think they're angry at me, either. They just liked me the way I was, where I was, how I was. They're moving on with their lives now, starting their family. We're moving on with ours. Some friends don't come along with you on every journey."

"Some friends do, though," Calli whispered. "Remember that."

"It's different with you," I protested as she stood, hopping on her knee scooter.

"I know," she said, winking at me as she scooted over to start unloading a shelf. "I wasn't talking about me."

"So," Olivia asked with a smirk as I handed the binder-clipped manuscript back to her. "What'dya think?"

"It honestly was pretty enjoyable," I said, taking a seat across from her.

"Oh come on, Abra!" Olivia cackled. "I never expected you to be one to candy-coat things!"

"I liked it!" I insisted. "It's weird as fuck, sure, but…I dunno, the part in the anti-gravity chamber was…what's the academic way to say, 'pretty hot'?"

"Provocative," Olivia informed me. "You really don't have to pretend to have liked it; I wrote it years ago, I'm not going to be hurt."

"I'm not pretending!" I laughed. "It was actually a fun read. Why did you give up on it? Maybe it wouldn't have shaken the foundations of the literary world, but it could have been a fun airport book."

"Honestly?" Olivia asked. I nodded in reply. "I threw my entire life into that book for years. My husband was an asshole, but I can't really blame him for getting sick of listening to me go on and on about the insane backstory I was crafting for the Euridians. This was going to be a series, you know."

"I had a feeling," I interjected.

"I kept getting tangled up in my own lore," Olivia said, putting her feet up on her desk. "Then, one night, I found myself up at two in the morning, televised poker on the TV, finishing up a lengthy description of the Euridian's system of parliamentary government. I was jotting down how a vote would be decided in case of a tie, when a thought occurred to me for the first time."

"What was it?" I asked.

"Why the hell would purple aliens from beyond our time and space have genitals compatible with our own?" Olivia asked, smacking her hand against the top of her thigh. "I realized I'd developed an entire society for the characters in my thinly veiled erotica, but hadn't thought about how they'd actually go about fucking. Then I realized that I was going to have to sit down and write out a logic behind their genitals being able to interact with a human's, and at that point I realized that this wasn't a dream anymore, it was a prison I had built myself. A prison of purple-junked aliens!"

"They…they could have been shapeshifters," I suggested, trying not to laugh.

"See, this is why I need you around," Olivia said, shaking her head. "Well, let me be your cautionary tale then, Miss Abra: When setting out to write the feminist sci-fi novel that will define a generation, make sure you don't let yourself get bogged

down in purple dongs."

"Jesus, where were you when I was picking out a senior quote?" I said, through peals of laughter.

"Right here, Abra," Olivia said, gesturing to the room around her. "Bogged down in purple dongs."

"I…I really want to thank you for putting this together," I said, sitting down next to Crystal as Calli played and sang *Have Yourself a Merry Little Christmas* for the crowd, all of them enraptured by her.

"Of course, Abra," Crystal said. "It's the least I could do. You cut me a hell of a deal. And you know I like you, right? I know I can come off like a bitch, but it's just my way. Besides, your girl up there is incredible. Why didn't anyone tell me she could sing like this? I would have booked her every week!"

"Maybe you can have her play when we visit," I suggested. "We'll come through every now and then."

"No, you won't," Crystal smirked.

"Yeah," I sighed. "You're probably right. I like the way the new music section looks. Taking down the shelves on the north wall really opened the room up."

"Thanks," Crystal said. "You sure cleared out of there fast."

"Half off/make an offer sale," I said. "Works every time. Got everything left over on eBay."

"So what are you going to do in Seattle?" she asked, as Calli hit the part about whether or not the fates will allow. "I know Calli has her new shop, but…."

"I'll find something," I shrugged. "Maybe I'll find a vintage shop to work for. They have more than one there. Maybe I'll start one of those puzzle room companies. Who knows?"

"You'll crush it, whatever you do," Crystal said, patting me on the back hard enough to jar me as Calli finished, to a round of applause. Crystal jumped out of her seat and gestured for me to follow her to the stage area.

"Jesus Christ that was good," she announced into the microphone as Calli stood up from the piano. "Can this girl sing, or can she sing?"

The whole place burst into applause again.

"So, as you know," Crystal continued, "this is a special night for Cluster. A sad night, but a special one. Our fearless leader, Abra Collins, who somehow managed to hook this little firecracker that you just got done listening to, is headed off for bigger, better things.

The crowd, mainly made up of regulars, let out a lengthy "aw."

"I know, I know," Crystal shushed the crowd. "And she's leaving Cluster in the hands of some trashy bitch she knows, too."

The crowd laughed as Crystal gestured to herself.

"We'll get Calli back up here before we let these two cuckoos fly the nest, but let's give them a break for a while and listen to the much less melodic sound of my band. Come on up, War Bitch!"

The crowd burst into applause as three other rough-looking women joined Crystal on stage, taking up their instruments and bursting into a hard rock version of O Come All Ye Faithful.

"I've got to give it to her, she knows how to work a crowd," Calli said, as we slid back to our table.

"So do you," I told her, over the noise from the band. "That was beautiful."

"Aw shucks," Calli blushed, giving Lindsee a smile as she set a latte down next to her in a ceramic mug. "How are you doing?"

"Honestly, I'm okay," I nodded, watching Crystal and her cronies rock out on stage. "I thought I was going to hit this moment of panic and would want to forget everything else and just stay, but…."

"Honestly, I figured you might, too," Calli smirked. "If you still do, it's okay; I planned for it."

"You planned for it?" I asked, raising an eyebrow.

"Of course," Calli nodded. "I was going to take you off to the side and talk you through the panic, remind you of all of the things that drove you crazy about this place and all of the reasons that you told me you want to leave Brahmton."

"That's…way more reasonable than I was expecting," I admitted.

"That was phase one," Calli shrugged. "If that didn't work, I was going to burn the building down."

"There we go," I laughed. "It would have been the right call. No, I'm doing okay. I'm happy, actually. Cluster gets to go its direction, we get to go ours. So how are you doing?"

"Finished up my last tattoo at Black Needles this morning," Calli said, before taking a sip of her coffee. "It was an infinity symbol that said 'hugs and kisses' for some reason. Yeah, I'm done here."

"Can you do one for me?" I asked, laughing. "I want it to say, 'infinity symbol.' Ink it on my ribs, too, so I can do one of those 'covering my boobs with one arm while totally just showing off my new tattoo, honest' photos."

"I…I wish that didn't sound so hot," Calli said, starting to laugh. Suddenly, she froze, her eyes bulging open.

"Calli, I was joking," I smirked.

"No, it's not that, it's just…." She said, staring over my shoulder, toward the door. I started to turn to look, but she shook her head, as a feeling of dread fell over me.

"Abra," she said, looking me square in the eyes. "I need you to take a deep breath, okay?"

"Okay," I complied, confused but trusting her. Air filled my lungs and then slowly escaped. "What? What is it?"

Calli didn't say anything, but gestured toward the door and this time let me look. There, over the heads of the crowd, stood someone I hadn't seen in two years.

"Hi," Neal mouthed over the noise from the band, holding up a hand in a tiny wave. I stood up, not realizing I had told my body to do so, and waved back.

5 THE THIRD THING

This is actually happening," I muttered in awe as Neal, Lore, Drew and I entered the vacant strip mall that would become Cluster for the first time. "It's actually fucking happening."

"Jesus," Drew said, looking around what would soon be our coffee shop, "the best thing one of my professors ever gave me was a half-hearted recommendation letter."

"So you want to knock this wall down, right?" Lore asked, tapping on the garish yellow wall between the abandoned coffee shop and the abandoned insurance agent's office.

"Most of it," I confirmed. "And the one on the other side, too."

"I'm going to go check out the auto shop," Drew said. "See how much work it'll take to get it converted. Can I borrow the keys, Abby?"

"Sure," I said, sliding the key to the auto shop off the ring Monica had provided me and tossing it to him. "The rest of you want to check out the office on the other side with me? I think that's where I'm going to set up my vintage shop."

"I'll be over in a minute," Lore said, peeking behind the coffee shop counter. "I want to see how many of this place's hookups still work."

"Okay," I said. "Neal?"

"You bet," Neal responded, following me out the door and to the adjoining office.

"Well, we're ripping up this carpet, that's for sure," I said as we entered, looking down at the hideous blue and white floral print. "Set some shelves along that wall.... Wait, what are you staring at?"

"You," Neal laughed. "You just...I like seeing you this happy."

"It's just so...big. I never thought this would happen," I said, trying to take

the whole shop in at once. "Not for real."

"Well," Neal said, looking up at the ceiling. "Here you are."

"Hey, you're here, too, you know," I said, walking next to him and bumping my hip into his.

"Yeah, but...what can I do?" Neal asked with a shrug. "Lore and Drew have the business side of things covered, Lore has barista experience, Drew knows music. You could sell Plan-B to the Pope. I think I'll probably have to just be your most regular customer."

"Neal," I said, shifting my voice to serious. "No. You're part of this. If you want to be, I mean. I'm not going to start doing things without you. I don't even know how that would work. What if you...like...graphic designed for us? Am I using that right?"

"Close enough," Neal smirked. "Well...you are going to need a sign."

"We'll need several signs!" I exclaimed. "Come on Neal; we're all in this. What, you thought I'd drop you just because I'm a high-powered business woman now?"

"No," Neal said as I turned back to examine the ethernet hookups on the wall. "Not because of that."

It took me a long time to question what he meant by that. By the time I did, it was too late.

Neal and I stepped into the roped off section that had, up until recently, been Cadabra's Corner, away from the crowd. I'd brought him over with a gesture; we still hadn't spoken to each other. The space between us was only about ten feet. The distance was immeasurable. I spoke first.

"Hi," I said, warbling the word as my heart and lungs pounded in my chest.

"Hi," Neal responded, sounding even worse than I did. "I...I got married."

"I heard," I said, still having trouble keeping the words steady. "Lore and Drew told me. I got engaged."

"I know," Neal said. "Lore and Drew told me, too. Congratulations."

"You, too." I said.

Silence descended again, the two of us just staring at each other. He looked just as I remembered him. I wondered if I still looked the same to him, or if he now saw me as twisted and awful. Finally, the quiet got too much for me.

"Did you ever think we'd get to this point," I blurted, tears filling my eyes. "Where we'd have to find out about each other's engagements and marriages second-hand?"

"No," Neal shook his head. "Did you ever think we'd go a single day without seeing each other, much less two years?"

"No," I barely spoke, my legs feeling weak under me. "I miss you so much, Neal."

"I miss you, too," Neal said, his eyes wet as well. "I hate this."

"I hate it, too," I agreed.

"So," Neal said, letting it hang.

"So," I repeated, trying to think of something clever, or meaningful, or even coherent to say after that, but my brain failed me. Instead, a writhing, burning urge propelled my body forward, at the same time he seemed overtaken by the same force.

"I'm so sorry," I cried, as we embraced with so much momentum we almost sent each other to the floor. "I'm so, so sorry. I never should have told you to leave. I miss you so fucking much!"

"You weren't wrong," Neal said back, holding my head to his shoulder. "You weren't wrong at all."

We eased apart, both of us ugly-crying, the crowds thankfully still turned toward War Bitch instead of over at the "UNDER CONSTRUCTION" section. I looked out toward the rest of Cluster, catching Calli's eye. She gave me a wink and a slow nod, and then turned back to the show.

"This is so…I don't…," I stammered. "Why are you here?"

"Lore and Drew called me right after they talked to you about selling Cluster, getting engaged and moving." Neal said, wiping his eyes. "They're…worried."

"Are you?" I asked, biting the inside of my cheek.

He shook his head. "You were always going to go your own way. I just missed you, and I knew that it would only get harder the longer we let pass. I knew where you were, here. Seattle's a big place."

"We never got to go," I said, slumping my shoulders.

"I'm not dead, Abra," Neal smiled through the tears.

"You're far away, though," I said, leaning against the wall that Crystal had stripped the shelves off of but not yet done anything else with. "And I feel like we barely know each other anymore. You've been gone so long."

"You told me to go," Neal said, a hint of resentment creeping into his voice.

"You needed to go," I responded.

"You told me to go," Neal repeated.

"Because I loved you too much to let you stay!" I insisted. "Not because I didn't want you to stay!"

"You told me to go," Neal said one more time.

"I know," I whispered, sliding down the wall until I was sitting on the floor. "I've hated myself for it every day since."

"I haven't," Neal said, leaning on the wall next to where I was sitting. "I just...you told me to go. I never thought you'd do that. I knew you'd never feel the same way about me. I imagined you telling me that. I imagined you telling me that we needed to spend less time together. I imagined you one day telling me you were in love with someone else, or that you were engaged, or even married. But I never imagined you'd tell me to leave."

"I didn't either," I admitted. "And I didn't want to! But you were drowning in me, Neal! You can deny it all you want, but you were drowning in me! Everyone else could see it except you. You—"

"Of course I saw it," Neal cut me off. "Of course I did, Abra. No one ever seemed to realize I was okay with that. I knew what I was to you, and I liked it. I was okay not being anything more. I was okay being stuck."

"I couldn't let you do that, Neal!" I yelled from the floor. "I couldn't be the millstone around my best friend's neck! Did you ever think of how that made me feel? To look at you every day and know that I'm the reason you were sad? To know that I was slowly poisoning you just by my presence? To have to look at you and see the awful thing I was doing to the person I loved the most? Did you?"

Neal slid down the wall this time, sitting next to me.

"No," he whispered. "I didn't."

"I've missed you so fucking much," I said again. "Every damn day. I'm not sad, I'm not alone, I'm not depressed...I just miss you. I have good days, and I think about how much better they could have been if you had been a part of them."

"I feel the same way," Neal said, dropping his head down. "I've almost called or written you a thousand times. The night I got engaged, I had nine digits of your phone number dialed before I chickened out."

"I've tried writing you more emails than I can count," I admitted. "I'm bad on the phone."

"I know," Neal said, with a stifled laugh. "But I'm bad at writing out my feelings."

"So, you came to see me," I said, looking out toward the other wall of what was once my lair. "Long way to fly to visit the bitch that sent you packing."

"You're not a bitch," Neal sighed. "I'm...I'm technically on my honeymoon. We were headed for Spokane to visit Lore and Drew, but veered this way instead."

"How does your husband feel about that?" I asked.

"He's...alright with it," Neal said, finally.

"That doesn't sound like the whole story," I chuckled.

"Well, how does Calli feel about me?" Neal asked.

"She likes you," I said. "Maybe a bit too much. But she doesn't know what to do with our relationship any more than we do, I think. She wanted me to reach out to you, though."

"She and Dan could have some conversations," Neal laughed. "Are you...Drew and Lore are worried."

"I know," I rolled my eyes. "They told me. She's not the person she was when they knew her before. I'm not either, really. Or maybe we both are, and we just never let anyone see it back then. Either way, they just...I think they locked both her and me into these roles they were comfortable with us in, and now they won't let us out."

"Ouch," Neal said.

"That came off as harsher than I wanted," I shook my head. "I don't think they meant to. I just think...they've moved on."

"I kinda get that," Neal nodded. "I love them, and I always will, but it wasn't the hardest decision I ever made to not visit them this trip. They have, like, farmer's market friends."

"I heard," I said. "Can you imagine Drew trying to make it through a conversation about artisanal soaps?"

"How about Lore making small talk about gender-reveal parties?" Neal laughed.

"Gender-reveal parties? What the hell are those?" I asked.

"Her friend Laurel had one. It's where an expectant mother gets all of her friends together and has some goofy ritual where she reveals if her baby will be a boy or a girl," Neal explained.

"Gee, I should have had one of those," I muttered, getting a burst of laughter from Neal. I forgot how much I liked the sound of that.

"Yeah, I think they're moving on," Neal said with a sigh. "I'm going to miss them."

"Me, too," I said, putting my head back against the wall. "But I'm happy for them."

"So…that leaves us, then," Neal said. "We've…kinda moved on, too. Haven't we?"

"Yeah," I admitted. "It looks that way. You're part of an old married couple now. Living the dream in New York."

"Can I be honest?" Neal asked, turning away from me.

"You always have been before," I shrugged.

"It's not much of a dream."

"What do--?"

"Not Dan," Neal clarified, quickly. "He's amazing. I…I really do need to thank you for that. Leaving you was the hardest thing I ever did, but I wouldn't have him without you having pushed me out."

"Pushing you out was the hardest thing I ever did," I said. "But Calli and I wouldn't have gotten to know each other—for real—if I hadn't. But if it's not Dan, what's--?"

"I hate my job," Neal confessed. "I hate it. It's just like my old graphic design gigs but with superheroes. I don't own my characters anymore, Abra! The company does. There are deadlines and focus groups and 'editorial input.' I've had so many storylines shot down in favor of safe, bland retellings of the same tales that have been spun in comics since before Superman could fly! I feel so fucking stupid, Abra: I uprooted my whole life and moved for my 'dream job' that turned into a nightmare."

"I'm sorry, Neal," I said, putting an arm around his shoulders. "But I kinda know what you're going through. Sometimes dreams just…fade away."

"What are we, Abra?" Neal blurted, jumping the conversational train tracks. "I love seeing you again. I love talking with you, it feels incredible. But what are we?"

"We're…friends," I said, my voice sounding less sure than I hoped.

"Are we, though?" Neal asked. "We haven't spoken in two years. We've…we've changed, Abra. You just said so yourself. Are we really friends anymore?"

"Were we ever, really?" I asked, my voice hollow and weak. "We were more than that. We weren't romantic, but we weren't…not. I don't know what we were."

"Me either," Neal said. "Maybe that says more than anything."

"Yeah."

"Yeah."

"Do you not…want…to be in each other's lives anymore?" I asked, in a voice far below a whisper.

"I do," he responded. "But…if you're not you anymore, and I'm not me…."

"Yeah," I barely said, my mouth dry and eyes wet. "So…this is it?"

"I…I worry it might need to be," Neal said, putting his face in his hands. We sat there, both crying, for several minutes, Crystal's band roaring in the background, crowds cheering, hands clapping. There was no silence anywhere but between us. We'd come all this way, found each other when we thought we were gone forever, just to say goodbye. God fucking dammit.

Finally, Neal dared say something else.

"We're here now, though," Neal said, touching my hand.

I nodded, unable to make words.

"I'd…I'd still like to hear how you've been doing," Neal said. "I still love you, Abra. Even if we're both different people. Even if we make no sense anymore."

"I love you, too," I whispered, my heart in such a deep, dark cave that I couldn't even hear its echo. I didn't know what else to say, so I told him the only thing I could think of.

"I…I figured out the maze," I stammered.

"No way," Neal said, perking up. "When?"

"Few days ago," I said, still sunken. "That tombstone…the worn one. There was one thing we never tried."

"What was it?" Neal asked, leaning around to look me in the eye. "I thought we tried everything."

"Talk," I said, my voice a little stronger.

"I…I thought we were," Neal stammered.

"No," I shook my head. "Talk. The talk command. Talk to the tombstone. We hit it, we used it, we examined it, we tried every item we had on it, but we never talked to it."

"For fuck sake," Neal sighed. "Talk. What…what happens when you talk to it?"

"A compartment slides open," I said, my mouth less dry. "There's a key inside."

"A key!" Neal exclaimed. "For the tapestry room!"

I nodded, coming close to smiling.

"Jesus Christ," Neal chuckled, wiping his eyes. "Talk to the tombstone. Those game designers should be tried for war crimes. How did you figure it out?"

"Calli and I went to the cemetery," I said. "To see Gwen. I…I introduced Calli. Talking to Gwen's urn tripped something in my brain."

Neal looked down and smiled for a good amount of time.

"Okay," he said. "I'm not worried."

"What do you mean?" I asked.

"Lore and Drew told me you've been acting impulsively," Neal said. "They worried you were rushing into things with Calli because you were feeling lost and this was all just some…expression of that. But you wouldn't bring her to meet Gwen if it wasn't real."

"No, I wouldn't," I said. "*You* were worried?"

"I'm sorry," Neal laughed. "They're pretty wound up. But I think everything is risky and impulsive to the farmer's market crowd. I'm…that makes me really happy, Abra. I liked Calli, what I knew of her."

"I know she was a bit odd back then," I admitted.

"That's what I liked about her," Neal said. "Tell me that hasn't changed."

"No, she's still wonderfully, amazingly strange," I told him, finally meeting his eyes again. "But all the best people are."

We both laughed, more out of exhaustion than anything, both of our heads coming to rest against each other.

"I don't want to not be with you," I finally said.

"Me, either," Neal sighed. "I don't care about all the other shit."

"So…is Dan going to be okay with that?" I asked. "I don't want to fuck anything up. More than I already have."

"He'll be okay with it," Neal nodded. "He's always called us The Third Thing."

"The what now?"

"Third thing," Neal laughed. "Like, we're not friends, we're not lovers, we're a third thing. Who the fuck knows what that is?"

"Honestly?" I said, leaning over and kissing him on the cheek. "Who the fuck cares?"

"He may not like that you did *that,*" Neal laughed.

"Sorry," I blushed.

"I'm kidding," Neal said, leaning over and kissing me on the forehead. "So…Seattle, huh?"

"Yeah," I said. "Seattle. Calli's old mentor is setting up a new shop and recruited her. I'll…I don't know. Eat a lot of Thai food, probably."

"You know when you're going to get married?" Neal asked.

"Sometime after the move," I answered. "Just a courthouse thing, like Lore and Drew did."

I paused, my face getting red for reasons I couldn't quite explain.

"If you…if you wanted to come, I'd—we'd—love you to be there," I said, looking down at the floor.

"I'll be there," he said, leaning against me. "I'm so sorry I didn't get you at mine. That was me being an idiot. I'm sorry."

"I think we've both been sorry enough for today," I said. "You going back to New York after your honeymoon?"

"Probably," Neal shrugged. "Wish I wasn't, though. It's…very loud."

"Are you thinking of moving?"

"Always," Neal sighed. "Dan has been great. His company is willing to let him stay on and telecommute, send his pages in from wherever. Mine is…less kind. But fuck, I just want to burn it all down and move. Problem is, I don't know where."

"Well…Seattle?" I offered.

"Are we there yet?" Neal asked, looking me in the eyes.

"I don't know," I admitted. "Yes. No. Probably both. Just a thought."

"A good one," Neal said. "Could be a bad one, though."

"True," I nodded.

"So what happens after the maze?" Neal asked, out of nowhere.

"What?"

"Well, you take the key to the keyhole behind the tapestry, right?" Neal said. "Is that the end of the maze, or…?"

"No, that's the end," I said. "You open a secret door and you're out of the maze."

"So what happens next?" Neal asked.

"I don't know," I confessed. "I didn't go any further. I don't know what happens next."

Neal laughed, and the two of us kept talking. We talked about what we thought the game would throw at the player next. We talked about games we played at kids, and the secret crush he apparently had on my sister during middle school. We talked about missing Drew's cooking and Lore's smile. We commiserated over what assholes his parents and my father were. I told him about Calli getting Snooty Crow back for me, and the stuffed bird's final resting place. He told me about his parents being told off by Dan one night when they called to "see if he had seen the light" yet. We remembered the one night we had that could have been called a date.

I could have kept going after the maze. Calli wanted to, and part of me did, too. Just like I could keep going on here. I could tell the story of how Olivia's old house burned down almost instantly after it sold, the victim of the new owner's hotplate. I could talk about how hard it was for Calli and me to get use to Seattle, how I ended up managing a comic book shop while she worked for Sera, and how both of us felt completely in over our heads for the first year. I could tell you about her breakdown on a Wednesday afternoon that ended with her in the psychiatric unit and me sobbing in the waiting room. I could tell you about her recovery, about mine, too. I could go on and on about the fight we had one New Year's Day, the result of me being an asshole, the one that almost ended us. I would say more about our reconciliation a month later. There's plenty to say about our 'simple' wedding; her parents showed up. Not to celebrate. I'd rather talk about our good times, though, our late-night walks, the cooking classes we took together. The video games we beat. How we felt utterly lost when we were apart for more than a few hours.

Maybe I could say something about the Cluster reunion we had, though Cluster wasn't Cluster anymore, it was renamed Epiphany, and it was booming. Lore and Drew brought their baby, Una, who is adorable. They weren't as far gone as Neal and I had feared. We made it to their restaurant in Spokane, too. I could go into great detail about how delicious my namesake dish was.

More interesting, though, would be the story of the marriage of Neal and Dan, who had their relationship almost end on the same New Year's Day Calli and I did, and yes, there's a story there, too. But I could also tell about how they reconciled, faster than Calli and I, and eventually adopted a child from foster care. His name is Evan, and he's adorable, too.

I could go on, through all of these stories, just like I could have gone on through *Unwelcome.* But I don't need to. Just like I knew everything I needed to know about that infernal computer game I discovered when I spoke to a tombstone and revealed a key, everything anyone could ever really need or want to know about me and Neal happened right there that night in the remains of Cadabra's Corner.

Sorry to have kept you for so long.

--Abra Collins, Founding Member, Society of the Heart of Crows

ACKNOWLEDGMENTS

Many thanks to the numerous people who contributed to the creation of this novel. To Ian Arbuckle, the most brilliant writer I know, who never stopped encouraging me to tell my stories. To my loyal beta-readers, Phoenix and Will McCollough, who set aside their lives whenever their unhinged friend runs at them with a 200-page manuscript and yells, "Look! I made this! With my brain!" To my wife, Beth, who patiently put up with me while I frantically typed out yet another "one last chapter." To my mother, who supported me no matter what and figured out how to use a Kindle so she could read an early draft of this novel. Thank you all for your unwavering help, support, and acceptance.

ABOUT THE AUTHOR

Jessica Conwell lives in Washington State with her wife and their daughter. When not doing horrible things to characters she has come to love, she can usually be found surrounded by a dozen unfinished art projects. You can read her various musings and random thoughts on Twitter @pairofclaws . She is transgender (She/her).

Made in the USA
Lexington, KY
29 April 2019